ALSO BY BRITTAINY CHERRY

THE ELEMENTS SERIES
The Air He Breathes
The Fire Between High & Lo
The Silent Waters
The Gravity of Us

THE *Air* HE *Breathes*

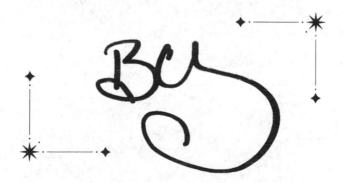

THE *Air*
HE
Breathes

BRITTAINY CHERRY

Copyright © 2015, 2024 by Brittainy Cherry
Cover and internal design © 2024 by Sourcebooks
Cover design by Stephanie Gafron/Sourcebooks
Cover images © Owen Smith/Getty Images, ilbusca/Getty Images
Internal design by Laura Boren/Sourcebooks
Internal artwork © Diana Dworak
Internal image © vectortatu/Getty

Sourcebooks and the colophon are registered trademarks of Sourcebooks.

The characters and events portrayed in this book are fictitious or
are used fictitiously. Any similarity to real persons, living or dead,
is purely coincidental and not intended by the author.

All brand names and product names used in this book are trademarks,
registered trademarks, or trade names of their respective holders.
Sourcebooks is not associated with any product or vendor in this book.

Published by Sourcebooks Casablanca, an imprint of Sourcebooks
P.O. Box 4410, Naperville, Illinois 60567-4410
(630) 961-3900
sourcebooks.com

Originally published in 2015 by Brittainy Cherry.

Cataloging-in-Publication Data is on file with the Library of Congress.

Printed and bound in Canada.
MBP 10 9 8 7 6 5 4 3 2 1

To all the white feathers,
thank you for the reminder.

Dear Reader,

May Tristan & Lizzie
heal parts of you that
you didn't know were
broken. Don't forget
to breathe.

♡
BC
do

PROLOGUE
Tristan

APRIL 2ND, 2014

Do you have everything?" Jamie asked, biting her nails as she stood in the foyer of my parents' house. Her beautiful blue doe eyes smiled my way, reminding me how lucky I was to call her mine.

I walked over and wrapped my arms around her, pulling her petite body closer to mine. "Yup. I think this is it, babe. I think this is our moment."

Her hands draped around my neck, and she kissed me. "I'm so proud of you."

"Of *us*," I corrected her. After a few too many years of being wishers and dreamers, my goal of building and selling my handcrafted furniture pieces was coming to life. My father was my best friend and business partner, and we were both on our way to New York to meet with a few businessmen who had showed a big interest in partnering with the two of us. "Without you supporting me, I would be nothing. This is our chance at getting everything we ever dreamed of."

She kissed me again.

I'd never known I could love someone so much.

"Before you go, I think you should know I got a call from Charlie's teacher. He got in a little trouble at school again, which isn't surprising seeing as how he takes after his father so much."

I smirked. "What did he do this time?"

"Mrs. Harper said he told a girl who was making fun of his glasses that he hoped she would choke on a toad because she looks like a toad. Choke on a toad—can you believe that?"

"Charlie!" I called toward the living room. He came walking out with a book in his hands. He wasn't wearing his glasses, which I knew had to do with the bullying.

"Yeah, Dad?"

"Did you tell a girl she should choke on a frog?"

"Yes," he said matter-of-factly. For an eight-year-old, he seemed to have surprisingly little concern about his parents getting upset with him.

"Buddy, you can't say things like that."

He replied, "But she looks like a freakin' toad, Dad!"

I had to turn away to laugh. "Come give me a hug, dude." He hugged me tight. I dreaded the days when hugging his old man would be something he wasn't interested in. "You be good for your mom and your grandma while I'm gone, all right?"

"Yeah, yeah."

"And put your glasses back on while you're reading."

"Why?! They are stupid!"

I bent down and tapped his nose. "Real men wear glasses."

"You don't wear glasses!" he whined.

"Yeah, well, real men don't wear glasses too. Just put on those glasses, buddy," I said. He grumbled before running off to continue reading his novel. The fact that he was more into reading than video games made me pretty damn happy. I knew he got his love of reading from his mom the librarian, but I still liked to think that my reading to her stomach before he was born had something to do with his love of books.

"What's the plan for you guys today?" I asked Jamie.

"This afternoon we are going to the farmer's market. Your mother wants to get some new flowers. She's probably going to buy Charlie something he doesn't need too. Oh, and Zeus chewed your favorite pair of Nikes, so I'm going to track down a new pair for you."

"God! Whose idea was it to get a dog anyway?"

She laughed. "I blame you for this. I didn't even want a dog, but you didn't know how to say no to Charlie. You and your mother have a lot in common." She kissed me again before pulling up the handle of my luggage. "Have a great trip, and go make our dreams come true."

I laid my lips against hers and smiled. "When I come home, I'm building you your dream library. With tall ladders and everything. And then I'm going to make love to you somewhere between *The Odyssey* and *To Kill a Mockingbird*."

She bit her bottom lip. "Promise?" she asked.

"Promise."

"Call me when your plane lands, okay?"

I nodded in agreement as I walked out of the house to meet Dad, who was already waiting in the taxicab for me.

"Hey, Tristan!" Jamie called toward me as I was loading the luggage into the trunk of the car. Charlie was standing beside her.

"Yes?"

They cupped their hands around their mouths and shouted, "WE LOVE YOU!"

I smiled and yelled the same thing back to them.

On the plane ride, Dad kept talking about what a big opportunity this was for us. When we touched down in Detroit for our layover, we both turned on our cell phones to check our emails and text Jamie and Mom to let them know we were okay.

When our phones turned on and we each had tons of messages from Mom, I knew something was wrong. The messages made my gut turn inside me. I almost dropped my phone as I read.

> **Mom:** There was an accident. Jamie and Charlie are in
> bad shape.
> **Mom:** Come home.
> **Mom:** Hurry!!

In the blink of an eye, in one moment's time, everything I knew about life changed.

CHAPTER 1

Elizabeth

JULY 3RD, 2015

E ach morning I read love letters written for another woman. She and I had much in common, from our chocolate eyes to the blond tone of our hair. We shared the same kind of laugh that was quiet yet grew loud in the company of the ones we loved. She smiled out of the right corner of her mouth and frowned out of the left, the same way my lips did.

I found the letters abandoned in the garbage can, resting inside a heart-shaped tin box. Hundreds of notes: some long, some short, some happy, others heartbreakingly sad. The dates of the letters went far back in years, some older than my entire existence on this earth. Some letters were initialed KB, others, HB.

I wondered how Dad would've felt if he'd known Mama threw all of them away.

Then again, lately it had been hard for me to believe she was the one who felt the way those letters said she felt.

Whole.

Complete.

A part of something divine.

Recently she seemed the complete opposite of all of those things.

Broken.

Incomplete.

Lonely all the time.

Mama became a whore after Dad died. There wasn't any other way to put it. It didn't happen right away, even though down the street Miss Jackson had been flapping her lips to everyone who would listen, saying Mama had always spread her legs, even when Dad was alive. I knew that wasn't true, though, because I'd never forgotten the way she'd looked at him when I was a kid. The way Mama stared was the way a woman gazed when she only had eyes for one man. When he'd go off to work at the crack of dawn, she would have his breakfast and lunch packed with snacks for the in-between hours. Dad always complained about getting hungry right after he was full, so Mama always made sure he had more than enough.

Dad was a poet and taught at the university an hour away. It wasn't surprising that the two left each other love notes. Words were what Dad drank in his coffee, and he tossed them into his whiskey at night. Even though Mama wasn't as strong with words as her husband, she knew how to express herself in each letter she wrote.

The moment Dad walked out the door in the mornings, Mama smiled and hummed to herself as she cleaned up around the house and got me ready for the day. She'd talk about Dad, saying how much she missed him, and would write him love letters until he came home at night. When he came home, Mama would always pour them both a glass of wine while he hummed their favorite song, and he'd kiss her against her wrist whenever she drew close enough to his mouth. They would laugh with one another and giggle as if they were kids falling in love for the first time.

"You're my love without end, Kyle Bailey," she'd say, pressing her lips to his.

"You're my love without end, Hannah Bailey," Dad would reply, spinning her in his arms.

They loved in a way that made fairy tales envious.

So on that sizzling August day years ago when Dad died, a part of Mama left too. I remembered in some novel I'd read the author said, "No soul mate leaves the world alone; they always take a piece of their other half along with them." I hated that he was right. Mama didn't get out of bed for months. I had to make her eat and drink each day, just hoping she wouldn't fade away from sadness. I'd never seen her cry until she lost her husband. I didn't show too much emotion around her because I knew that would only make her sadder.

I cried enough when I was alone.

When she finally did get out of bed, she went to church for a few weeks, taking me alongside her. I remember being twelve and feeling completely lost sitting in a church. We weren't really a praying kind of family until after bad things happened. Our church trips didn't last very long, though, because Mama called God a liar and scorned the townsfolk for wasting time on such deceit and empty promises of a promised land.

Pastor Reece asked us not to come back for a while, to let things smooth out a bit.

I hadn't known people could be banished from a holy temple until that very moment. When Pastor Reece said come one, come all, I guessed he met a different kind of "one" and a special kind of "all."

Nowadays, Mama had moved on to a new pastime: different men on the regular. Some she slept with, others she used to help pay the bills, and then some she kept 'round because she was lonely and they kind of looked like Dad. Some she even called by his name. Tonight there was a car parked in front of her little house. It was a deep navy blue, with shiny metallic silver frames. The inside had apple-red leather seats, a man sitting with a cigar between his lips, and Mama in his lap. He looked like he'd walked right out of the 1960s. She giggled as he whispered something to her, but it wasn't the same kind of laugh she'd always given Dad.

It was a little vacant, a little hollow, a little sad.

I glanced down the street and saw Miss Jackson surrounded by the other gossipy women, pointing at Mama and her new man of the week. I wished I were close enough to hear them so I could tell them to keep their yaps shut, but they were a good block away. Even the kids who were tossing a ball in the street, hitting it around with a few broken sticks, stopped their actions and stared wide-eyed at Mama and the stranger.

Cars that cost as much as his never traveled down streets that looked like ours. I'd tried to convince Mama she should move to a better neighborhood, but she refused. I thought it was mainly because she and Dad had bought the house together.

Maybe she hadn't completely let him go yet.

The man blew a cloud of smoke into Mama's face, and they laughed together. She was wearing her nicest dress, a yellow dress that hung off her shoulders, hugged her small waist, and flared out at the bottom. She wore so much makeup that it made her fifty-year-old face look more like a thirty-year-old's. She was pretty without all that gunk on her cheeks, but she said a little blush made a girl turn into a woman. The pearls around her neck were from Grandma Betty. She'd never worn those pearls for a stranger before tonight, and I wondered why she was wearing them now.

The two glanced my way, and I hid behind the porch post where I was spying from.

"Liz, if you're planning on hiding, at least do a better job at it. Now come on over and meet my new friend," Mama shouted.

I stepped from behind the post and walked over to the two of them. The man blew another puff of smoke, and the smell lingered around my nostrils as I took in his graying hair and deep-blue eyes.

"Richard, this is my daughter, Elizabeth. Everyone we know calls her Liz, though."

Richard eyed me up and down in a way that made me feel less like a person. He studied me as if I were a porcelain doll he wanted to watch shatter. I tried not to show my discomfort, but it seeped through as my eyes shifted to the ground. "How do you do, Liz?"

"Elizabeth," I corrected, my voice hitting the concrete I'd been staring down at. "Only people I know call me Liz."

"Liz, that is no way to speak to him!" Mama scolded, her slight wrinkles deepening in her forehead. She would've had a fit if she'd known her wrinkles were showing. I hated how whenever a new man came around, she was quick to back them up instead of standing up for me.

"It's all right, Hannah. Besides, she's right. It takes time to get to know somebody. Nicknames need to be earned, not given out freely." There was something so slimy about the way Richard stared at me and puffed on his cigar. I was wearing a pair of loose jeans and a plain, oversized T-shirt, but his eyes made me feel exposed. "We were about to go grab a bite to eat in town, if you want to join us," he offered.

I declined. "Emma's still sleeping." My eyes glanced back at the house, where my baby girl was lying on the pullout sofa she and I'd been sharing for one too many nights since we'd moved back in with Mama.

Mama wasn't the only one who'd lost the love of her life.

Hopefully I wouldn't end up like her.

Hopefully I'd just stay in the sad phase.

It'd been a year since Steven passed away, and still each breath was hard to swallow. Emma's and my true home was back in Meadows Creek, Wisconsin. It was a fixer-upper place where Steven, Emma, and I had taken a house and created a home. We fell deeper in love, into fights, and back in love, over and over again.

It became a place of warmth just by us being within its walls, and after Steven passed away, a drift of coldness filled the space.

The last time he and I were together, his hand was around my waist in the foyer and we thought we had forever to keep doing things like that.

Forever was much shorter than anyone would ever like to believe.

For the longest time, life flowed in its accustomed stream, and one day it all came to a shocking stop.

I'd felt the suffocation of the memories, of the sadness, so I'd run off to stay with Mama.

Going back to the house would ultimately be me facing the truth that he was really gone. For over a year, I'd been living in make-believe, pretending he'd gone out for milk and would be walking through the door anytime now. Each evening when I lay down to sleep, I stayed on the left side and closed my eyes, pretending Steven was against the right.

But now, my Emma needed more. My poor Emma needed

freedom from pullout couches, strange men, and gossiping neighbors who said words that should never fill a five-year-old's ears. She needed me too. I'd been walking through the darkness, only being half the mother she deserved, so maybe facing the memories of our house would help bring me more peace.

I headed back inside the house and looked down at my sleeping angel, her chest rising and falling in a perfect pattern. She and I had much in common, from our dimpled cheeks to the blond tone of our hair. We shared the same kind of laugh that was quiet yet grew loud in the company of the ones we loved. She smiled out of the right corner of her mouth and frowned out of the left, the same way my lips did.

But there was one big difference.

She had his blue eyes.

I lay beside Emma, placing a gentle kiss against her nose before I reached into the heart-shaped tin box and read another love letter. It was one I'd read before, yet it still tugged at my spirit.

Sometimes I pretended the letters were from Steven.

I always cried a little.

CHAPTER 2
Elizabeth

A re we really going home?" asked sleepy Emma when morning came through the living-room window, spilling light against her sweet face. I picked her up from the bed and placed her and Bubba— her teddy bear and all-time favorite companion—on the closest chair. Bubba wasn't simply a teddy bear, he was a mummified teddy bear. See, my little girl was a little weird, and after she saw the movie *Hotel Transylvania*—which involved zombies, vampires, and mummies— she decided that maybe a little scary and maybe a little weird was perfect.

"We are." I smiled toward her as I folded up the pullout. The night before, I hadn't slept a wink and had stayed up packing all our belongings.

Emma had a goofy grin on her face that matched her father's. She screamed, "YAY!" and told Bubba we were really going home.

Home.

That word stung a little in the back of my heart, but I kept smiling.

I'd learned to always smile in front of Emma because she had a way of growing sad whenever she thought I was sad. Even though she gave me the best butterfly kisses when I was feeling down, she didn't need that kind of responsibility.

"We should make it back in time to see the fireworks from our rooftop. Remember how we used to watch the fireworks on the roof with Daddy? Do you remember that, babe?" I asked her.

She narrowed her eyes as if going deep into her mind, searching. If only our minds were like file cabinets and we could simply retrieve our favorite memories from a neatly organized system whenever we chose. "I don't remember," she said, hugging Bubba.

That breaks my heart.

I smiled anyway.

"Well, how about we stop at the store on the way and pick up some Bomb Pops to eat on the roof?"

"And some Cheetos Puffs for Bubba!"

"Of course!"

She smiled and screamed once more. That time the grin I gave her was nothing but real.

I loved her more than she'd ever know. If it hadn't been for her, I would've definitely lost myself to the grief. Emma saved my soul.

I didn't say goodbye to Mama because she never came home from her dinner date with Casanova. When I first moved in with her and she didn't come home, I would call and call, worried about her whereabouts, but often she would yell at me, telling me she was a grown woman doing grown woman things.

So I left her a note.

Going home.

We love you.

We'll see you soon.

—E&E

We drove for hours in my broken-down car, listening to the *Frozen* soundtrack enough times for me to consider pulling out my eyelashes one at a time. Emma somehow listened to each song a million times yet had a way of making up her own words to every line. To be honest, I liked her version of the songs the best.

When she fell asleep, *Frozen* slept with her, leaving me with a car full of silence. My hand reached out toward the passenger seat, palm up, waiting for another hand to lock my fingers with theirs, but the touch never found me.

I'm doing good, I told myself over and over again. *I'm so good.*

One day, it would be true.

One day, I'd be good.

As we merged onto the I-94 freeway, my gut tightened. I wished I could take back roads to get to Meadows Creek, but this was the only way into town. It was quite busy for the holiday, but the new smooth pavement of the once-broken roadway made for easy travels. Tears formed in my eyes as I remembered watching the news.

Pileup on I-94!

Chaos!

Mayhem!

Injuries!

Casualties!

Steven.

One breath.

I kept driving, and the tears that tried to escape failed. I forced my body to go numb, because if I wasn't numb, I'd feel everything. If I felt everything, I'd fall apart, and I couldn't fall apart. The rearview mirror showed me my small bit of strength as I stared at my baby. We made it across the freeway, and I took another breath. Each day was one breath at a time. I couldn't think much further than that, otherwise I'd choke on the air.

On a polished, white piece of wood was a sign that read "Welcome to Meadows Creek."

Emma was awake now, staring out the window. "Hey, Mama?"

"Yes, baby?"

"Do you think Daddy will know that we moved? Do you think he'll know where to leave the feathers?"

When Steven passed away and we moved to stay with Mama, there were white bird feathers scattered around the front yard. When Emma asked about them, Mama said they were small signs from the angels, letting us know they were always close by, watching over us.

Emma had loved the idea, and whenever she would find a feather, she would look up to the sky, smile, and whisper, "I love you too, Daddy." Then she would take a picture with the feather to add to her collection of "Daddy and Me" photos.

"I'm sure he'll know where to find us, sweetie."

"Yeah," she agreed. "Yeah, he'll know where to find us."

The trees were greener than I remembered, and the little shops in downtown Meadows Creek were decked out with reds, whites, and blues for the festivities. It was so familiar yet foreign all at once. Mrs. Fredrick's American flag flapped in the wind as she fixed the patriotically dyed roses in her flowerpot. Pride bloomed from her entire existence as she stepped back to admire her home.

We got stuck behind the one traffic light in town for ten minutes. The wait made no sense at all, but it did give me time to take in everything that reminded me of Steven. Of us. Once the light switched over, I placed my foot on the gas pedal, wanting nothing more than to get home and ignore the shadows of the past. As the car took off down the street, from the corner of my eye I saw a dog dashing toward me. My foot moved quickly to the brake, but my old, beat-up car hiccupped and hesitated to stop. By the time it finally did, I heard the loud yelp.

My heart leaped into my throat and stayed there, blocking the ability for me to inhale my next breath. I slammed the car into park. Emma asked what was happening, but I didn't have time to reply. I swung my door open, reaching the poor dog right as a man raced up to me. His wide-eyed stare locked with mine, almost forcing me to train in on the intensity of his stormy grayish-blue eyes. Most blue eyes came with a warm, welcoming feeling attached to them, but not his. His were intense, just as his stance was. Icy and private. Around the rims of his irises were profound blues, but silver and black strands of coloring were woven in and out, which added to the shrouded look in his stare. His eyes matched the shadows of the sky right before a thunderstorm was about to pass through.

Those eyes were so familiar to me. Did I know him? I could've sworn I'd seen his stare somewhere before. He looked both terrified and livid as he moved his eyes to what I was assuming was his dog, which was lying still. Around the stranger's neck were huge headphones that were attached to something resting in his back pocket.

He was decked out in workout clothes. His long-sleeved white shirt hugged his muscular arms, his black shorts showed his built legs, and sweat was brewing along his forehead. I assumed he'd been taking his dog for a run when he lost hold of his leash, but the man wasn't wearing any shoes.

Why wasn't he wearing shoes?

That didn't matter. Was his dog okay?

I should've been paying closer attention.

"I'm so sorry. I didn't see..." I started to say, but the man grunted harshly at my words, almost as if they offended him.

"What the hell?! Are you fucking kidding me?!" he shouted, his voice making me jump a bit. He lifted his dog into his arms, cradling the pet as if it were his own child. As he stood, I stood. As he searched around, I searched around.

"Let me drive you to the vet," I said, my body shaking from seeing the dog trembling in the stranger's arms. I knew I should've been annoyed with the tone he'd taken with me, but when someone was in panic mode, you couldn't really blame them for their behavior. He didn't speak back, but I watched the hesitation in his eyes. His face was framed with a very thick, dark, untamed beard. His mouth was hidden somewhere in the wildness resting against his face, so all I had to rely on was the story he told with his eyes. "Please," I begged. "It's too far to walk."

He nodded once and only once. He opened the passenger-side door, sat inside with his pet, and closed the door behind him.

Hopping into the car, I started driving.

"What's going on?" Emma asked.

"We are just going to take the pup to get checked out, honey. Everything's fine." I really hoped I wasn't lying to her.

It was a twenty-minute drive to the closest twenty-four-hour animal hospital, and the car ride didn't exactly go the way I'd thought it would.

"Take a left on Cobbler Street," he ordered.

"Harper Avenue will be faster," I disagreed.

He grunted, his annoyance shining through. "You don't know what the hell you're talking about; take Cobbler!"

I took a breath. "I know how to drive."

"Do you? Because I think your driving is the reason we're sitting here."

I was five seconds from kicking the rude jerk out of my car, but his whimpering dog was the only reason I didn't. "I already apologized."

"That doesn't help my dog."

Asshole.

"Cobbler is the next right," he said.

"Harper is the next, next right."

"Don't take Harper."

Oh, I'm taking Harper just to annoy the living shit out of this guy. Who does he think he is?

I turned right onto Harper.

"I can't believe you just fucking took Harper," he groaned. His infuriation made me smile a little, until I hit the construction zone and "Closed Street" signs. "Are you always so ignorant?"

"Are you always…always…always…" I started stuttering, because unlike some, I wasn't great at arguing with people. I actually sucked at it and normally ended up crying like a child because words didn't form in my head at the speed that fights normally functioned. I was the awkward person who thought of the best comebacks three days after the argument took place. "Are you always…always…"

"Always what? Spit it out! Use words!" he ordered.

I swung my steering wheel around, making a U-turn, and headed for Cobbler Street. "Are you always a…"

"Come on, Sherlock, you can do it," he said mockingly.

"A DICK!" I screamed, turning on Cobbler.

The car went silent. My cheeks heated up, and my fingers gripped tightly around the wheel.

When I pulled into the driveway, he opened the door and, without any words my way, lifted his dog and rushed into the emergency room. I debated if that was where we should part ways, but my mind wouldn't be able to calm down until I knew the dog was okay.

"Mommy?" Emma asked.

"Yes, baby?"

"What's a dick?"

Parenting fail number five-hundred-and-eighty-two of today.
"Nothing, babe. I said tick. A tick is a bug."

"So you called that person a bug?"

"Yup. A big bug."

"Is his puppy going to die?" she asked next.

I really hope not.

After unbuckling Emma, we headed into the emergency hospital. Stranger was slamming his hands against the receptionist's desk. His lips were moving, but I couldn't hear anything he was saying.

The receptionist grew more and more uncomfortable. "Sir, I'm just saying I need you to fill out the forms and provide us with a reliable credit card, or we cannot proceed with looking into your pet's injuries. Furthermore, you cannot just walk in here with no shoes. Also, your attitude isn't needed."

Stranger banged his fists against the desk once more before pacing back and forth, his hands running through his long, black hair and landing against his neck. His breaths were heavy and uneven, his chest rising and falling quite hard. "Does it fucking look like I am currently traveling with credit cards? I was on a run, you idiot! And if you aren't going to do anything, then get me someone else to talk to."

The woman flinched at his words and anger, as did I.

"They're with me," I said, walking over to the receptionist. Emma clung to my arm and Bubba clung to hers. Reaching into my purse, I pulled out my wallet and handed the woman my card.

She narrowed her eyes, unsure. "You're with *him*?" she asked, almost insultingly, as if Stranger was someone who deserved to be alone.

No one deserved to be alone.

I looked at him and saw perplexity in his eyes, along with the anger, which still remained. I wanted to break our stare, but the misery swimming in his irises seemed way too familiar to pull away from. "Yes." I nodded. "I'm with him." She hesitated some more, and I stood up straight. "Is that a problem?"

"No, no. I just need you to fill out this form."

I took the clipboard from her grip and walked over to the sitting area.

The overhead television was tuned to Animal Planet, and there was a train set in the far corner, which Emma and Bubba quickly occupied. Stranger kept staring at me, his stance hard and distant. "I need some information," I said. He approached slowly, sat down beside me, and rested his hands in his lap.

"What's his name? Your pet?" I asked.

He parted his lips and paused before saying, "Zeus."

I smiled at the name. Such a perfect name for a large golden retriever.

"And your name?"

"Tristan Cole."

After finishing the paperwork, I handed it back to the receptionist. "Anything Zeus needs, just put the charges on my card."

"Are you sure?"

"Absolutely."

"It could add up quickly," she warned.

"Then add it up quickly."

I sat back down beside Tristan. His hands started tapping against
his shorts and I observed the nerves rushing through him. When I
looked at him, he was staring with the same confusion that'd been
there since we'd crossed paths.

His lips started muttering something as his fingers rubbed against
each other quickly before he put his headphones against his ears and
hit play on his cassette tape.

Emma walked over to me every now and then, asking when we
could go home, and I'd tell her a little longer. On her way back to
the train set, she stared at Tristan, taking in all of his features. "Hey,
mister." He ignored her. She placed her hands on her hips. "Hey,
mister!" she said, raising her voice. A year staying with Mama had
made my mini-me a sassy monster. "Hey, mister! I'm talking to you!"
she said, tapping her feet. Stranger looked down at her. "You're a big,
fat, giant TICK!"

Oh my gosh.

I shouldn't have been allowed to parent. I sucked at the parent
thing.

I went to scold her, but for a second I saw a tiny smile creep behind
Tristan's thick beard. It was almost nonexistent, but I swore I saw his
bottom lip twitch. Emma had a way of making even the darkest souls
smile; I was living proof.

Another thirty minutes passed before the vet came out to inform us that Zeus would be fine, just a few bruises and a fractured front leg. I thanked the vet, and as he walked away, Tristan's hands loosened and his body stood still. Every inch of him began to shake. With one deep inhale, the angry asshole disappeared and was replaced with despair. He lost himself in his emotions, and when he exhaled, he began to sob uncontrollably. He wailed, his tears harsh, raw, and painful. My eyes watered over, and I swore a part of my heart broke right along with his.

"Hey, Tick! Hey, Tick! Don't cry, Tick," Emma said, tugging on Tristan's T-shirt. "It's okay."

"It's okay," I said, echoing my sweet girl's words. I placed a comforting hand against his shoulder. "Zeus is okay. He's good. You're good."

He tilted his head toward me and nodded as if he kind of believed me. A few deep breaths were taken, and he pinched his fingers over his eyes, shaking his head back and forth. He tried his best to hide his embarrassment, his shame.

His throat cleared, and he moved away from me. We stayed at a distance until the vet brought Zeus out to leave. Tristan wrapped his hands around his dog, who was tired but still managed to wag his tail and give his owner puppy kisses. Tristan smiled, and it was almost impossible to miss this time. It was a big smile of relief. If love was a moment, this would be where it existed.

I didn't invade their space. Emma took my hand, and we walked a few steps behind Tristan and Zeus as they exited the hospital.

Tristan began to walk away with Zeus in his arms, uninterested in a ride back into town. I wanted to stop him, but I had no real reason to ask him to turn back. I buckled Emma into her seat and as I closed her door, I jumped out of my skin when I saw Tristan standing a few inches from me. His eyes locked in with mine. My eyes wouldn't look away. My breathing became jagged, and I tried my best to remember the last time I'd stood that close to a man.

He stepped in closer.

I stayed still.

He took a breath.

I took one too.

One breath.

That's all I could manage.

Our proximity made my stomach knot, and I was already prepared to say "you're welcome" for the "thank you" I was certain he was going to give me.

"Learn how to drive a fucking car," he hissed before he walked off.

Not a "thank you for picking up the bill," not a "thank you for driving me," but a "learn how to drive a fucking car."

Well then.

With a small whisper, I responded into the wind that swept against my chilled skin. "You're welcome, Tick."

CHAPTER 3
Elizabeth

W ell, it took long enough for you two to get here!" Kathy smiled, walking out of the front door of the house. I hadn't a clue that she and Lincoln would be meeting us at the house, but it made complete sense seeing as how they hadn't seen us in so long and only lived about five minutes away.

"Grammy!" Emma shouted as I unbuckled her from her car seat. She jumped out of the car and dashed toward her grandmother, happier than ever. Kathy wrapped her arms around Emma and lifted her up for a big hug. "We're back home, Grammy!"

"I know! And we are so happy to hear that," Kathy said, giving Emma kisses all over her face.

"Where's Poppi?" she asked, referring to Lincoln, her grandfather.

"Looking for me?" Lincoln said, walking out of the house. He looked so much younger than his actual age of sixty-five. Kathy and Lincoln would probably never truly grow old—they had the youngest hearts in the world and were more active than most people my age. Once I'd gone on a run with Kathy and died after about thirty minutes—and she said we were only one-fourth of the way in to the jog.

Lincoln grabbed Emma from his wife and tossed her up in the air. "Well, well, well, who do we have here?"

"It's me, Poppi! Emma!" She laughed.

"Emma? No way! You look too big to be my little Emma."

She shook her head back and forth. "It's me, Poppi!"

"Well, if that's so, prove it. My little Emma always gave me special kinds of kisses. Do you know them?" Emma leaned in and wiggled her nose against each of Lincoln's cheeks before giving him butterfly kisses. "Oh my gosh, it is you! Well, what are you waiting for? I've got some red, white, and blue popsicles with your name on them. Let's get inside!" Lincoln turned my way and gave me a welcome-home wink. The two of them hurried toward the house, and I took a second to look around.

The grass was tall, with weeds and wish-makers, as Emma liked to call them. The fence we'd started putting up was only half-finished, a job Steven was never able to complete. We'd wanted to fence in the property to keep Emma from wandering too close to the street, or into the huge forest in our backyard.

The extra white wooden pieces were stacked up against the side of the house, waiting for someone to complete the task. I glanced toward the backyard for a moment. Beyond the half-built fence were the trees that led to the miles of forested land. A part of me wanted to run, get lost in those woods, and stay there for hours.

Kathy walked over and wrapped her arms around me, pulling me into a tight hug. I collapsed against her, holding her closer. "How are you holding up?" she asked.

"Still standing."

"For Emma?"

"For Emma."

Kathy squeezed me right before she separated from our hug. "The yard is a mess. No one has been up here since…" Her words faded off, along with her smile. "Lincoln said he'll handle it all."

"Oh no, don't. Really, I can handle it all."

"Liz—"

"Really, Kathy. I want to. I want to rebuild."

"Well, if you're sure. At least you aren't the messiest yard on the block," she joked, nodding toward my neighbor's house.

"Someone lives there?" I asked. "I didn't think Mr. Rakes's place would ever sell after all the rumors of it being haunted."

"Yep. Someone actually bought the place. Now, I'm not one to gossip, but the guy who lives there is a bit weird. Rumor has it he is on the run for something he did in his past."

"What? You mean, like a felon?"

Kathy shrugged. "Marybeth said she heard things about how he stabbed a person. Gary said he killed a cat for meowing the wrong way."

"No way. What? Am I living beside a psychopath?"

"Oh, I'm sure you're okay. Ya know, just small talk in this small town. I doubt the rumors have any truth to them. But he does work at oddball Henson's shop, so you know the guy can't be all right in the head. So mainly, just lock your doors at night."

Mr. Henson owed the shop Needful Things in downtown Meadows Creek, and he was one of the weirdest people I'd never met. I only knew about his weirdness based on what others said about him.

The townspeople were some of the best at gossiping and living the small-town lifestyle. People were always on the go, but no one ever really got anywhere.

I looked across the street and saw three people gossiping outside a house. Two women power-walked past my house, and I listened to them talking about my return to town—they didn't say hello to me or anything, but they spoke about me. Right around the corner came a father who was teaching his little girl to ride her bike for what appeared to be the first time without training wheels.

A smile crept across my face. It was all so stereotypical, the small-town life. Everyone knew everyone's business, and it spread fast.

"Anyhow." Kathy smiled, bringing me back to reality. "We brought some barbeque and things for dinner. Stocked up your fridge too, so you wouldn't have to worry about grocery shopping for a week or two. Plus, we already put the blankets on top of the roof for the fireworks, which should be starting right about…" The sky filled with blues and reds, igniting the world with color. "Now!"

I looked up at the rooftop to see Lincoln carrying Emma in his arms as they got comfortable and shouted "Ooo! Ahh!" each time the night lit on fire.

"Come on, Mama!" Emma yelled, not taking her eyes away from the display of colors.

Kathy wrapped her arm around my waist and we walked toward the house. "After Emma goes to bed, I have a few bottles of wine with your name on them."

"For me?" I asked.

She smiled. "For you. Welcome back home, Liz."

Home.

I wondered when that sting would disappear.

Lincoln wanted to put Emma to bed, and when he seemed to be taking longer than normal, I went to check on them. Emma had a way of giving me a hard time each night when I put her to bed, and I was sure she was giving him the same issues. I tiptoed down the hallway and didn't hear screaming, which was a good sign. Peeking into the room, I found the two spread out sound asleep in the full-sized bed, with Lincoln's feet hanging over the end of the bed frame.

Kathy giggled, walking up behind me. "I don't know who's more excited to be reunited, Lincoln or Emma." She walked us to the living room, where we sat in front of the two biggest wine bottles I'd ever seen.

"Are you trying to get me drunk?" I laughed.

She grinned. "If it makes you feel better, I might just have to." Kathy and I had always been so close. After growing up with a mom who wasn't the most stable mother, when I got together with Steven, meeting Kathy was such a breath of fresh air. She welcomed me in with arms wide open and never let me go. When she found out I was pregnant with Emma, she cried even more than I did.

"I feel awful that I kept them apart for so long," I said, sipping at my glass of wine and staring down the hallway toward Emma's room.

"Honey, your life was turned upside down. When tragedies happen and there are children involved, you don't think, you just act. You do what you think is best—you go into survival mode. And you can't blame yourself for that."

"Yeah. But I feel like I ran away for me, not for Emma. It was just too much for me to handle. Emma probably would've been better staying here. She missed it." My eyes watered over. "And I should've visited you and Lincoln. I should've called more. I'm so sorry, Kathy."

She leaned in toward me, resting her elbows against her kneecaps. "Now listen to me, darling. The time right now is 10:42 p.m., and right now, at 10:42 p.m., you stop blaming yourself. Right now is the moment you forgive yourself. Lincoln and I understood. We knew you needed space. Don't feel as if you owe us an apology because you don't."

I wiped away the few tears that slipped out from my eyes. "Stupid tears." I laughed, embarrassed.

"You know what makes the tears stop?" she asked.

"What's that?"

She poured me another big glass of wine. *Smart woman.*

We stayed up for hours chatting, and the more we drank, the more we laughed. I forgot how warming it felt to laugh. She asked about my mom, and I couldn't help but wrinkle my nose. "She's still lost, somehow walking in circles, making the same mistakes with the same types of people. I wonder if there's a point where people can never be found anymore. I think she's always going to be this way."

"You love her?"

"Always. Even when I don't like her."

"Then don't give up on her. Even if you need your space for a while. Love her and believe in her coming around from a distance."

"How did you get so wise?" I asked. She smiled a wolfish grin and tipped her wineglass toward me, then poured herself another glass. *Very smart woman.* "Do you think you can watch Emma for me tomorrow? I'm going to go into town and look for some work, maybe see if Matty needs an extra hand or two at the café."

"How about we keep her for the weekend? It could be great for you to have a few days to yourself. We can even start up our Friday-night sleepovers again. Anyway, I don't think Lincoln is planning on giving her up anytime soon."

"You'd do that for me?"

"We'd do anything for you. Plus, every time I go into the café,

Faye says, 'How's my best friend? Is my best friend back yet?' So I'm guessing she'll want some one-on-one time with you."

I hadn't seen Faye since Steven had passed away. Even though we talked almost daily, she understood that I needed the space. I hoped she would understand that now I needed my best friend to make it through this new beginning.

"I know this might be a bad time to ask, but have you thought about getting your business up and running again?" Kathy asked.

Steven and I had started In & Out Design three years before. He handled the exterior of homes while I worked on the interior designs for individuals and businesses. We had a shop right in downtown Meadows Creek, and it was some of the best times of my life, but the truth of the matter was that Steven's lawn work skills brought in most of the money for our business, along with his business degree. There would be no way for me to run things on my own. Having an interior design degree in Meadows Creek pretty much gave me the opportunity to work at a furniture store selling people overpriced recliners, or I could go back to my college roots and work in food service.

"I don't know. Probably not, though. Without Steven it just doesn't seem possible. I just need to find some steady work and try to let go of that dream."

"I understand. Don't be afraid to start dreaming new dreams, though. You were really good at your job, Liz. And it made you happy. You should always hold on to the things that make you most happy."

After Kathy and Lincoln decided to head home, I fumbled with the locks on my front door that Steven and I were supposed to have changed months before. With a yawn, I headed toward my bedroom and stood in the doorway. The bed was perfectly made, and I hadn't found the strength to enter the room yet. It seemed almost like a betrayal to crawl into the bed and close my eyes without him beside me.

One breath.

One step.

I walked in and went to the closet, opening it wide. All of Steven's clothes hung on the hangers, and my fingers brushed against them before I started shaking. Taking all of the clothes off the hangers, I tossed them on the ground, tears burning the back of my eyes. I opened his drawers and pulled out the rest of his items. Jeans, T-shirts, workout clothes, boxers. Every single article of clothing Steven owned found its way to the ground.

I lay in the pile, rolling through his slight scent, which I pretended was still there. I whispered his name as if he could hear me, and I hugged the thought of him kissing me and holding me in his arms. The tears of my pained heart released on the sleeve of Steven's favorite T-shirt, and I fell more and more into my sorrow. My cries were wild and thick with ache, like a creature in indescribable pain. Everything hurt. Everything was broken. As the minutes went by, I grew more and more exhausted from my own feelings. The profound tranquility of my dreadful seclusion took me away into a deep sleep.

When I opened my eyes, it was still dark outside. A beautiful little girl and her Bubba were lying beside me, with a tiny part of her blanket resting over her body, and the rest covering me. Every time a moment like this one appeared, I felt a little like my mother. I remembered taking care of her when I should've been a child myself. It wasn't fair for Emma. *She needs me.* I snuggled in closer to her, kissed her forehead, and promised myself I wouldn't fall apart anymore.

CHAPTER 4
Elizabeth

The next morning, Kathy and Lincoln showed up bright and early to pick up Emma for their weekend adventures. Once they were gone, I cleaned up the mess I'd made the night before, carefully hanging up Steven's clothes in the closet and folding the rest, placing it back in the dresser. Right as I was about to walk out of my house, I heard pounding on my front door. Opening it, I pasted on my biggest fake smile as I stared at three women who lived on my block—three women I hadn't missed one bit. "Marybeth, Susan, Erica, hi."

I should've known it wouldn't be long before the three most dramatic and gossipy women in town were standing on my porch. "Oh, Liz," Marybeth gasped, pulling me into a hug. "How are you doing, darling? We heard rumors that you were coming back into town, but you know us, we hate gossip, so we had to see for ourselves."

"I made you a meatloaf!" Erica exclaimed. "After Steven died, you left so fast that I wasn't able to make you any comfort food, so now I was finally able to make you this meatloaf to help you mourn."

"Thanks, ladies. I was actually just on my way out to—"

"How's Emma handling everything?" Susan cut in. "Is she deal-ing? My Rachel was asking about her and wondering if they can have their playdates again, which would be great." She paused and leaned in. "But just to be clear, Emma's not suffering from depression, is she? I hear that can be quite contagious with other kids."

I hate you, I hate you, I hate you. I smiled. "Oh no, Emma's good. We're good. Everything's good."

"So you'll be back at our book club meetings? Every Wednesday at Marybeth's. The kids stay in the basement playing while we chat it up about a novel. This week we're reading *Pride and Prejudice*."

"I—" ...*really don't want to go.* Their eyes zoned in on me, and I knew if I said no, I would be causing myself more trouble than it was worth. Plus, it would be nice for Emma to be around other girls her age. "I'll be there."

"Perfect!" Marybeth's eyes glanced around the yard. "Your yard has quite a personality." She said it with a grin, but what it really meant was, *When are you cutting your grass? You're embarrassing all of us.*

"I'm working on it," I explained. I took the meatloaf from Erica and placed it inside before hurrying out and locking my door, trying my best to give them the signal that I was on my way out. "Well, thanks for stopping by, ladies. I better get going into town."

"Oh? What are you doing in town?" Marybeth questioned.

"I'm actually looking to see if Matty needs an extra hand at Savory & Sweet."

"Even though they just hired someone? I doubt they'll have room to add you on," Erica explained.

"Oh, so the rumors were true that you aren't starting up your company again? It makes sense that you wouldn't, without Steven," Marybeth said.

Susan nodded in agreement. "He was quite the businessman. And I know you only had the interior design degree. It must be sad to go from something so great to something so…mundane, like being a waitress. I know I couldn't do it. What a step backward."

Screw you, screw you, screw you. I smiled. "Well, we'll see. It was great running into you. I'm sure we'll see each other soon enough."

"Wednesday at seven!" Susan smirked.

Pushing myself past them, I couldn't help but roll my eyes as I listened to them whisper about how it looked like I'd gained a few pounds and how heavy the bags under my eyes were.

I walked toward Savory & Sweet Café, and I tried my best to shake the nerves. What if they didn't need any help in the café? What would I do to make money? Steven's parents told me not to worry about those kinds of things, saying they would help us out for a while, but I couldn't help it. I needed to find a way to stand on my own. Pushing open the door to the café, I smiled when I heard the loud shout from behind the counter.

"Please tell me I'm not dreaming and my best friend is back!" Faye screamed, leaping over the counter and tackling me in a bear hug. She didn't let me go and turned to Matty, the owner of the shop. "Matty, tell me you're seeing this too and I'm not just screwed up from the crazy amount of drugs I took before coming to work."

"She's really there, crazy." He smirked. Matty was an older guy, and the way he dealt with Faye's loud, vibrant personality was normally with eye rolls and smirks. His brown eyes locked with mine and he nodded once. "Good to see you, Liz."

Faye snuggled her head against my breasts, as if they were her pillow. "Now that you're here you can never, ever, ever leave again." Faye was beautiful in all the perfect, unique ways. She had silver-dyed hair—unique for a twenty-seven-year-old—with strands of pinks and purples running through it. Her nails were always dressed with vibrant colors, and her dresses always hugged her curves in all the right places. The thing that made her so beautiful, though, was her confidence. Faye knew she was stunning, and she also knew that it had not one thing to do with her looks. Her feeling of pride for herself came from within; she didn't need the approval of anyone else whatsoever.

I envied that in her.

"Well, I actually came in to see if you guys were currently hiring. I know I haven't worked here since college, but I could use the work."

"Of course we are hiring! Hey, you, Sam!" Faye said, pointing to a server I didn't know. "You're fired."

"Faye!" I shouted.

"What?!"

"You can't just fire people," I scolded, seeing the fear in Sam's eyes. *Poor guy.* "You're not really fired," I said.

"Oh, yes you are."

"Shut up, Faye. No, you're not. How could you even fire people?"

She stood up tall and tapped against her name tag, which read Manager. "Someone had to step into the role of management, woman."

I turned to Matty, a bit of shock in my stare. "You made Faye a manager?"

"I think she drugged me." He laughed. "But if you really need some work, we always have room for you. It might just be part-time."

"Part-time would be great, really, anything." I smiled at Matty, thanking him.

"Or we could fire Sam," Faye offered. "He already has another part-time job! Plus, he's kind of creepy."

"I can hear you," Sam said shyly.

"It doesn't matter if you can hear me; you're fired."

"We aren't firing Sam," Matty said.

"You're no fun. But you know what is fun?!" She took off her apron and yelled, "Lunch break!"

"It's nine thirty in the morning," Matty scolded.

"Breakfast break!" Faye corrected, pulling me by the arm. "We'll be back in about an hour."

"Breaks are thirty minutes."

"I'm sure Sam will cover my tables. Sam, you're no longer fired."

"You were never fired, Sam." Matty smiled. "One hour, Faye. Liz, make sure to have her back on time or she'll be the one who's fired."

"Is that so?" Faye asked, placing her hands on her hips, almost… flirtatiously? Matty smirked at her, his eyes traveling over her body almost…sexually?

What the…?

We walked out of the building, Faye's arm linked with mine, confusion about the odd interaction between her and Matty still clouding my thoughts. "What was that?" I asked, arching an eyebrow in Faye's direction.

"What was what?"

"*That,*" I said, pointing back toward Matty. "The little sexually intense tango you two just performed?" She didn't reply, but she began chewing on her bottom lip. "Oh my God… You *slept* with *Matty*?!"

"Shut the hell up! Do you want the whole town to know?" She blushed, looking around. "It was an accident."

"Oh? Was it? Was it an accident? Were you casually walking down Main Street and then Matty started walking toward you and his penis accidentally tumbled out of his pants? Then did a strong whoosh of wind pass through, knocking said penis into your vagina? Was it *that* kind of accident?" I mocked.

"Not exactly like that." She pushed her tongue against the inside of her cheek. "The wind kind of pushed the penis toward my mouth first."

"OH MY GOSH, FAYE!"

"I know! I know! This is why people shouldn't go out on windy days. The penises are on rampage on the windy days."

"I cannot believe you right now. He's like twice your age."

"What can I say? I have daddy issues."

"What are you talking about? Your dad's amazing," I said.

"Exactly. No guy our age could ever live up to that! But Matty..." She sighed. "I think I like him."

That was shocking. Faye never used the word "like" when it came to a guy. She was the biggest woman-whore I'd ever met. "What do you mean you like him?" I asked, my voice soaked with hope that my friend was finally planning on settling down.

"Whoa, slow your roll there, Nicholas Sparks. What I mean is, I like the dick. I even gave it a nickname. Do you want to hear it?"

"For the love of everything good in the world, no."

"Oh, I'm going to tell you."

"Faye." I sighed.

"Fatty Matty," she said, her wolfish grin growing deep.

"You know what, these kinds of things you don't have to share with me. Ever. Like, never ever."

"I'm talking like two bratwursts combined kind of Fatty Matty. It's almost as if the sausage god is finally listening to my prayers. Remember Pinky Peter and Unclipped Nick? Well, this is so much better! Fatty Matty is the promised land of sausages."

"There's seriously vomit rising up from my gut. So if you would please stop talking."

She laughed and pulled me closer to her. "Gosh, I missed you. So, what do you say? Should we head to our regular hangout location?"

"Oh, most definitely."

As we walked for a few blocks, Faye had me laughing each and every moment, and I wondered why I'd stayed away for so long. Maybe a part of me felt guilty knowing that if I stuck around, I would slowly start feeling better, and the idea of feeling better was kind of terrifying to me. But right then laughing felt like exactly what I needed. When I laughed, I didn't have much time to cry, and I was so tired of the tears.

"It's kind of weird being here without Emma," Faye said, sitting on the teeter-totter at the playground. We were surrounded by kids with their parents and nannies, running around and playing while we went up and down on the teeter-totter. One kid stared at us as if we were insane for hanging out at a kids' playground, but Faye was quick to scream at him, "Never grow up, kid! It's a goddamn trap!"

She was so ridiculous all the time.

"So how long has this thing with Matty been going on?" I asked.

She blushed. "I don't know, like a month. Or two."

"Two months?"

"Maybe seven. Or eight."

"Eight?! What? We've been talking every day. How has this not come up?"

"I don't know." She shrugged. "You were going through so much with Steven, you know? And it seemed kind of heartless to talk to you about my sexlationship." Faye never had relationships, but she was a pro at sexlationships. "My shit was small, yours was…" She frowned and stopped pushing on the teeter-totter, leaving me hanging high in the air. There weren't many moments when Faye grew serious, but Steven had been like a brother to her. They'd fought and bickered more than any pair of siblings I'd ever met, and they'd cared for one another so much. She'd actually introduced us to one another during college. They'd known each other since the fifth grade and were the best of friends. I hadn't really seen her eyes grow sad since he'd passed away, but I was almost certain that they did often. I was probably living in my own world of despair, missing the fact that my best friend had also lost her best nonrelated brother. She cleared her throat, giving me a tight smile. "My shit was small, Liz. Yours wasn't."

She pushed up into the air. "Well, I want you to always feel like you can tell me everything, Faye. I want to know all about the wild old man sexcapades you're having. Plus, there's nothing about your life that's small. I mean, for the love of God, look at your boobs."

She laughed wildly, tossing her head back. When Faye laughed, the whole universe felt her happiness. "I know! These tits are no joke."

"We should probably get you back to work before you're fired," I suggested.

"If he fired me, he would be hiring blue balls into his life."

"Faye." I blushed, looking around at all the people staring our way. "You need a filter."

"Filters are for cigarettes, not for humans, Liz," she joked. We started walking back toward the café, her arm linked with mine, our footsteps matching each other's. "I'm happy you're kind of back, Liz," Faye whispered, laying her head on my shoulder.

"Kind of back? What do you mean? I'm here, I'm back."

She looked up at me with a knowing smile. "Not yet. But soon enough, you'll get there, babycakes."

The way she could see my hurt under the surface was remarkable. I pulled her closer to me, certain I wouldn't let her go anytime soon.

CHAPTER 5
Elizabeth

L iz, you have some nerve leaving like you and Emma did without even giving me a call!" Mama scolded me through the telephone. Emma and I had been back in our house for two days and Mama was just now calling me. It was either because she was upset with me for only leaving her a note, or because she'd been off running around town with some stranger and had just now returned home after all that time.

I was leaning toward the second option.

"I'm sorry, but you knew we were planning on leaving… We needed a new start," I tried to explain.

"A *new* start in your *old* house? That doesn't make much sense."

I didn't expect her to understand, so I changed the subject. "How was dinner with Roger?"

"Richard," she scolded. "Don't pretend like you don't remember his name. And it was amazing. I think he could be the one."

I rolled my eyes. Each guy she saw was the one—until they weren't.

"Are you rolling your eyes at me?" Mama asked.

"No."

"You are, aren't you?! You're so disrespectful sometimes."

"Mama, I need to get to work," I lied. "Is it okay if I call you back later?"

Maybe tomorrow.

Maybe next week.

I just need space.

"Fine. But don't forget who was there for you when you had no one, baby girl. Sure, Steven's parents are probably helping you now, but there's going to come a point when you realize who your real family is, and who it isn't."

I'd never been so thankful to end a phone call.

Sometimes I stood in the backyard and stared out into the wild bushes and tall grass, trying to remember what it had used to look like. Steven had made the place beautiful. He'd always had an eye for details when it came to landscaping, and I could almost imagine the smell of the flowers he'd planted, which were now all dead.

"Close your eyes," Steven whispered, walking up to me with his hands behind his back. I did as he said. "Name this flower," he said. The smell hit my nose and I smiled.

"Hyacinth."

I smiled wider when I felt his lips kiss mine. "Hyacinth," he echoed. My eyes opened. He placed the flower behind my ear. "I was thinking of planting a few by the pond in the backyard."

"It's my favorite flower," I said.

"You're my favorite girl," he replied.

I blinked, and I was back, missing the smells of the past.

My eyes shifted to my neighbor's house, whose lawn was even worse off than mine. The house was made of reddish-brown bricks and had ropes of ivory wrapping around each side. Their grass was ten times longer than mine, and on the back porch I saw a garden gnome that was shattered into pieces. A plastic yellow kid's baseball bat was hidden in the ever-growing strands of grass, along with a toy dinosaur.

A small table saw was set up by the shed, its red paint peeling. Stacks of wood were leaning up against the shed, and I wondered if anyone actually lived in the house at all.

It seemed more abandoned than ever, and I couldn't help but wonder about the mindset of my neighbor.

Behind all the houses on our block was the beginning of Meadows Creek's forest. The area was surrounded with trees. I knew deep within those trees there was a narrow river hidden in the darkened woods that ran for miles and miles. Most people didn't know it actually existed, but when I was in college, I'd discovered it with Steven. In the narrow river was a tiny rock. On the tiny rock were the initials ST and EB. Those initials had been carved into the tiny rock resting in the narrow river in the darkened woods when Steven had asked me to marry him. Without much thought, I found myself walking into the woods, and before long I sat within the trees, staring down at my reflection in the water.

One breath.

The small fish swam downstream peacefully until the water began to ripple from a big splash. I turned my head to my left to see what the commotion was, and my cheeks blushed as I saw Tristan standing in the river wearing no shirt and a pair of running shorts. He bent down to the water and began washing his face, scrubbing his fingers against his rough, wild beard. My eyes danced across his tanned chest, which was covered with hair, and he began tossing water against his body, cleaning himself. Tattoos covered his left arm and wrapped across his pec. I studied the markings on his body, unable to look away. There were more than I could count, yet my eyes tried to take in each one. *I know those tattoos.* Each a different masterpiece from classic children novels. Aslan from *Narnia*. A monster from *Where the Wild Things Are*. The boxcar from *The Boxcar Children*. Across his chest were the words "We're all mad here" from *Alice's Adventures in Wonderland*.

My insides exploded from the brilliance of it all. There was nothing more stunning than a man who not only knew the most classic stories of all time but also found a way to make his body his own personal bookshelf.

Water from his wet hair dripped down his forehead and fell to his chest. All of a sudden I was frozen in place. I wondered if he knew how handsome yet frightening he was. My thoughts very much matched those old Tootsie Roll Pop commercials as I gazed at his body. *"Mister Owl, how long can I stare at this man before it becomes socially inappropriate?" "I don't know, Liz. Let's find out. One...Two...Three..."*

He hadn't taken notice of me, and my heart was pounding against my rib cage as I stepped away from the river, hoping to not be seen.

Zeus was tied up to a tree, and when he saw me, he instantly started barking.

Shoot!

Tristan looked up toward me, his eyes as untamed as before. His body froze, water dripping from his chest down to the edge of his shorts. I stared for a moment too long, then realized I was staring straight at his package. My eyes shifted back up to his wild stare. He hadn't moved an inch. Zeus kept barking and wagging his tail, trying to break away from the tree.

"Following me?" he asked. His words were short, not leaving much room for a conversation, very straight to the point.

"What? No."

He arched an eyebrow.

I kept staring at his tattoos. *Oh, Dr. Seuss's Green Eggs and Ham.* He noticed my staring.

Crap. Stop, Liz.

"Sorry," I muttered, my face heating up from nerves. What was he doing out there?

He arched his other brow and didn't blink once as he looked my way. Even though he could speak, it seemed he found it much more fun to make me uncomfortable and anxious. He was hard to look at because he was so broken, but every scarred part of his existence seemed to draw me in.

I watched his every move as he untangled Zeus's leash from the tree and headed in the direction I'd just come from. I started behind him to get back to my house.

He paused.

A slow turn in my direction.

"Stop following me," he hissed.

"I'm not."

"You are."

"Not."

"Are."

"Not not not!"

He cocked his brow again. "You're like a five-year-old." He turned back around and kept walking. I started my steps up too. Every now and then he would glance back and grunt, but we didn't speak another word. When we reached the edge of the woods, he and Zeus walked up to the wild yard beside my house.

"I guess we're neighbors," I said with a chuckle.

The way he glared at me made my stomach flip. There was a high level of discomfort in my chest, yet behind it was still that familiar ting in my gut that arrived when he looked me in the eyes.

We both walked into our houses without a goodbye.

I ate dinner alone at the dining-room table. When I looked across the room, through my dining-room windows, I saw Tristan sitting at his table eating too. His house seemed so dark and empty. Lonely. When he looked across and saw me, I straightened up. I gave him a simple smile and a small wave. He stood from his chair, walked over to his windows, and closed his blinds.

It didn't take long for me to realize that our bedroom windows were also right across from one another, and he was quick to shut those curtains too.

I called to check in on Emma, who from the sound of it was hyped up on candy and grandparents time. Around eight o'clock I was sitting on the living-room sofa, staring into space, trying not to cry when Faye texted me.

Faye: You okay?

Me: I'm fine.

Faye: Interested in company?

Me: Not tonight. Tired.

Faye: Interested in company?

Me: Sleeping...

Faye: Interested in company?

Me: Tomorrow.

Faye: Love you, tits.

Me: Love you, boobs.

The pounding on the front door that followed after our last

message wasn't that surprising. I figured there was no way Faye wouldn't stop by because she knew when I said I was okay, I was normally far from being okay. What was surprising was when I opened the front door to see a slew of people. *Friends.* The leader of the pack was Faye, holding the biggest bottle of tequila known to mankind.

"Interested in company?" She grinned.

I stared down at my pajamas and then glanced once more at the tequila. "Absolutely."

"I really thought you would've slammed the door in all of our faces," a familiar voice said from behind me as I stood in the kitchen, pouring out four shots. I turned to see Tanner staring my way, and I leaped into his arms for a tight hug. "Hey, Liz," he whispered, pulling me into a tighter grip.

Tanner was Steven's best friend, and for a long time they'd had the kind of bromance that made me think my husband might leave me for a man. Tanner was a built guy with dark, dark eyes and blond hair. He worked at the auto shop he'd taken over after his dad became sick. He and Steven became best buddies when they were paired as roommates their freshman year of college. Even though Tanner stopped going to school after the first year in order to work for his dad, he and Steven stayed close.

Tanner gave me his friendly smirk and let me go. He lifted two of the shots I poured. He handed one to me, and we downed them together. Then he lifted the other two, and we downed those also. I smiled. "You know, all four of those were for me."

"I know. Just saving your liver a little." I watched as he reached into his pocket, pulling out a quarter. The same quarter he would always flip between his fingers nonstop. It was a weird habit that he'd been doing way before we even met.

"I see you still have that coin of yours." I laughed.

"Never leave home without it," he replied with a chuckle before placing it back into his pocket.

I studied his face, concern filling me up inside. He probably didn't know it, but sometimes his eyes looked so sad. "How are you?"

His shoulders rose and fell. "It's just nice to see your face again. It's been a while, buddy. Plus, you kind of just vanished after..." His words faded off. Everyone's words always faded off when they were about to mention Steven's death. I thought that was a good thing.

"I'm back." I nodded and poured us four more shots. "Emma and I are here to stay. We just needed a bit of air, that's all."

"You still driving that piece-of-shit car?" he asked.

"I definitely am." I bit my bottom lip. "I hit a dog the other day."

His mouth dropped open. "No!"

"Yup. The dog's okay, but my crappy car hiccupped and ran into the thing."

"I'll check it out for you," he offered.

I shrugged. "It's okay. I can pretty much walk everywhere now that I'm in town. No big deal."

"It will be a big deal when winter comes along."

"Don't worry, Tanner Michael Chase, it will be all right."

A smirk found his lips. "You know I hate when you use my full name."

I laughed. "That's exactly why I do it."

"Well, we should make a toast," Tanner offered. Faye came crashing into the room and lifted one of the shots high.

"I'm all about toasts when tequila is involved." She giggled. "Or vodka, whiskey, rum, rubbing alcohol..."

I laughed, and the three of us held the shot glasses in the air. Tanner cleared his throat. "To old friends making new beginnings. We missed you and Emma, Liz, and we are so damn happy to have you back. May the next few months be easy on you, and may you remember that you're never alone."

With one swift movement, we downed the shots.

"So, random question. I want to change all the locks in the place just for a new start. Do you know anyone who can do that?"

"Definitely, Sam can."

"Sam?"

"You know the guy I fired so I could hire you? The socially awkward kid at the café? His dad has a shop that Sam works at part-time for that kind of stuff."

"Seriously? You think he'll help me out?"

"Of course. I'll tell him he has to, or else I'll fire him." Faye winked. "He's weird as all get-out, but he's good at his job and quick."

"Since when do you like quick guys?" I joked.

"Sometimes a girl just needs a dick, a beer, and reality television all within thirty minutes. Never underestimate the power of a quickie." Faye poured herself another shot and danced away.

"Your best friend might be the first woman I've ever met who actually thinks like a man," Tanner joked.

"Did you know that she and Matty are—"

"Fucking? Absolutely. After you left, she needed a girlfriend to complain to in person, and somehow she decided I looked like I had a vagina. She showed up at the auto shop every day with a story about Fatty Matty—which, by the way, made me extremely uncomfortable."

I giggled. "You mean you aren't interested in her nicknames for her sexlationships?"

He leaned in. "Flakey Frankie? Is that a real thing?"

"Faye's far from a liar."

"Well, that's unfortunate for poor Frankie." I smiled, maybe because of the alcohol, maybe because Tanner reminded me of some of the best memories. He leaped onto the countertop and patted a spot beside him, which I accepted. "So, how's Miss Emma doing?"

"Sassy as ever." I sighed, thinking of my baby.

"Just like her mother." He laughed.

I lightly shoved him in his shoulder. "I still think she received the loud sass from her father."

"True, he was quite the handful. Remember when we went out for Halloween and Steven thought he could fight anyone because he was dressed as a ninja? He kept yelling at anyone and everyone he came across, but instead of being an awesome real-life ninja, he ended up with a black eye and got us kicked out of three bars." We laughed together, remembering how much of a terrible drunk my husband had been.

"If I remember correctly, you weren't the best influence on him. You always drank a bit too much and became the jerk that egged on the people who always ended up beating up my husband."

"Truth. I'm not the nicest person when I have one too many drinks, but Steven understood that. Damn. I miss the asshole." He sighed. We stopped laughing, my eyes growing heavy. His eyes grew heavy too, and we sat silent, missing him together.

"Well," Tanner said, changing the subject. "The landscape around this place looks like complete shit. I can come by and cut the grass for you if you want. And maybe toss up the fence to keep the place a bit more private."

"Oh, no. Actually, I think I'm going to take care of it all. I'm only working part-time, so it will give me something to do until I find more steady work."

"Have you thought about getting back into interior design?"

The question of the week. I shrugged. "I haven't really thought much about anything for the past year."

"Completely understandable. Are you sure you don't want a hand around this place? It's no big deal for me to help you out."

"Yeah, I'm sure. There comes a point when I have to start doing things for myself, you know?"

"I hear ya. But I think you should stop by my shop on Sunday. I have something I want to give you."

I smiled. "A gift?"

"Something like that."

Nudging him in the shoulder, I told him we could meet up on Sunday morning if Emma could join us.

He nodded, then lowered his voice, staring my way. "What's the hardest part?"

That was a very easy question for me to answer. "There are times when Emma does the funniest thing, and I'll call into the other room for Steven to come see her. Then I pause and remember." The hardest part about losing someone you loved was the fact that you also lost yourself. I placed my thumb between my teeth and chewed on my nail. "Enough depressing stuff. What about you? Still dating Patty?"

He cringed. "We don't really talk anymore."

I wasn't surprised. Tanner was as into commitment as Faye was.

"Well, aren't we just two sad, single peas in a pod."

With a laugh, he lifted the bottle of tequila, pouring us another shot. "Here's to us."

The rest of the night kind of faded together. I remembered

laughing at things that probably weren't funny, crying over things that weren't even sad, and having the best night I'd had in quite some time. When I woke up the next morning, I was lying in my bed, not exactly sure how I got there. I hadn't slept in the bed since the accident. I reached for Steven's pillow and hugged it to my body. With a deep inhale of the cotton pillowcase, my eyes fluttered closed. Even if I didn't feel it yet, there was no denying the fact that this was home. This was my new normal.

CHAPTER 6
Elizabeth

Sam stopped by to change out the locks around the house later that week. I knew Faye called him creepy, but there was something so easy and friendly about him. He had blond hair that he spiked and rectangle glasses that somewhat hid his sweet, brown stare. His voice was always low when he spoke to me, and so sweet. If he thought he offended me—which he never did—he always kind of backtracked and apologized with a bit of a stutter.

"Some of these locks are extremely crappy, but others are in pretty great shape, actually, Elizabeth. Are you sure you want to change them all up?" he asked. "Sorry, that was a stupid question. You wouldn't have asked me here if you didn't need them changed. So sorry," he apologized.

"No, it's fine." I smiled. "I just want a completely new start, that's all."

He pushed his glasses up his nose and nodded. "Of course. Well, I can be done here in a few hours or so."

"Perfect."

"Oh! Also, let me show you something." He ran to his car and came back with a tiny thing in his hand. "My dad also just got a new security camera bundle deal if you're interested. The cameras are this small and could easily be hidden. A few cameras could go up around the place for extra security. I know if I were a pretty woman living alone with my daughter, I would want the extra protection."

I smiled, this time warily. "I think I'll hold off on that for a while. Thanks again, Sam."

"No problem at all." He laughed. "The only person to buy these so far was Tanner, so I doubt they will be big sellers like my dad hoped for."

He worked fast and was good at what he did. Before I knew it, all of the locks in the house were brand-spanking-new. "Anything else I can help ya with?" he asked.

"Nope! That's it. I better get going actually. I have to be at the café in about ten minutes, and my car pretty much gave up on life, so I have to walk there."

"No way. I'll give you a ride."

"No, no. I can walk."

"It's already starting to drizzle with rain. You don't want to get caught in that. It's really no big deal."

My nose scrunched up. "Are you sure?"

"Of course." He held the passenger door of his truck open. "No problem at all."

As we drove into town, Sam asked me why I thought Faye didn't like him, but I tried my best to explain that Faye hardly liked anyone at first. "Give her some time, you'll grow on her."

"She said I have all the characteristics of a psychopath," he joked.

"Yeah. She's a bitch like that."

"And your best friend."

I smirked. "The best friend I've ever had."

The rest of the way into town, Sam pointed out everyone we saw, telling me anything and everything he knew about them. He told me since most people thought he was weird, they ignored him, but that made it easy for him to eavesdrop on all the gossip around the town. "That right there is Lucy," Sam said, pointing toward a girl on her cell phone. "She's the best speller in town. Even won the annual spelling bee contest every year for the past five years. And over there is Monica. Her pops is a recovering alcoholic, but between you and me, I know he drinks out by Bonnie Deen's house on Friday nights. And over there is Jason. He kicked my ass a few months ago because he thought I called him somethin' I didn't call him. He apologized, though, saying he was on some bad drugs."

"Wow, you really do know everything about everyone."

He nodded. "You'll have to let me take you out some time to a town meeting or something. Then I can show you the craziness that happens around this place."

I smiled. "That would be awesome." As we pulled up to the café, my gut tightened as I stared across the street. "What about him?" I asked, seeing Tristan running down the street with his headphones on. When he reached Mr. Henson's store, he took off his headphones and stepped inside. "What's his story?"

"You mean Tristan? He's an asshole. And a bit crazy too."

"Crazy?"

"Well, he works for Mr. Henson. You have to be a bit of a nutjob to deal with him. Mr. Henson practices voodoo and stuff in his back room. It's freaky. It's a good thing Tanner has been trying to get the shop shut down."

"What?"

"You didn't hear? Tanner wants to expand his auto shop, and Mr. Henson's store is the only thing keeping him from doing so. He's been trying to start protests to get Mr. Henson to give up his store. He says it's a waste of space since nobody ever goes into the place."

I couldn't help but wonder what the story behind Mr. Henson's store truly was, and I couldn't help but wonder why Tristan found himself working there.

During my shift, every now and then I glanced across the street at Mr. Henson's shop where Tristan was moving things around. The store was packed with all kinds of magical things. Crystals, tarot cards, wands…

"Do you have a vibrator?"

As the words left my best friend's mouth, I was snapped from my mental wandering. I almost dropped the three plates of burgers and fries I was trying to balance. "Faye!" I whisper-shouted, my cheeks turning red instantly.

She glanced around the café, shocked by my response to her not-so-appropriate question. "What? You act as if I just asked if you had herpes. Vibrators are a normal thing nowadays, Liz, and I was just thinking the other day about your poor, dry, grandma vagina."

My face was on fire. "How thoughtful of you." I laughed, setting the plates in front of three elderly ladies who were giving me the rudest looks of distaste. "Anything else I can get you?" I asked.

"Maybe your friend could use a filter."

"Trust me, I've tried." I smiled and walked over to Faye, begging her to keep the vagina talk on the quiet side.

"Listen, Liz, all I'm saying is it's been a long time since you had any action. What is it like down there? Is it kind of like *George of the*

Jungle meets *The Golden Girls*? Is there more hair down below than up here?" she asked, tapping my head.

"I'm not answering that." She reached into her apron pocket and pulled out her little black book, which had always brought about trouble in the past. "What are you doing?" I asked warily.

"I'm finding a penis to help you tonight."

"Faye. I don't think I'm ready for that kind of emotional connection with someone."

"What the hell does sex have to do with emotions?" she wondered, completely serious. I didn't even know how to tackle that question. "Anyway, I know this guy who can help you clean up your garden of weeds. His name is Edward. He's a creative genius when it comes to that stuff. Once, he drew hearts down there on me for Valentine's."

"You're so disturbing."

She smiled. "I know. But I can set up an appointment with Edward Scissorhands for you, and then you can pick any guy in my book to have a nice, easy one-night stand with."

"I don't do one-night stands."

"Okay. You can lie down to do it if you want." She winked. "But seriously, Liz. Have you thought about dating? Just getting out there around a few guys. It doesn't have to be anything serious, but I think it could be good for you. I don't want you to stay stuck in neutral."

"I'm not stuck in neutral," I argued, slightly offended. "It's just—I have a daughter. And it's only been a year since Steven's death."

Wow.

I was somewhat impressed by how it had rolled off my tongue without any backlash of emotion.

"I didn't mean it in a harsh way. You know I love you, and you know how much Steven meant to me."

"I know…"

"Look, I'm a woman-whore, but even woman-whores get their hearts broken sometimes, and for me, when things are hard to move on from, sex always helps."

I laughed. "I don't think I'm ready for that just yet, but I'll keep it in mind."

"I understand, sweetie. But if there comes a point when you feel as if you need my little book, you just let me know."

I smiled. "Your book seems so small now. I could've sworn it was bigger before."

Her hand dove into her apron again, and she pulled out two more books. "Don't be silly. I was just trying to seem ladylike by only displaying one at a time."

During my break, curiosity got the best of me, and I found myself stepping foot in Mr. Henson's shop. Within a few seconds, it was easy to tell that Mr. Henson pretty much sold anything and everything magical. Half of the store was a coffee shop while the other half was set up like a closet that was filled with things I'd seen in many supernatural stories.

As I entered, the bell dinged above the door, causing Mr. Henson and Tristan to look at one another with confusion in their eyes. When they turned my way, I tried my best to act normal as I explored the store, even though I could still feel their eyes on me.

I paused for one moment, reaching to the top shelf of one of the bookcases for a book. A book of spells? *Okay then.* The binding was tied together with string, and it was covered in dust. I picked up another book. Both pieces looked older than dirt but still somewhat beautiful. Dad had always loved finding old gems like those in vintage shops. He'd had a huge collection of old books in his study that were in different languages or on subjects he hadn't any idea about, but he just loved how the covers felt and looked.

"How much for these two?" I asked Mr. Henson. He remained silent. I arched an eyebrow. "I'm sorry. Are you closed?" When my stare met Tristan's, I held the books to my chest and my cheeks blushed over. "Hi."

Mr. Henson cut in to the conversation, which was probably for the best.

"Oh! No, no. We're open. We just don't get that many visitors. Especially visitors as easy to look at as you are," Mr. Henson said, sitting down on the edge of the countertop. "What's your name, darling?" His comment broke my stare away from Tristan, and I cleared my throat, somewhat pleased by the distraction.

"Elizabeth. And you?"

"I'm Mr. Henson. And if I weren't four hundred times your senior and very engrossed in the male anatomy, I might think about taking you out dancing at the old barn house."

"Dancing? What makes you think a girl like me would be interested in dancing?"

Mr. Henson kept the look of pleasure on his face and didn't answer. I walked over and sat beside him. "This is your store?"

"It is. Every inch, every square. Unless you want it." Mr. Henson laughed. "Because if you want it, then it's yours. Every inch, every square."

"That's very tempting. But I have to say, I have read every Stephen King book ever published five times over, and the idea of taking on a store called Needful Things is a bit alarming."

"Between you and me, I thought about calling it Answered Prayers, but I'm not much of a religious guy."

I snickered. Tristan did too.

I looked over at him, pleased that we were laughing at the same time, so he stopped.

My eyes fell to the books. "Is it okay if I take these off your hands?"

"They're yours, free of charge."

"Oh, no… I want to pay."

Going back and forth, the two of us argued about me taking the books for free, but I wouldn't let up. Mr. Henson ultimately folded.

"And this is why I stick to my men. Women are too much like me. Come back in another day and I'll give you a free tarot reading."

I smiled. "That sounds like fun."

He stood up and walked toward the storage room. "Tristan, ring her up, will you?" He turned to me and gave a slight nod before he disappeared into the back.

Tristan went to the cash register, and I followed.

I slowly laid the books on the counter. My eyes moved to the tan-and-black photos of the forest framed against the wall behind me. "Beautiful," I said, staring at the pictures.

Tristan punched in made-up numbers for the books. "Thanks."

"You took these?"

"No," he said, glancing at the pictures. "I carved them out of wood, then added the black ink."

My mouth hung open in disbelief, and I moved closer. The closer I looked, the more I could tell that the "photos" were actually wood carvings.

"*Beautiful*," I muttered again. When my eyes locked with his, my stomach twisted with nerves. "Hi," I repeated, this time with a sigh. "How are you?"

He rang my items up, ignoring my question. "Are you going to fucking pay or what?"

I frowned, but he didn't seem to care. "I'm sorry. Yes. Here you go," I said, handing him the money. I thanked him, and before I walked out of the store, I looked at him once more. "You act like such a jerk all the time, and the town only knows you as this callous man, but I saw you in the waiting room when you found out that Zeus was going to be okay. I saw you break down. I know you're not a monster, Tristan. I just don't understand why you pretend to be."

"That's your biggest mistake."

"What is?" I asked.

"Pretending for a second that you know any damn thing about me."

CHAPTER 7
Tristan

APRIL 2ND, 2014
FIVE DAYS UNTIL GOODBYE

*W*hen the taxi dropped Dad and me off at the hospital, I ran all the way to the emergency room. My eyes darted around the space, searching for something, someone familiar. "Mom," I shouted in the waiting room, making her look up. I took off my baseball cap and hurried toward her.

"Oh, honey," she cried, rushing to wrap her arms around me.

"How are they? How are...?"

Mom started sobbing harder, her body trembling. "Jamie...Jamie's gone, Tristan. She was holding on for so long, but it was too much."

I pulled away and pinched the bridge of my nose. "What do you mean gone? She's not gone. She's fine." My eyes moved to Dad, who was shocked. Confused. Hurt. "Dad, tell her. Tell her that Jamie is fine."

He lowered his head.

My insides were set on fire.

"*Charlie?*" *I asked, almost sure I didn't want to know the answer.*

"*He's in intensive care. He's not doing great, but he's—*"

"*Here. He's here.*" *I ran my fingers through my hair. He was okay.* "*Can I see him?*" *I asked. She nodded. I hurried over to the nurses' station and they took me to Charlie's room. My hand wrapped around my mouth as I stared at my little boy, hooked up to more machines than I'd ever thought possible. A tube was down his throat, IVs ran through his arms, and his face was bruised and battered.* "*Jesus...*" *I muttered.*

The nurse gave me a wary smile. "*You can hold his hand.*"

"*Why the tube? W-w-why is there a tube down his throat?*" *I stuttered, my mind trying to stay with Charlie, but the truth of Jamie was slowly creeping in. Jamie's gone, Mom said. She was gone. But how? How could she be gone?*

"*During the car accident, his left lung collapsed, and he's been having a hard time taking in air and breathing. It's to help him breathe.*"

"*He's not breathing on his own?*"

She shook her head.

"*Will he be okay?*" *I asked, staring into the nurse's eyes and seeing her guilt.*

"*I'm not his doctor. Only they can—*"

"*But you can tell me, can't you? If you were me, and you'd just lost your wife—*" *The words forced emotion out of me, and I choked it back down.* "*If that little boy was all you had, and you were all he had left, you would want to know how much hope there was, right? You would beg for someone to tell you what to do. How to act. What would you do?*"

"*Sir—*"

"*Please,*" *I begged.* "*Please.*"

Her eyes faltered to the ground before she met my stare. "*I would hold his hand.*"

I nodded once, knowing she had just told me more truth than I was ready to hear. I walked over to the chair beside Charlie's bed and took his hand in mine. "Hey, buddy. It's Dad. I'm here, okay? I know I haven't been around as much as I should've been, but I'm here now, okay? Dad's here, and I need you to fight for me. Can you do that, buddy?" Tears rolled from my eyes onto his cheeks as my lips rested against his forehead. "Daddy needs you to work on your breathing. We gotta get you better because I need you. I know people say that the kid needs the parent, but that's a lie.

"I need you to keep me going. I need you to keep me believing in the world. Buddy, I need you to wake up. I can't lose you too, okay? I need you to come back to me... Please, Charlie... Come back to Dad."

His chest rose high and when he tried to exhale, the machines started beeping rapidly. The doctors came rushing in, and they pulled my hand away from Charlie, who was shaking uncontrollably. They all began shouting at each other, saying words I didn't understand, doing things I couldn't comprehend.

"What's happening?!" I shouted, but no one heard me. "What's going on?! Charlie!" I yelled as two nurses tried to pull me out of the room. "What are they doing? What's... Charlie!" I said, louder and louder, as they pushed me from the room. "CHARLIE!"

Late Friday night, I sat at my dining-room table and dialed a number that had previously been so familiar to me but hadn't been used as much in recent days. As it rang, I held the phone to my ear. "Hello?" the voice said, smooth and soft. "Tristan, is that you?" The alertness in her sounds made my stomach twist. "Son, please say something," she whispered.

I pounded my fist against my mouth, but I didn't reply.

I hung up the phone. I always hung up. I sat alone in the darkness for the rest of the night, allowing it to swallow me whole.

CHAPTER 8
Elizabeth

Saturday morning, I was certain I was seconds away from waking up the whole neighborhood as I tried to start the lawnmower, which kept backfiring every few seconds. Steven had always made it look so easy when he handled the lawn work, but I wasn't having the same luck.

"Come on." I yanked the chain to start the engine one more time, and after a few sputters, it went ahead and died. "Jesus Christ!" I kept trying over and over again, my cheeks blushing over when a few neighbors from across the street started staring at me from their homes.

When a hand landed against mine as I was about to yank the chain yet again, I jumped in fright.

"Stop," Tristan scolded me, his brows narrowed and his eyes filled with irritation. "What the hell are you doing?"

I frowned, staring at his tight lips. "Mowing my lawn."

"You're not mowing your lawn."

"Yes I am."

"No, you're not."

"Then what am I doing?" I asked.

"Waking up the whole fucking world," he grumbled.

"I'm sure people were already awake in England."

"Just stop talking." *Hmm*. It seemed he wasn't a morning, after-noon, or night kind of person, so he had that going for him. He pushed the lawnmower away from me.

"What are you doing?" I asked.

"Cutting your grass so you will stop waking up the whole fucking world, minus England."

I didn't know if I should laugh or cry. "You can't cut the lawn. Besides, I think it's broken." Within a couple seconds after he yanked the cord, the lawnmower started up. *Well, this is embarrassing.* "Seriously, though. You can't cut my grass."

He didn't turn back once to look at me. He just went to complete his job—the same job I'd never asked him to do. I was seconds away from continuing arguing with him, but then I remembered how he'd killed a cat for meowing wrong, and well, I liked my sad little life enough and didn't want to risk dying.

"You did a great job with the lawn," I said, watching Tristan shut off the lawnmower. "My husband…" I paused, taking a breath. "My late hus-band used to cut the grass in diagonals. And he would say, 'Babe, I'm raking up the grass clippings tomorrow. I'm too tired now.'" I chuckled to myself, looking at Tristan, but not really seeing anything anymore. "The clippings would stay there for at least a week, maybe two, which is weird because he always handled others' lawns so much better. But still, I liked the clippings." My throat tightened and the burning of tears entered my eyes. I turned my back to Tristan and wiped away the few that fell. "Anyway, I like how you did diagonal lines." *Stupid memories.* I grabbed the white metal handle and opened the screen door, but my feet paused when I heard him.

"They sneak up on you like that and knock you backward," he whispered like an abandoned soul kissing their loved ones goodbye. His voice was smoother than before. It was still deep with a bit of gruff to it, but this time there was a slight bit of innocence that existed in his sounds. "The little memories."

I turned to face him, and he was leaning up against the lawnmower. His stare had more life to it than I'd ever witnessed, but it was a sad kind of life. Broken, stormy eyes. I inhaled just to keep from falling. "Sometimes I think the little memories are worse than the big ones. I can handle remembering his birthday or the day of his death, but remembering the little things like the way he cut the grass, or how he only read the comics in the newspaper, or how he only smoked one cigarette on New Year's Eve..."

"Or the way she tied her shoes, or puddle jumped, or touched the palm of my hand with her pointer finger and always drew a heart..."

"You lost someone too?"

"My wife."

Oh.

"And my son," he whispered, quieter than before.

My heart shattered for him. "I'm so sorry. I can't even imagine..." My words faded off as he stared at the newly cut grass. The idea of losing both the love of my life and my baby girl was too much; I would've given up.

"The way he said his prayers, the way he wrote his *R's* backward, the way he broke his toy cars just so he could fix them..." Tristan's voice was shaky, along with his body. He wasn't speaking to me anymore.

We were living in our own worlds of little memories, and even though we were both separate, somehow we managed to feel for one another. Lonely often recognized lonely. And today, for the first time, I began to see the man behind the beard.

I watched the poor soul's eyes swell with emotion as he placed his headphones on his ears. He began to rake up all the grass clippings, not speaking another word my way.

People in town called him an asshole, and I could see why. He wasn't nice, he wasn't stable, and he was broken in all of the wrong and right places, but I couldn't blame him for his coldness. Truth was I sort of envied Tristan's ability to escape reality, to shut himself off from the world around him. It must have been nice to feel empty every now and then—Lord knew I thought about losing myself daily, but I had Emma to keep me sane.

If I had lost her too, I would've been emptying my mind of all emotion, of all the hurt.

When he finished with his work, his feet stopped moving, but his chest kept rising and falling hard. He turned toward me, his eyes red, his thoughts probably scattered. His hand wiped against his brow and he cleared his throat. "Done."

"Do you want some breakfast?" I asked, standing. "I made enough for you."

He blinked once before he began to push the lawnmower back toward my porch. "No." He walked toward his porch, disappearing from my view. As I stood there alone, I closed my eyes, placed my hands over my heart, and for a small moment, I lost myself too.

CHAPTER 9
Elizabeth

The next morning, I knew I had to stop by Tanner's auto shop for the surprise he'd mentioned to me earlier that week. Emma, Bubba, and I skipped into town, her singing her own version of the *Frozen* soundtrack, me pulling out my eyelashes, and Bubba being a pleasantly silent stuffed animal.

"Uncle T!" Emma yelled, bum-rushing Tanner, whose head was under the hood of a car. Tanner turned around, his white shirt covered in oil stains and his face dressed with the same substance.

He lifted her in his arms and spun her around before pulling her into a close hug. "Hey, munchkin. What's that behind your ear?" he asked her.

"I don't have anything behind my ear!"

"Oh, but I think you're wrong." He pulled his faithful quarter from behind Emma's ear, making her laugh and laugh, which in turn made me smile. "How have you been?"

Emma smiled and went into a deep, thought-provoking story about how I let her dress herself that day, which ended with a purple tutu, rainbow socks, and a T-shirt with zombie penguins.

I smiled. Tanner stared her way as if truly interested in her story. After a few minutes, Tanner sent Emma off with a few dollar bills to go attack the candy machine with one of his workers, Gary. The whole way, I could hear Emma rehashing the story to poor Gary of how her outfit had come to life.

"She's cuter than I remember." Tanner smiled. "She has your smile."

I grinned and thanked him, even though her smile reminded me more of Steven.

"So, I have something for you. Come here." He led me to the back room where a sheet was covering a car. When he pulled it off, my legs almost buckled beneath me.

"How?" I asked, walking around the Jeep, running my fingers across it. Steven's Jeep looked newer than ever. "It was totaled."

"Ah, bumps and bruises can always be healed."

"This had to cost you a fortune."

He shrugged. "Steven was my best friend. You're one of my best friends. I just wanted you to have something familiar to come home to."

"You always knew I would come back?"

"We all hoped." Tanner bit his bottom lip as he stared at the Jeep. "I still can't stop blaming myself. The week before the accident, I begged him to stop into my shop so I could give the car a tune-up. He said he would be good for a few more months. I can't help but think that maybe I could've noticed something was wrong with the car if he stopped in to see me. If he had let me get under the hood, then maybe he would still..." He pinched the bridge of his nose and stopped talking.

"It wasn't your fault, Tanner."

He sniffled and gave me a tight smile. "Yeah, well. The thought just passes through my mind every now and then. Now come on, hop inside."

I stepped into the driver's seat and sat. My eyes closed, and I took a few deep breaths as I lay my hand across to the passenger seat, waiting for that touch, the warmth of another's hand to hold. *Don't cry. Don't cry. I'm good, I'm good.* Then I felt the hold from another, and when my eyes opened, I saw Emma's small hand sitting in mine, chocolate all over her face. She smiled wide, causing me to do the same.

"You okay, Mama?" she asked.

One breath.

"Yes, baby. I'm good."

Tanner walked over to me and placed the keys in my hand. "Welcome home, ladies. Remember, if you need me to help with the lawn and stuff, just give me a call."

"Tick already did it!" Emma exclaimed.

Tanner arched an eyebrow. "What?"

"I actually ended up hiring a guy to do it. Well, kind of. I owe him some kind of payment."

"What? Liz, I could've done it for free. Who did you hire?"

I knew he wouldn't like the answer. "His name is Tristan…"

"Tristan Cole?!" Tanner ran his fingers over his face, which was turning red. "Liz, he's an asshole."

"He's not." *Yeah, okay, he is.*

"Trust me, he is. He's a fucking nutjob too. Did you know he works for Mr. Henson? He's the freaking case study of insanity."

I didn't know why, but Tanner's words made me feel as if he were speaking about me. "That's really harsh, Tanner."

"He's insane. And Tristan is dangerous. Just…let me handle the work around the house. God. I hate that he lives next door to you."

"He did a great job. It's really not a big deal."

"It is. It's just, you're too trusting. You need to use your head a little more than your heart. You have to think." *Ouch.* "I don't like this at all, Liz. And I doubt Steven would've either."

"Yeah, well. He's not really around anymore," I hissed, feeling a bit embarrassed and a lot hurt. "I'm not an idiot, Tanner. And I can handle this. Just..." I paused, forcing out a smile. "Thank you for this. For the Jeep. You have no clue how much it means to me."

He must have seen through my fake smile because he placed a hand on my shoulder. "Sorry. I'm an asshole. I just worry. If anything happened to you..."

"I'm fine. We're safe. I swear."

"Okay. Well, get out of here before I say something else I'll regret." He smirked. "Emma, take care of your mama, all right?"

"Why? I'm the kid, not her," Emma sassed. I couldn't help but laugh because she was one hundred percent right.

CHAPTER 10
Elizabeth

Each Friday after I dropped Emma at her grandparents' house, I walked into town for the farmers' market. All of the townspeople came to the center of downtown Meadows Creek to sell and trade their products. The smells of the fresh breads, the displays of the flowers, and the small-town gossip always made the journey worth it.

Steven and I had always come to the market to check out the fresh flowers, so when Friday came around with the fresh roses, I always stood in the middle of it all, breathing in the memories and breathing out the hurt.

During my weekly trip to the farmers' market, I always noticed Tristan walking around. We hadn't spoken since he'd cut my grass, but I couldn't stop thinking about his sad eyes. I couldn't stop thinking about his wife and son. When had he lost them? And how? How long had Tristan been living his current nightmare?

I wanted to know more.

Sometimes, I would see him walk out to the shed in his backyard, and he would stay there for hours. The only time he came out was when he would cut wood with his table saw, and then he would go back inside and stay hidden.

Whenever he walked past me, my cheeks flushed and I'd turn away as if I hadn't seen him. Even though I had. I *always* saw him, and I wasn't exactly sure why.

Everyone told me he was callous, and I believed them. I'd seen the harsh realities that lived in Tristan. But I'd also seen another side of him that many didn't notice. I'd seen him fall apart when he learned that Zeus would be okay. I'd seen him slowly open up about the loss of his wife and son. I'd seen a gentle, broken side of Tristan that many seemed to miss.

Currently, in the middle of the farmers' market, I was so intrigued by another side of Tristan. Each week, he would walk around as if he didn't see anyone. He was focused on his mission, which was always to buy bags of groceries and fresh flowers. Then he would disappear up the hills, stopping by the bridge where he always handed all the groceries and flowers to a homeless man.

As he handed the bags off to the guy, I was only a few feet away from him because I was heading back to the house. As I approached him, I couldn't stop the smile that was overtaking me. He started walking in the direction of his house.

"Hey, Tristan."

He looked my way with a blank stare.

He continued walking.

It was as though we were back to day one. I hurried my footsteps to keep up with his long strides. "I just wanted to say I thought that was really nice. It's really sweet what you do for that man. I think it's really—"

He shot around and stepped toward me. His jaw clenched and he narrowed his eyes. "What the hell do you think you're doing?"

"What?" I stammered, confused by his tone.

He stepped closer. "You think I don't see the way you look at me?"

"What are you talking about?"

"I want to make something clear to you," he whispered harshly. Tristan blinked once before his stormy eyes reappeared. "I don't want to be involved with you in any way, shape, or form. Okay? I cut your fucking grass because you annoyed the living shit out of me. That's all. I want nothing to do with you again. So stop with the damn looks."

"You th—you think I'm hitting on you?!" I cried out as we reached the top of the hill. He cocked an eyebrow and gave me a hell-yes-I-think-you're-hitting-on-me look. "I thought it was nice, okay?! You give the guy food, you prick! And I wasn't trying to ask you out or hit on you. I was trying to have a conversation with you."

"Why would you want to have a conversation with me?"

"I don't know!" I said, my words somersaulting off my tongue. I was truly unsure why I would have wanted to be in a conversation with someone who was so hot and cold on a daily basis. One day he was opening up about his demons, and the next he was shouting at me for saying hello. *I can't win.* "Stupid me for thinking we could've been friends."

His eyebrows furrowed. "Why would I want to be your friend?"

A shiver ran across my body. I wasn't sure if it was due to the light breeze or due to Tristan intruding on my personal space.

"I don't know. Because you seem lonely and I'm lonely. And I thought—"

"You didn't think."

"Why are you so mean?"

"Why are you always watching me?"

My lips parted to speak, but no reply came to mind. We stared at each other, so close that our bodies were almost linked, so close that our lips were almost touching.

"Everyone in this town is afraid of me. Do I scare you, Elizabeth?" he whispered, his breaths brushing against my lips.

"No."

"Why not?"

"Because I see you."

The coldness in his stare softened for a split second, almost as if he was confused by those four words. But I did see him. I saw past the hate in his stare and noticed the hurt in his frown. I saw the broken parts that somehow matched my own.

Without thought, Tristan pulled me to his body, his lips pressing hard against mine. The confusion swimming around in my head began to fade as his tongue slipped between my lips and I kissed him back. I kissed him back, and maybe even kissed him more than he kissed me. God, I missed that. I missed kissing. The feeling of falling into someone who was holding you up from hitting rock bottom. The feeling of warmth washing against your skin as another person supplied you with your next few breaths.

I missed being held, I missed being touched, I missed being wanted…

I missed Steven.

Tristan's kisses were angry and sad, apologetic and agonizing, raw and authentic.

Just like mine.

My tongue slid across his bottom lip, and I pressed my hands against his chest, feeling his rapid heartbeat flying through my fingertips—flying into my own body.

For a few seconds, I felt like I had felt before.

Whole.

Complete.

A part of something divine.

Tristan hastily yanked his mouth away from mine and turned away, leading me back to my current, dark reality.

Broken.

Incomplete.

Lonely all the time.

"You don't know me, so stop acting like you do," he said. He started walking again, leaving me standing, perplexed.

What was that?!

"You felt it too, didn't you?" I asked, watching him walk away. "It felt like...it felt like they were still here. It felt like Steven was here. Did it feel like your wife—"

He turned with a fire burning in his stare. "Don't ever speak about my wife as if you know anything about her or me." He began to hurry away once again.

He felt it.

I knew he did.

"You can't...you can't just walk away, Tristan. We can talk to each other. About them. We can help each other remember." My biggest fear was the idea of forgetting.

He kept walking.

I hurried beside him once more. "Besides, that's the point of becoming someone's friend. To get to know them. To have someone to talk to." My chest was rapidly rising and falling as I became more and more upset with him for walking away in the midst of our conversation. In the midst of the most painful and satisfying kiss my lips had ever experienced. He was helping me remember what it had been like to feel happy, and I hated him for walking away. I hated him for taking that small moment of lust that faintly reminded me of the love that had been taken away from me. "God. Why do you have to be such a…such a…*monster*?!"

He turned to me, and a split second of misery tinged his eyes before his jaw and his facial expression hardened. "I don't want you, Elizabeth." He tossed his hands up in frustration and stepped toward me. "I don't want anything to do with you." He stepped closer. I stepped back. "I don't want to talk to you about your fucking dead husband." Another step closer. "I don't want to tell you shit about my dead wife." Step, step. Back, back. "I don't want to touch you." Closer. Backward. "I don't want to kiss you." Step. "I don't want to lick you." Back. Back. Step. Step. "And I damn sure don't want to be your fucking friend. So leave me alone and *just shut the hell up!*" he hollered, standing over me, his voice rocketing from his mouth like a clap of thunder, making me jump with fright.

As I took one final step backward, the heel of my shoe skidded over a rock, causing me to tumble down the hill. I felt every bump and thump through my body the whole way down.

Tristan was standing over me within an instant. "Shit," he muttered. "Are you okay? Here," he said, reaching his hand out to me.

I refused his offer and stood on my own. Minus a few bruises and a ton of embarrassment, I was fine. His eyes were filled with concerns, but I didn't care. They would probably be filled with hate within a moment's time.

Seconds before the fall, he had told me to shut up, so that was exactly what I'd do. I gave him exactly what he wanted. I limped back home in silence, not once looking his way, even though I could see his pathetic stare out of the corner of my eye.

"He pushed you down a hill?!" Faye shouted into the phone. The moment I'd returned from my interaction with Tristan, I'd called her. I needed my best friend to tell me that no matter what, I was right and Tristan was wrong.

Even if I had called him a monster.

"Well, not exactly. He yelled at me, and I kind of tripped."

"After he kissed you?"

"Yes."

"Ugh. I hate him. I hate him so much."

I nodded. "I hate him too."

That was a lie, but I couldn't tell her my true thoughts about Tristan. About how he and I had so much in common. I couldn't tell anyone. I hardly even told myself.

"But since we are on the subject, tell me..." Faye said, and I could almost see her grin through the phone. "Did he use tongue? Did he growl? Was he shirtless? Did he motorboat you? Did you touch his abs? Did you lick his sharp jaw? Is he the size of a horse? Did you giddy up? Did you find his Nemo? Did you Grace his Frankie? Did you Justin his Timberlake?"

"I can't handle you." I chuckled, but my mind was still thinking about the kiss and what it meant. Maybe it meant nothing. Or perhaps everything.

She sighed. "Come on, give me something. I'm currently trying to get laid here, and this phone call is killing my vibe."

"What do you mean you're trying to get laid?" I gasped. "Faye, are you having sex right now?"

"What do you mean? Like, sex-sex?"

"Yes, sex-sex!"

"Well, if you mean is there a penis currently sitting in my vagina, then yes. I guess you could semi call that sex."

"Oh my God, Faye! Why the hell would you answer the phone?!"

"Um, because chicks before dicks? Like, literally." She laughed. I gagged.

"Hi, Liz," I heard Matty call from the background. Gag again. "I put you on the work schedule for thirty hours next week."

"I'm hanging up."

"What? No. I have plenty of time right now."

"You're disturbing."

"Ow, stop, Matty. I told you not to bite that." Oh my fucking gosh, my best friend was a freak. "Okay, babycakes, I gotta get going. I think I'm bleeding. But as for you, at least find some time to meditate and clear your head."

"And by meditate you mean…?"

"Tequila. Top-shelf, burns in the belly, aids in bad decisions, tequila."

That sounded about right.

CHAPTER 11

Tristan

APRIL 3RD, 2014
FOUR DAYS UNTIL GOODBYE

I stood on my parents' back porch staring at the pouring rain hammering against the swing set Dad and I had built for Charlie. The tire swing swayed back and forth against the wooden frame.

"How are you holding up?" Dad asked, walking outside to join me. Zeus followed behind him and found a place to sit and stay dry in the corner. I turned to Dad and stared at a face that resembled mine in almost every way, except that there were a few more years of age and wisdom in his eyes.

I didn't reply to his question but turned back to the rain.

"Your mom said you were having trouble writing the obituaries?" he asked. "I can help."

"I don't need your help," I growled lightly, my fingers forming fists, my nails digging into my palms. I hated how angry I felt each passing day. I hated how I blamed the people around me for the accident. I *hated that I was becoming colder each passing moment. "I don't need anyone."*

"Son." He sighed, placing his hand on my shoulder.

I pulled away. "I just want to be alone."

His head lowered, and he ran his fingers across the back of his neck. "Okay. Mom and I will be inside." A second later he turned away and opened the screen door. "But, Tristan, just because you want to be alone, doesn't mean you are alone. Remember that. We are always here when you need us."

I listened to the screen door slam and huffed at his words.

We are always here when you need us.

The truth of the matter was "always" had an expiration date.

Reaching into my back pocket, I pulled out the piece of paper I'd spent the past three hours staring at. I'd finished Jamie's obituary early that morning, but Charlie's was still blank in my hand, with only his name attached to it.

How was I supposed to do it? How was I supposed to write his life story when his life hadn't even had a chance to begin?

The rain began to slam against the paper, and tears climbed into my eyes. I blinked a few times before shoving the paper back into my pocket.

I wouldn't cry.

Fuck the tears.

My feet led me down the steps of the porch, and within seconds I was soaked from head to toe, becoming a part of the dark storm that was brewing.

I needed air. I needed space. I needed to escape.

I needed to run.

I started running with no shoes, with no thought, and with no direction. Zeus began to run behind me. "Go home, Zeus!" I shouted toward the dog, who was just as soaking wet as I was. "Go away!" I hollered, wanting to be left alone. I ran faster, but he kept up. I pushed so much that my chest burned and breathing became a chore. I ran until my legs quit and my body fell to the ground. Lightning struck above us, painting the sky with its scars, and I began to sob uncontrollably.

I wanted to be alone, but Zeus was right there. He'd kept up with my crazed mind, he was right beside me when I hit rock bottom, and he wasn't going to leave me. He was in my face, giving me kisses, giving me love, giving me himself to hold when I needed someone the most.

"Okay." I sighed, tears still falling as I held him close to me. He whimpered, almost as if he too was heartbroken. "Okay," I said again, kissing the top of his head and rubbing his side.

Okay.

I loved to run barefoot.

Running was something I was good at.

I liked when my feet ran away.

I liked when they cracked and bled from the pressure they felt hammering against the concrete streets.

I liked when I was reminded of my sins through the pains of my body.

I love to hurt.

But only myself. I loved to hurt myself. No one else had to be hurt by me. I stayed away from people so I wouldn't hurt them.

I'd hurt Elizabeth, and I didn't want to.

I'm sorry.

How could I apologize? How could I fix it? How did one kiss make me remember?

She fell down the hill because of me. She could've broken bones. She could've cracked her head open. She could've died…

Dead.

Jamie.

Charlie.

I'm so sorry.

That night I ran more. I ran through the woods. Fast. Faster. Hard. Harder.

Go, Tris. Run.

My feet bled.

My heart cried, slamming against my rib cage over and over again, rocking my mind, poisoning my thoughts as buried memories began to resurface. She could've died. It would've been my fault. I would've caused it.

Charlie.

Jamie.

No.

I pushed them down.

I fell into the pain racing through my chest. The pain was nice. It was welcomed. I deserved to hurt. No one else, only me.

I'm so sorry, Elizabeth.

My feet hurt. My heart hurt. It all hurt.

The pain felt scary, dangerous, real; it felt good. It felt so damn good in such an ugly way. God, I loved it. I loved it so much. I fucking loved the hurt.

The night grew darker.

I sat in my shed, trying to figure out a way to apologize to her without her finding the need to be my friend. People like her didn't need people like me complicating their lives.

People like me didn't deserve friends.

Her kiss, though…

Her kiss made me remember. It had felt good to remember for a moment, but then I'd ruined it because that's what I did. I couldn't get the image of Elizabeth falling down the hill out of my mind. What the hell was wrong with me?

Maybe I always ended up hurting people.

Maybe that was why I'd lost everything I cared about.

But I was only trying to get her to stop talking to me so I could avoid her getting hurt.

I shouldn't have kissed her. But I wanted to kiss her. I needed to kiss her. I was selfish.

I didn't leave my shed until the moon was high above me. As I stepped out, I paused and listened to the sound of…giggling?

It was coming from the woods.

I should've left it alone. I should've minded my own business. But instead, I followed the sound to find Elizabeth stumbling through the woods, laughing to herself with her fingers wrapped around a bottle of tequila.

She was pretty. And by pretty, I meant the beautiful kind of pretty. The kind of beautiful-pretty that was effortless and didn't take much upkeep. Her blond hair had loose waves, and she wore a yellow dress that looked almost as if it were made only for her body. I hated that I thought she was the beautiful kind of pretty because my Jamie had been the same kind of beautiful-pretty too.

Elizabeth kind of danced as she stumbled. A drunken waltz of sorts.

"What are you doing?" I asked, grabbing her attention.

She waltzed my way, on her tiptoes, and placed her hands on my chest. "Hi, stormy eyes."

"Hi, brown eyes."

She laughed again, snorting this time. She was wasted. "Brown eyes. I like that." She bopped my nose. "Do you know how to be funny? You always seem so unfunny, but I bet you can be funny. Say something funny."

"Something funny."

She laughed, loud. Almost annoyingly so. But it wasn't. It wasn't annoying at all. "I like you. And I have no clue why, Mr. Scrooge. When you kissed me, it reminded me of my husband. Which is stupid because you're nothing like him. Steven was sweet, almost sickeningly so. He always took care of me, and held me, and loved me. And when he kissed me, he meant it. When he pulled away from kisses, he always moved in for another. And another, like he always wanted me against him. But you, stormy eyes...when you pulled away from the kiss, you looked at me as if I was disgusting. You made me want to cry. Because you're mean." She stumbled backward, almost falling to the ground until my arms wrapped around her waist, pulling her to a standing position. "Hmph. Well, at least you caught me this time." She smirked.

My gut twitched when I saw the bruise against her cheek and the cut from her fall earlier. "You're drunk."

"No. I'm happy. Can't you tell that I'm happy? I'm displaying all of the happy signals. I'm smiling. I'm laughing. I'm drinking and dancing merrily. Th-th-that's what happy people do, Tristan," she said, poking me in the chest. "Happy people dance."

"Is that so?"

"Y-y-yes. I wouldn't expect you to understand, but I'll try to explain." She kept slurring her words. She stepped back, took a swig from the tequila, and started to dance again. "Because when you're drunk and dancing, nothing else matters. You're twirling, twirling, twirling, and the air gets lighter, the sadness gets quieter, and you forget what it feels like to feel for a while."

"What happens when you stop?"

"Oh, see, that's the one tiny problem with dancing. Because when you stop moving"—her feet froze and she released the glass bottle from her hand, sending it crashing to the ground—"everything shatters."

"You're not as happy as you say you are," I said.

"That's only because I stopped dancing."

Tears fell from her eyes as she started lowering herself to the broken glass. I stepped in, stopping her. "I'll get it."

"Your feet are bleeding," she said. "Did the bottle cut you?"

I looked down at my feet, bruised and battered from my run. "No."

"Well then, you just have really unfortunate, ugly feet." I almost smiled. She definitely frowned. "I'm not feeling too good, stormy eyes."

"Yeah, well. You drank enough tequila for a small army. Come on, I'll get you some water." She nodded once before bending over and vomiting all over my feet. "Or, you know, just throw up on me."

She giggled as she wiped her hand against her mouth. "I think that's karma for you being rude to me. Now we're even."

Well, that seemed fair enough.

I carried her back to my house right after the vomit incident. After I washed my feet in the hottest water known to mankind, I found her sitting on my living-room couch, staring around at my place. Her eyes were still heavily drunk. "Your house is boring. And dirty. And dark."

"I'm glad you like what I've done with the place."

"You know, you could use my lawnmower for your yard," she

offered. "Unless you were going for the whole beast's-palace-before-he-met-beauty thing."

"I couldn't give two shits about my yard looking a certain way."

"Why's that?"

"Because unlike some, I could care less what my neighbors think of me."

She giggled. "That means you care what people think. What you meant was you *couldn't* care less what they thought."

"That's what I said."

She kept giggling. "That's not what you said."

God, you're annoying. And beautiful. "Well, I *couldn't* care less what people think of me."

She huffed. "Liar."

"That's not a lie."

"Yes, it is." She nodded before biting her bottom lip. "Because everyone cares what others think. Everyone cares about the opinion of others. That's why I haven't even been able to tell my best friend that I find my neighbor highly attractive, even though he's an asshole. Because widows aren't supposed to feel any kind of feelings for anyone anymore—you're just supposed to be sad all the time. But not *too* sad because that makes other people super uncomfortable. So the idea of kissing someone and feeling it between your thighs, and finding that the butterflies still exist…that's a problem. Because people would judge me. And I don't want to be judged because I care what they think."

I leaned in closer to her. "I say fuck it. If you think your neighbor Mr. Jenson is hot, so be it. I know he's like one hundred years old, but I've seen him do yoga in his front yard before, so I totally get your attraction to him. I think I've even had a tingling in between my legs for the dude."

She burst out in a fit of laughter. "He's not exactly the neighbor I was referring to."

I nodded. I knew.

Her legs crossed, and she sat up straight. "Do you have any wine?"

"Do I seem like the type to have wine?"

"No." She shook her head. "You seem like the type who drinks the darkest, thickest kind of beer that grows hair on your chest."

"Exactly."

"Okay. I'll take a hairy-chest beer, please," she said.

I walked out of the room and returned with a glass of water. "Here, drink up."

She reached for the glass, but her hand landed against my forearm, and she left it there as she studied my tattoos. "They're all children's books." Her fingernail traced *Charlotte's Web*. "Your son's favorites?"

I nodded.

"How old are you?" she asked.

"Thirty-three. You?"

"Twenty-eight. And how old was your son when he…?"

"Eight," I said coldly as her lips turned down.

"That's not fair. Life isn't fair."

"Nobody ever said it was."

"Yeah…but we still all hope it is." She kept her eyes on the tattoos, traveling up to Katniss Everdeen's bow and arrow. "Sometimes I hear you, you know. Sometimes I hear you shouting in your sleep at night."

"Sometimes I hear you cry."

"Can I tell you a secret?"

"Yes."

"Everyone in town expects me to be the same girl I was before

Steven died. But I don't know how to be that girl anymore. Death changes things."

"It changes everything."

"I'm sorry I called you a monster."

"It's okay."

"How? How is that okay?"

"Because that's how death changed me; it made me a monster."

She pulled me closer, making me kneel in front of her. Her fingers ran through my hair, and she stared deeply into my eyes. "You're probably going to be mean to me again tomorrow, aren't you?"

"Yes."

"I thought so."

"But I won't mean it."

"I thought that too." Her finger ran against my cheek. "You're beautiful. You're a beautiful, broken kind of monster."

My finger grazed against her bruised face. "Does it hurt?"

"I've felt worse pain."

"I'm so sorry, Elizabeth."

"My friends call me Liz, but you made it pretty clear that we are not friends."

"I don't know how to be a friend anymore," I whispered.

She closed her eyes and placed her forehead to mine. "I'm really good at being a friend. If you ever want me to, I can give you a few pointers." She sighed, lightly pressing her lips to my cheek. "Tristan."

"Yes?"

"You kissed me earlier."

"I did."

"But why?" she asked.

My fingers moved to the back of her neck, and I slowly pulled her closer to me. "Because you're beautiful. You're a beautiful, broken kind of woman."

She smiled wide, and her body shook slightly. "Tristan?"

"Yes?"

"I'm going to throw up again."

Her head had been in the toilet for over an hour now, and I stood behind her, holding her hair up. "Drink some water," I said, handing her the glass sitting on the sink.

She sat back and took a few sips. "Normally I'm better at this drinking thing."

"We've all had these kinds of nights."

"I just wanted to forget for a while. To let go of everything."

"Trust me," I said, sitting across from her. "I know what that's like. How are you feeling?"

"Dizzy. Silly. Stupid. Sorry about, you know, vomiting on your toes."

I felt the corner of my mouth turn up. "Karma, I guess."

"Was that a smile? Did Tristan Cole just smile at me?"

"Don't get used to it," I joked.

"Dang it. Too bad. It's kind of nice." She went to stand up, and I followed her movements. "Your smile was the highlight of my day."

"What was your dark moment of the day?" I asked.

"Your frown." She exhaled as her eyes locked with mine. "I should get going. But thank you for controlling my drunkenness."

"I'm sorry," I said with a thickness in my throat. "I'm sorry for making you fall earlier."

She pressed her fingers to her lips. "It's okay. I already forgave you."

She headed back toward her house, much more sober but still moving on her tiptoes. I made sure she made it inside the house before I headed to bed. When we both got to our bedrooms, we took a few moments to stand by our windows and stare at each other.

"You felt it, too, didn't you?" she whispered across to me, speaking of our kiss.

I didn't reply, but yeah.

I felt it.

CHAPTER 12
Elizabeth

That night after Tristan and I left our windowsills, I lay down in my bed, still a little tipsy, and I imagined him and his wife. I imagined what she'd been like. I wondered if she'd smelled like roses or lilies, I wondered if she'd been a cook or a baker, I wondered how much he loved her. I imagined her with him, and for a moment I even pretended that I heard her whisper she loved him against his thick beard. I felt his fingers pulling her closer, the gentle touch to her spine as she curved into his body, the way she called out his name.

Tristan...

My hand glided against my neck, and I pretended it was her neck he was touching. He warmed her up without saying a word; he loved her quietly with his hands. His fingers trailed down her neck, and she moaned as he reached the curves of her breasts. *Tristan...* My breaths picked up as I felt him taste her skin, his tongue gliding from his mouth and slowly licking her nipple before he placed it between his lips and sucked, nibbled, massaged. She was surrendering herself to him. *Tristan...*

My hands moved lower across my skin as Tristan filled my mind. He lowered her panties as I lowered mine. His hand glided between her pulsing thighs as I slowly slid a finger inside myself. I gasped, almost surprised by the feeling Tristan brought to me, my thumb massaging my clit as I kept imagining.

But she was gone now.

It was only him and me.

His rough beard brushed against my stomach before his tongue danced around my belly button. I moaned slightly, feeling another finger slip into me. His fingers moved faster, fell deeper, and pushed harder as he worked me up to a sweat. I whispered his name as he owned mine, and when I felt his tongue taste me, I was seconds away from losing myself to him. My hips thrust against his tongue, my lips begged for more, and he gave me more, faster, deeper, harder. Caringly, gently, forcefully. *Oh my God, Tristan...*

My mouth parted and I pumped my fingers faster, feeling myself hanging from the cliff of forever and moments away from falling into the depths of never. He fed my imagination, he rocked my insides, he begged for me to come apart against his lips, and I did. I collapsed with his touch inside me and released with a feeling of bliss, unable to remember the last time I'd been able to feel alive.

I'm good.

I'm good.

I'm so fucking good.

And then I opened my eyes and saw the darkness of my bedroom.

My hand slid from between my thighs. My panties moved back up my legs, and the feeling of bliss dissipated.

I'm not good.

I looked over at Steven's side of the bed, and a level of disgust filled me inside. For a moment, I swore I saw him lying beside me, staring my way with confusion. I blinked once and reached out to touch him, but he was gone.

Because he'd never really been there.

What did I just do? How could I do such a thing? What is the matter with me?

Pulling myself up from the sheets, I headed to the bathroom and turned on the shower. I stepped inside with my bra and panties still on, and I fell to the ground as the water washed over me. I begged the water droplets to drag my guilt down the drain, to make the disappointment I'd been feeling leave my body. But it didn't.

The shower rained over me, mixing with my own tears, and I stayed there until the water ran cold. I shivered in the tub and closed my eyes.

I'd never felt so alone.

CHAPTER 13
Elizabeth

Despite Tanner's protests, I chose to keep having Tristan come to care for the lawn. Every Saturday he would come over, cut the grass, and head into town to work with Mr. Henson. Sometimes he worked in the mornings, other times, late into the night. We hadn't spoken since my drunken night, at least, not besides the occasional small talk. But I thought that was all right. Emma always played with Zeus in the front yard as I sat on the porch, reading a romance novel. Even when your heart was hurting, there was something so hopeful about reading a book filled with love. The pages were somewhat of a reminder that maybe one day I would be okay again. Maybe one day I would be all right.

Each week, I tried to give Tristan money, but he declined it. Each week, I invited him to stay for a meal, and each week he said no.

One Saturday, he arrived right as Emma was in the middle of an emotional breakdown, and he stood at a distance, trying his best not to interrupt.

"No! Mama, we have to go back! Daddy doesn't know where we are!" Emma cried.

"I'm sure he does, baby. I think we just have to wait a little while. Give Daddy time."

"No! He never takes this long! There's no feathers! We have to go back!" she hollered as I tried to pull her into a hug, but she yanked away from me and hurried into the house.

I sighed, and when I looked up at Tristan, I saw his scowl. I shrugged my shoulders. "Kids." I smiled. He kept his grimacing look.

He turned to walk back toward his house.

"Where are you going?"

"Home."

"What? Why?"

"I'm not going to sit out here and listen to your damn kid whine all morning."

Mean Tristan was back in full force. "God. Sometimes I start to make believe that you're a decent person, but then you just go ahead and remind me of how much of a jerk you are."

He didn't reply but disappeared once more into his darkened home.

"Mama!" The next morning, I was awakened to a hyper Emma bouncing up and down on my bed. "Mama! It's Daddy! He came!" she screamed, pulling me up to a sitting position.

"What?" I muttered, rubbing the sleep from my eyes. "Emma, we sleep in on Sundays, remember?"

"But, Mama! He showed up!" she exclaimed.

I sat up straighter when I heard a lawnmower outside. Tossing on a pair of sweatpants and a tank top, I followed my excited girl to the front of the house. When we stepped outside, a small gasp left my lips as I stared at the porch, which was covered with white feathers.

"See, Mama! He found us!"

My hands covered my mouth as I stared at the white feathers that were starting to float around the space from the bursts of wind.

"Don't cry, Mama. Daddy's here. You said he would find us and he did," Emma explained.

I smiled. "Of course, honey. Mama's just happy, that's all."

Emma started picking up the feathers and smiled. "Picture?" she asked. I hurried inside to get Steven's old Polaroid camera to take the usual picture of Emma holding the feather for her "Daddy and Me" box. When I came back, Emma was sitting on the porch with her bright smile and dozens of feathers surrounding her.

"Okay, say cheese!"

"Cheeeeeseeee!" she screamed.

The picture printed out, and Emma ran inside to add it to her collection.

My eyes looked out at Tristan, who was cutting the grass as if he had no clue what was happening. Walking over to him, I shut off the lawnmower. "Thank you," I said.

"I don't know what the hell you're talking about."

"Tristan...thank you."

He rolled his eyes. "Can you just let me be?"

He went to turn it back on, but I placed my hand over his. His hands were warm—rough but warm. "Thank you."

When our eyes locked, I felt his touch grow even warmer. He smiled a true smile. A smile I hadn't known his lips were capable of creating. "It's no big deal. I found the freakin' feathers in Mr. Henson's shop. It didn't take much work." He paused. "She's good," he said, gesturing toward the house, speaking of Emma. "She's a good kid. Annoying as all get-out, but she's good."

"Stay for breakfast?" I asked.

He shook his head.

"Stop by for lunch."

He declined.

"Dinner?"

He bit his bottom lip. He glanced down at the ground, debating my request. When our eyes met again, I almost fell over from the single word he spoke. "Okay."

The neighbors all gossiped about what it meant, me having Tristan work on my lawn, but I was slowly starting to care less and less what others thought of me.

I sat on the porch, surrounded by the feathers as he finished the lawn work. Emma played fetch with Zeus.

And every now and then, Tristan remembered how to smile.

Later, we sat down at the dinner table, Emma yapping away about a dead bug she found on the porch that Zeus ate. She was being extra loud and extra messy with her spaghetti. I sat at the head of the table, and Tristan sat at the other end. Every now and then I would catch him staring my way, but most of the time he was smiling out of the corner of his mouth at Emma.

"And Zeus went CHOMP! Like it was the best thing ever! Now he has bug guts in his teeth!"

"Did you eat the bugs too?" Tristan asked.

"Ew! No! That's gross!"

"I hear they are a great source of protein."

"I don't care, Tick! That's gross!" She made a gagging face, making us all laugh. "Ooo ah! Oo ah ah!" she said, transitioning into her gorilla speech. For weeks now, she'd been exploring her gorilla roots after watching *Tarzan*. I wasn't sure how to explain it to Tristan, but within seconds, I understood that I wouldn't have to.

"Oo?" Tristan responded. "Ah? Ahhh! Ahhh!" He laughed.

I wondered if he knew he made my heart skip a few beats that day.

"All right, Jane of the jungle, I think it's time for you to go pick out some pajamas for tonight. It's getting past your bedtime."

"But!" she started to complain.

"No buts." I smiled, nodding her out of the room.

"Okay, but can I watch *Hotel Transylvania* in my room?"

"Only if you promise to fall asleep."

"Promise!" She hurried off, and as she left, Tristan stood up from his chair. I stood with him.

He nodded once. "Thanks for dinner."

"You're welcome. You don't have to go. I have wine…"

He hesitated.

"There's beer too."

That pulled him in. I kept myself from telling him that the only reason I'd bought beer was in hopes that one night he would stay for dinner. After I put Emma to bed, Tristan and I took our drinks outside and sat on the front porch with Zeus sleeping beside us. Every now and then one of the feathers would get picked up by a gust of wind and blow past us. He didn't talk a lot, but I was growing used to that fact. Being quiet with him was kind of nice.

"I was thinking of ways I can pay you back for helping me with my lawn work."

"I don't need your money."

"I know, but…well, I can help you with your house. With the interior," I offered. I went on to tell him that I'd gone to school for interior design and that it only made sense for me to help him out. His house always seemed so dark, and I loved the idea of adding a bit more life to it.

"No."

"Just think about it," I said.

"No."

"Are you always so hardheaded?"

"No." He paused and smiled a bit. "Yes."

"Can I ask you a question?" I wondered out loud. He turned my way and nodded.

"Why do you give food to that homeless man?"

He narrowed his eyes and placed his thumb between his teeth. "One day when I was running barefoot, I stopped near that bridge and fell apart. Memories were attacking me and I remember just becoming short of breath. An overwhelming panic attack. The man walked over to me and, um, he patted me on the back and stayed with me until I caught my breath. He asked if I was okay, and I said yes. Then he told me that I shouldn't worry too much about falling apart because the dark days only stayed dark until the sun came up. And then as I started to walk away, he offered me his shoes. I didn't take them of course, but…he had nothing. He lived under a damn bridge with a tattered blanket and a pair of broken-down shoes. But he still offered them to my feet."

"Wow."

"Yeah. Most people probably see a dirty druggie under that bridge, you know? A problem to society. But I saw someone who was willing to give his all to help a stranger stand."

"I just… That's so beautiful."

"He's a beautiful man. It turned out he fought in a war and when he came back, he suffered from PTSD, and his loved ones couldn't understand why he changed so much. He got a job, but lost it due to his panic attacks. He lost everything because he volunteered to fight for all of us. It's bullshit, you know? You're a hero until you take off your uniform. After that, you're just damaged goods to society."

My heart was breaking.

I'd walked by the man under the bridge millions of times and never stopped to find out his story. I'd thought the things Tristan mentioned about the man—how he was a drug addict, how he was something I preferred to look away from.

It was amazing how our minds crafted stories for strangers who probably needed love more than our close-minded judgments.

It was so easy to judge from the outside looking in, and I couldn't help but think that Emma was learning from me. I needed to be careful of how I treated others in passing because my daughter was always studying my every move.

I bit my lip. "Can I ask you another question?"

"I don't know. Is this going to become a regular thing? Because I hate questions."

"This will be the last one for tonight, I swear. What is it you listen to? With those headphones?"

"Nothing," he replied.

"Nothing?"

"The batteries died months ago, and I haven't found the nerve to change them yet."

"But what *were* you listening to?"

His thumb landed between his teeth and he bit it gently. "Jamie and Charlie. A few years ago, they recorded themselves singing, and I just held on to the tape."

"Why haven't you changed the batteries yet?"

His voice lowered. "I think hearing them again will kill me. And I'm already pretty much dead."

"I'm so sorry."

"Not your fault."

"I know, but still, I am sorry. But I can't help but think...if I had a chance to hear Steven's voice one more time, I would take it."

"Tell me about him," he whispered, which surprised me. He didn't seem the type to care, but any opportunity I could find to talk about Steven, I took. I didn't want to forget him anytime soon.

That night we stayed on that porch remembering. He told me all about Jamie and her silly humor, and I invited him into my heart to meet my Steven. There were stretches that passed where we didn't speak, and that seemed perfect too. Tristan was broken in all the same places I was shattered, yet even more so because he lost his wife and son. No parent should ever have to lose their child; it seemed like such a hideous kind of hell.

"So I have to ask. The wand on your pointer finger... What book is that?"

"Harry Potter," he answered matter-of-factly.

"Oh. I've never read those books."

"You've never read Harry Potter?" Tristan asked me, his eyes wide with concern.

I chuckled. "I'm sorry, is that some kind of issue?"

He looked at me as bewildered as possible, and he was definitely silently judging me. "No, it's just, you always have a book in your hand, and it's insane that you've never read Harry Potter. It was Charlie's favorite. I believe there are two things that exist in the world that everyone should read because they teach you pretty much everything you need to know about life: the Bible and Harry Potter."

"Really? Those are the *only* two things?"

"Yup. That's it. That's all you need. And well, I haven't read the Bible, but it's on my to-do list." He snickered. "That's probably part of the reason I'm currently failing at life."

Every time he laughed, a part of me came back to life.

"I've read the Bible, but not Harry Potter, so maybe we can give each other the CliffsNotes versions."

"You've read the Bible?"

"Yes."

"The whole way through?"

"Yes." Holding my hair up in a ponytail, I turned so he could see the three cross tattoos behind my left ear. "When I was younger, my mom used to date and ditch a lot of guys. At one point, I really thought she was going to settle down with this one guy named Jason. I loved him—he always brought me candy and stuff. He was a really religious guy, and Mama told me that if she and I read the Bible, then maybe he would love us and would be my new dad. He even moved in with us for a little while. So for weeks I sat in my bedroom reading the Bible, and one day I came running into the living room shouting, 'Jason! Jason! I did it, I read the Bible!'

"I was shaking with excitement because I wanted that, you know? I wanted a chance to have another dad, even though mine was the best. In my mind, if I had a new dad, then maybe my mama would be my mama again instead of someone I hardly knew anymore."

"What happened with Jason?"

I frowned. "When I got to the living room, I saw him loading his suitcases into the back of his Honda. Mama said he wasn't the one and had to leave. I remember getting so mad at her—screaming, crying, wondering why she would do that. Why she would mess it up. But that's what Mama does. She screws things up."

Tristan shrugged. "It seems like she did a decent job with you."

"Minus the lack of me reading Harry Potter."

"Your mom should date a wizard next time."

I laughed. "Trust me, it's probably next in her lineup."

Around three a.m. he stood to leave, and I hurried inside, bringing out a pair of double-A batteries for his cassette player. He hesitated at first but then placed them into his player. As he walked across the lawn with Zeus, he hit play on the music, placing the headphones over his ears. I watched his footsteps pause. He covered his face with the palms of his hands and his body shook.

I dropped down to my knees, watching the suffering that engulfed his spirit. A part of me wished I hadn't given him the batteries, but another part was happy that I had because his reaction meant he was still breathing.

Sometimes the hardest part of existing without your loved ones was remembering how to breathe.

He turned back my way and spoke. "Do me a favor?"

"Anything."

He gestured toward the house. "Hold her tight each day and night because nothing's promised to us. I just wished I would've held on tighter."

CHAPTER 14
Tristan

APRIL 4TH, 2014
THREE DAYS UNTIL GOODBYE

*T*his one's really nice if you are looking for something strong," the funeral home director, Harold, said to my mother and me as we stood staring at caskets. "It's full copper, which has excellent resistance to corrosion. It's stronger than stainless steel and provides a remarkable life for your loved ones."

"That's very nice," Mom said, as I stood completely uninterested.

"And over here, if you're looking for something a bit higher class, then you want to look into this beauty." Harold's fingers brushed against his goatee before he patted the inside of another casket. "This is solid bronze, which is the strongest and longest-lasting of any casket material. If you are looking to send your loved ones out in style, this is the way to go.

"There's also the option of the hardwood caskets. Now, they aren't as strong as these ones, but they are shock-resistant, which is nice. They *come in different types of hardwoods such as cherry, oak, ash, or walnut. Now, my personal favorite is the cherry finish, but that's just me."*

"Fucking creep," I muttered under my breath, my mom the only one to hear me.

"Tristan," she scolded, turning away from the funeral director. "Be nice."

"He has a favorite casket. That's fucking weird," I hissed, irritated with Harold, irritated with my mother, irritated that Jamie and Charlie were gone. "Can we get this over with?" I complained, looking into the empty caskets that would soon enough be filled with my everythings.

Come back to me.

Mom frowned but went ahead and handled the details that I wanted to pretend didn't exist.

Harold took us to his office, where he wore his creepy smile and talked about shit that annoyed me as each moment passed. "For the tombstones we also offer wreaths for the holiday season, vases for flowers, and blankets for the colder months—"

"Are you shitting me?" I murmured. Mom placed a comforting hand on my shoulder, almost as if to stop me from snapping at Harold, but it was too late. I was too far gone. "It must be really nice for you, huh, Harold?" I asked, leaning forward with my eyes narrowed and my fingers laced together. "It must be a good fucking job to offer sad fucks blankets for their loved ones. To get them to pour all their money into stupid shit that doesn't matter because they are in a vulnerable state. A blanket? A BLANKET?! They are fucking dead, Harold," I shouted, standing up from the chair. "The dead don't need blankets because they don't get cold. They don't need wreaths because they don't celebrate Christmas, and they don't need flowers because what's the point?!" I hollered, slamming my hands against his desk, sending papers flying.

Mom stood up and reached for me, but I yanked my arm away. My chest rose and fell, my breaths becoming harder and harder to control, and I could feel the wildness that was living within my eyes. I was losing it. I was falling apart more and more as each second passed.

I rushed out of his office and leaned my back against the closest wall. Mom apologized to Harold as my hands formed fists and began to slam against the wall behind me. Over and over again, I slammed my fists against the wall. My fingers were turning red, and my heart was turning cold as it all began to set in.

They were gone.

They were gone.

My mom walked out of the room and stood across from me, her eyes filled with tears.

"Did you get the blanket?" I asked sarcastically.

"Tristan," she whispered, the heartbreak audible within her soft words.

"If you did, you should've gotten Charlie a green one and Jamie purple. Those were their favorite colors…" I shook my head, not wanting to talk anymore. Not wanting Mom to try to make me feel better. Not wanting to breathe.

It was the first day that their deaths felt real. The first day I came to the realization that in three days I would have to say my final goodbye to my world. My soul was in flames, and every inch of me felt the burn. I shook my head more and more, cupped my hands over my mouth, and howled into my sadness.

They were gone.

They were gone.

Come back to me.

"CHARLIE!" I screamed, sitting up in my bed. It was still pitch-black outside, and my sheets were soaked in my own sweat. A slight breeze passed through my window as I tried to shake off the nightmare that was more real than ever before. My nightmares were my past memories that came to haunt me.

I watched as a light turned on across at Elizabeth's house. She walked over to the window and glanced my way. I didn't turn on my light. I sat on the edge of my bed, my body still burning hot. The light flooded over her face, and I watched her lips move.

"Are you okay?" she questioned, crossing her arms against her body.

She was so damn beautiful, and it annoyed me.

It also annoyed me that my shouts probably awakened her almost every night. I walked over to the window, my eyes still heavy with the guilt of not being there for Jamie and Charlie. "Go to sleep," I told her.

"Okay," she replied.

But she didn't move to her bed. She sat on the ledge of her windowsill, and I leaned against mine. We stared at one another until my heartbeat slowed, and her eyes fell shut.

I silently thanked her for not leaving me alone.

CHAPTER 15
Elizabeth

Rumor has it you're banging an asshole," Faye said over the phone a few days after I'd sat up with Tristan after his nightmare. I hadn't spoken to him since then, but I couldn't stop thinking about him.

"Oh my gosh, that is not a rumor."

"No, but it sounds more exciting than Tanner whining about some dude cutting your grass, even though I remember offering you a certain guy named Ed to trim your bushes. But really, though, are you okay? Should I be worrying like Tanner is?"

"I'm fine."

"Because that Tristan guy is a total dick, Liz." The worry on the end of each of her words was sad. I hated that she was worrying about me.

"I can talk to him," I said quietly. "About Steven, I can talk to him."

"You can talk to me about him too."

"Yeah, I know. But it's different. Tristan lost his wife and son."

Faye went silent for a moment. "I didn't know that."

"I doubt anyone does. People mainly judge him from the outside, I think."

"Listen, Liz. I'm just going to be uncool for a second because sometimes being a best friend means being truthful even when your bestie doesn't want to hear it. It's sad, really, about Tristan's family. But how do we know we can trust this guy? What if he made that story up?"

"What? He didn't."

"How do you know?"

Because his eyes are haunted the same way mine are.

"Please don't worry, Faye."

"Honey…" Faye sighed into the phone receiver. For a second, I contemplated hanging up on her, something I would've never done in the past. "You just got back into town a few weeks ago, and I know you're hurting. But this Tristan guy, he's mean. He's wild. And I think what you need is more stability in your life. Have you thought about talking to a therapist or something?"

"No."

"Why not?"

Because therapists were supposed to help you move on, and I didn't want to move on. I yearned to go backward. "Look, I gotta get going. We'll talk later, okay?"

"Liz—"

"Bye, Faye. I love you," I said, and meant it, even though I didn't like her very much right then.

"Love you too."

When I hung up, I went to the front window of the house and watched as the darkened skies started rolling in. A rainstorm was building right in front of me. Such a large part of me was excited for the rain too, because the rain meant the grass would grow faster, and that meant broken Tristan would be here again, standing right in front of broken Liz.

Saturday evening, I couldn't have been happier sitting and watching Tristan cut the grass. I sat on the front porch with Mama's heart-shaped tin box of love letters, going through all the words I'd already read millions of times. When Tanner's car pulled up toward my house, I placed the letters back into the box and shoved them to the corner of the porch. A weird sense of embarrassment washed over me knowing that Tanner was about to see Tristan cutting the grass.

As his engine turned off and Tanner hopped out of his car, I gave him a tight smile and stood up. "What brings you around here, buddy?" I asked. His eyes instantly locked on Tristan, and he frowned.

"Just was driving around after work and thought I would see if you and Emma wanted to grab some dinner or something."

"We already ordered pizza, and Emma is inside on her second round of watching *Frozen.*"

He stepped closer, his frown still remaining. "The grass doesn't seem like it was that long to begin with from what I can tell."

"Tanner," I warned, my voice low.

"Please tell me you aren't paying him cash, Liz. He's probably using it for drugs or something."

"Stop being ridiculous."

He cocked an eyebrow. "Ridiculous? I'm being realistic. We don't really know anything about this guy except that he works with Crazy Henson. And I mean, look at him; he has the look of some psychopath or killer, or Hitler or something. It's creepy."

"If you want to stop being a jerk, you can head inside and get some pizza. Otherwise, we should catch up later, Tanner."

His head shook back and forth. "I'm going to run inside and say hi to Emma, then I'll get out of your hair." He went inside the house with his hands stuffed in his jeans, and I sighed. When he came out, he gave me a wary smile. "There's something different about you, Liz. I can't put my finger on it, but you're acting strange ever since you came back. It's like I don't know who you are anymore."

Maybe you never did.

"We'll chat later, okay?"

He nodded and walked back to his car. "Hey," he hollered in Tristan's direction. Tristan turned and looked his way with narrowed eyes. "You missed a patch to your left." Tristan blinked once, then went back to what he was doing as Tanner drove off.

After Tristan finished, he walked over to the porch and gave me a semi-broken smile. "Elizabeth?"

"Yes?"

"Can I..." His words trailed off, and he cleared his throat, scratching at his beard. He stepped up closer to me. I watched the sweat sitting at his hairline began to fall against his forehead and such a big part of me longed to wipe it away.

"Can you what?" I whispered, staring at his lips longer than I should have.

He inched closer, making my heart rate increase. I stopped breathing and simply stared at him. My head tilted slightly as his blue eyes seemed to be staring at my mouth the same way I stared at his.

"Can I..." he muttered.

"Can you..." I echoed.

"Do you think..."

"Do I think..."

He looked into my eyes. My heartbeat somehow slowed yet sped up all at once. "Do you think I could use your shower? My hot water is out."

A small, low breath passed through my lips, and I nodded. "Yes. A shower. Yeah, of course." He smiled and thanked me. "You can borrow some of Steven's clothes, so you don't have to run over to your place."

"You don't have to do that."

"I want to." I nodded. "I want to." We headed inside, and I grabbed a plain white T-shirt and a pair of sweatpants from my bedroom for Tristan. Then I picked up some washcloths and towels for him to use. "Here you go. There's shampoo and soap in the shower already. I'm sorry, but most of it smells girly."

He chuckled. "Better than my current smell."

I hadn't heard him laugh often. It was such a welcomed sound. "Okay, well, anything you need can be found under the sink too. I'll be around."

"Thank you."

"Anytime," I said, and I meant it.

He began chewing on the inside of his cheek and nodded once before closing himself in the bathroom. A sigh left me as I disappeared to go put Emma to bed to keep myself busy until Tristan was done in the shower.

Walking down the hallway toward the bathroom, I paused when I reached the open door. Tristan was standing in front of the bathroom sink wearing only the sweatpants I'd given him.

Tristan ran his hands through his long, wet hair that he tossed into a man bun on his head. He brought a razor blade to his upper lip, making me twitch. "You're shaving?"

He stopped his movement and glanced my way once before he made his mustache cease to exist. He then trimmed his beard to the point that it was almost invisible.

"You shaved." I sighed, staring at a man who looked so different than mere minutes before. His lips looked fuller, his eyes brighter.

He broke his stare away from me and went back to studying his now nude face in the mirror. "I didn't want to look like a serial killer, or worse—Hitler."

My stomach dropped. "You overheard Tanner."

He didn't reply.

"You didn't look like Hitler," I said softly, making him turn and notice that I was gawking at his every move. Trying my best to gather my scattered thoughts, I kept speaking. "His comment didn't even really make sense because you know Hitler had the"—I placed my finger under my nose—"little mustache, and you had the"—I moved my hands all around my chin—"lumberjack-type beard. Tanner, he was just being…I don't know…protective of me in a weird way. He's like my big brother. But he was wrong to say those things. And out of line."

His face was stone as his gaze searched mine. He had such solid bone structure that made it almost impossible to look away from him. Tristan lifted the shirt from the countertop and slid it over his body before he walked past me, brushing against my shoulder. "Thanks again," he said.

"Again, anytime."

"Is it hard? Seeing me wearing his clothes?"

"Yes. But at the same time, it just makes me want to hug you because it would kind of be like hugging him."

"That's weird." He smiled playfully.

"I'm weird."

I didn't expect it, but when his arms wrapped around me, I slowly melted into him. What was shocking was how far away from sadness I felt in that moment. There was something about the way he softly massaged my back and gently rested his chin on my head that brought me a level of peace I hadn't seen in some time. I felt selfish, holding on to him tighter, because I wasn't ready to release the feeling of not being alone. Within those few minutes of Tristan holding me, my mind stopped reminding me how lonely I was. Within those few quiet moments, I found the comfort I'd been missing.

I hadn't even noticed I was crying until I felt his thumbs rubbing beneath my eyes, wiping the tears away. We were closer together, my hands twisted against the T-shirt, his hands pulling me closer to his body. When his lips separated, my own parted, and we breathed against one another. As his eyes closed, mine floated shut, and we stayed quiet together. I wasn't certain whose lips touched whose first, but we kept them pressed together. We weren't kissing but merely holding our mouths together, sending breaths into one another's lungs, holding each other up from falling into our own obscurity.

Tristan breathed in while I breathed out.

I thought about kissing him.

"My hot water isn't out," he said softly.

"Really?"

"Really."

I thought about kissing him again.

I looked up into his stormy eyes and saw a bit of life. My heartbeat quickened as I held on to him, not wanting to let go anytime soon.

"I should go," he said.

"You should go," I replied.

I thought about kissing him some more.

"Unless you stayed," I said.

"Unless I stayed," he replied.

"My best friend told me I should use sex to help me move on from losing Steven." I sighed against his lips. "But I'm not ready to forget. I'm not ready to move on. But I do want this." I studied his embrace of me. "I want you to be here with me because it helps me. It helps me remember what it felt like to be wanted. I just…" I lowered my head, almost embarrassed by my words. "I miss having someone to take care of me."

Tristan lowered his voice and brushed his lips against my ear. "I'll help. I'll help you hold on to him. I'll help you remember. I'll take care of you."

"We'll use each other to remember them?"

"Only if you want to."

"This sounds like a terrible idea in the best kind of way."

"There's still this giant part of me that misses Jamie every day. And holding you"—his tongue gently danced across my bottom lip—"helps me remember holding her."

"Feeling your heartbeat"—I placed my hand against his chest—"reminds me of his heartbeat."

"Running my fingers through your hair"—he tangled his hands through my blond locks, making me gasp lightly—"helps me remember her."

"Feeling your skin against my skin"—I slowly lifted his T-shirt—"reminds me of him." My head tilted to the left, and I studied his facial structure. The sharp lines of his jaw, the tiny creases in the corners of his eyes. His breaths sawed in and out. Everyone in town was convinced that he ran so much because he was trying to run from his past, but that was far from the truth. He was trying to hold on to it daily. He hadn't had any plans to become a true runner anytime soon. If he had been, his eyes wouldn't have looked so pained. "Pretend with me for a little while," I muttered before slowly brushing my lips across his. "Help me remember him tonight," I whispered, a bit shy.

His hips pressed against mine, his eyes dilated. He placed his right hand behind my lower back, forcing me to thrust my body against his. I felt his hardness against my inner thigh, and my body slowly began to grind against him. *Yes.* We moved to the closest wall. His left hand formed a fist and landed against the wall above my head. His brows drew closer and a deep, weighted sigh rolled through him. "We shouldn't…"

Yes.

This time my mouth parted, and I softly bit his bottom lip as my hand rolled against the fabric of his sweats. My thumb circled the tip of his hardness. *Yes, yes.* He emitted a low growl and tightened his grip on my back. I watched as his tongue slowly slid from his mouth, and it ran against my neck, making me shiver inside. *Do that again.*

His hand trailed up under my dress, his touch landing against my inner thigh, and when he rolled his fingers against my wet panties, my heartbeat soared. *Yes, yes, yes…*

I moaned as he pulled the fabric of my panties to the side and slid a finger inside me.

Our mouths crashed together and he whispered a name, but I wasn't certain that it was mine; I whispered one back, not positive that it was his. He was taking me all in as he kissed me hard, his tongue exploring every inch of me. He slid another finger deep inside me as his thumb circled my clit. "God, you feel so good…" he growled, feeling my tightness, my wetness…feeling me.

My hand slid into his boxers, and I began to stroke him up and down, squeezing lightly and listening to his growls of appreciation.

"Perfect," he stuttered, his eyes closed, his breaths growing shorter and shorter. "Fucking perfect."

It was bad.

But so, so good.

As my hand worked faster, his fingers sped up. We both panted together, losing ourselves, finding ourselves, losing our loved ones, finding our loved ones. In the moment, I loved him because it felt like loving Steven. In the moment, I hated him because it was nothing more than a lie. But I couldn't stop touching him. I couldn't stop needing him. I couldn't stop wanting him.

He and I together was a terrible idea. We were both unstable, we were both shattered, and there was no getting around it. He was thunder, I was lightning, and we were seconds away from creating the perfect storm.

"Mama," a small voice said behind me. I took a big leap away from Tristan's body, his fingers falling from me. I smoothed out my dress, flustered. My eyes shot down the hallway toward Emma, who was holding Bubba in her hand, yawning.

"Hey, baby. What's going on?" I asked, wiping my hand over my lips. I hurried to her side.

"I can't sleep. Can you come lie with Bubba and me?"

"Of course. I'll be right there, okay?"

She nodded and dragged her feet back to her bedroom. When I turned to Tristan, I saw the guilt in his eyes as he readjusted his pants.

"I should go," he whispered.

I nodded. "You should go."

CHAPTER 16
Tristan

We should've stopped that night. We should've realized how bad an idea it was for us to use each other to remember Steven and Jamie. We were our own ticking time bombs, and we were set to explode.

But we didn't care.

Almost every day, she stopped by and kissed me.

Almost every day, I kissed her back.

She told me his favorite color. *Green.*

I told her Jamie's favorite food. *Pasta.*

Some nights I climbed out of my bedroom window and straight into hers. Other nights, she crawled into my bed. When I entered her bed, she never turned the sheets down. She hardly allowed me on his side of the bed. I understood that more than anyone could've ever known.

She undressed me and made love to her past.

I slid into her and made love to my ghosts.

It wasn't right, yet somehow it made sense.

Her soul was scarred, and mine was burned.

But when we were together, the hurting hurt a little less. When we were together, the past wasn't as painful to take in. When we were together, I never for a second felt alone.

There were plenty of days when I was okay. There were a ton of times when the hurt was just hidden inside of me but not punching me in the gut. But then there were the days of the big memories. Jamie's birthday was one. It was Jamie's birthday, and that night I struggled.

The past demons that were buried deep within my soul were slowly creeping out. Elizabeth showed up to my bedroom. I should've pushed her away. I should've allowed the darkness to swallow me whole.

But I can't leave her alone.

Occasional flashes of tenderness and care traveled through the two of us as her body rested beneath mine. Her eyes shook me—they always did. Her hair fell against my pillow. "You're stunning," I whispered before wrapping my hand around her neck and lifting, allowing her mouth to find my lips.

That night, she was my ecstasy. My hallucinations.

I loved the taste of strawberry lip gloss on her lips.

Her nude body hid under me and my lips explored her neck as she arched her spine.

"Do you know how beautiful your eyes are?" I asked, sitting up with her pinned beneath me.

She smiled again. *That's beautiful too.* My finger outlined the curvature of her body, taking in every inch of her.

"They're just brown," she replied, combing her fingers through her hair.

She was wrong. They were more than that, and I noticed them more each night I held her against me. If I looked closely, I could see the few flakes of gold floating around the rims of her eyes.

"They're beautiful." There wasn't anything about her that wasn't beautiful.

My tongue washed against her hard nipple. She shivered. Dependency on my touch dripped from every fiber of her being as she begged me to explore her deepest fears and her sweetest tastes. I slid my hand behind her back and lifted her so we were both sitting up in my dark bedroom. I stared into those beautiful eyes as I spread her legs and positioned her against me. She nodded once, granting me permission to do exactly what she had come over to my place for.

I grabbed a condom from my nightstand and rolled it on. "How do you want it?" I asked.

"Huh?"

My lips rested against hers as I spoke in a whisper, my breaths filling her up inside. "I can be rough. I can be gentle. I can make you scream. I can make you cry. I can fuck you so hard that you won't be able to move. I can fuck you so slow that you'll think I'm in love with you. So tell me how you want it. You're in control." My finger circled her lower back. I needed her to be in control. I needed her to take charge because I was losing my grip on reality.

"Well, aren't you the gentleman?" she nervously said.

I cocked an eyebrow.

Sighing, she avoided eye contact. "Gentle and slow…like you love me," she whispered, hoping not to sound too desperate.

I didn't tell her, but that's exactly how I needed it.

That's exactly how I would've loved to love Jamie on her birthday.

God, my mind was fucked up.

What was scary was how Elizabeth's thoughts were almost a carbon copy of my own.

How did two people so broken find each other's shattered pieces?

I was slow to enter her at first, my eyes watching how her body reacted to my being inside her. Her eyes wanted to close as I pushed in deeper, her lips parting, allowing a small moan to escape. When my tongue ran across her bottom lip, I was in the strawberry fields, tasting all of her.

My hands were shaking, but I stopped the nerves by focusing on her eyes. She caught her breath, placing her hand over her heart for a moment. Her eyes were with mine, staring as if we'd never see one another again; it felt as if we were both terrified of losing that small bit of comfort.

Did she see him when she stared my way? Did she remember his eyes?

I could almost tell that her heart was beating as hard as mine, working as intensely.

"Can I stay the night?" she whispered as I lifted her thighs and placed her back against the headboard.

"Of course." I sighed, rolling my tongue against her ear, massaging her breasts in my hands. *She shouldn't stay the night.* But I wanted her to. I was so terrified of being alone with my thoughts that the reply fell from my mouth like I was begging. "We can pretend till morning," I offered.

She shouldn't stay here, my brain ordered me. *What are you doing?!* it scolded.

Harder. We both wanted it more and more now, our eyes locked the whole time. Our hips moved in harmony. "Oh my God," she muttered, breathless. Our heart rates intensified as we allowed our bodies to become one for a while. I slid into her tightness, and she arched her back for more.

"Steven…" she whispered, but I didn't even care.

"Jams…" I muttered back, and she didn't mind.

We were so fucking insane.

Deeper. I yanked on her hair as she wrapped her fingers in mine. Each second it grew a bit rougher, a bit wilder, a bit more untamed. "Fuck." I sighed, loving how it felt being between her legs, loving the sweat that rolled down her body. It felt good to be inside her; it felt safe.

Faster. I wanted to feel all of Elizabeth. I wanted to bury myself so deep inside her that she would never forget the way I made her skip reality. I wanted to fuck her as if she were my love and I was hers.

Lifting her right leg, I placed it over my shoulder. I allowed her to feel every inch of me as she told me to make love to her harder. Did she realize what she'd said? Had she really said *love*? I knew it was what we had agreed to, but hearing the words fall from her lips made me lose focus for a moment.

I wasn't him.

She wasn't her.

But my God, it felt good to lie to ourselves.

She was out of breath, and I liked the way her head fell back to the headboard. I also liked how her nails dug into my skin as if she never wanted to let me go. Then she blinked once, and when her eyes reappeared, they were holding back tears. The tension of struggling tears strived for an outlet, yet she took a breath instead.

Slower. She asked me once more if she could really stay the night. She was probably nervous that I'd kick her out afterward, and she would be forced back into the reality that she was alone. And I was alone. Pre-rejection was swimming in her eyes. But I'd promised I wouldn't. I could see it in those brown eyes of hers: she hated being by herself with her own thoughts.

We had something in common.

Gentler.

We had many things in common.

Laying her down on the mattress, I kept myself inside her but slowed my movements. "I'll stop," I said, seeing tears falling from her eyes.

"Please don't," she begged, shaking her head. She dug her fingers deeper into my back, as if she were trying to hold on to something that wasn't even there.

This is nothing more than a dream.

"We're dreaming, Elizabeth. We're dreaming. It's not real."

She pushed her hips up. "No. Keep going."

I wiped her tears away, but I didn't keep going.

It was wrong.

She was broken.

I was broken.

I removed myself from her warmth and sat up on the edge of the bed. My hands gripped the sides of the mattress. The sheets wrinkled with her every move. She sat up on the other side of the bed, her hands gripped to the sides of the mattress. Our backs faced one another, but I swore I could still feel her heartbeat.

"What's wrong with us?" she whispered.

My fingers brushed against my temple, and I sighed. "Everything."

"Was today one of the big moments?" she asked.

I nodded, even though she couldn't see me. "Jamie's birthday."

She chuckled. I turned around to see her wiping tears away. "I thought so." She stood up, slid on her panties, and tossed on her bra.

"How did you know?"

She moved over to me and stood between my legs. Her eyes studied my stare, and her fingers combed through my wild hair. She placed her hand against my chest, finding my rapid heartbeat. Her lips lay against mine, not kissing me, but feeling my breaths. "Because I could really feel how much you longed for her. In those stormy eyes I could see how disappointed you were that I wasn't her."

"Elizabeth," I said, feeling guilty.

She shook her head and pulled away from me. "It's okay," she promised. She picked up her T-shirt and tossed it onto her small frame. She slid her pajama shorts up her legs and walked over to my window to leave. "Because I'm guessing you could see how disappointed I was that you weren't him too."

"We should probably stop doing this," I said as she walked over to her window.

She pulled her hair back into a ponytail and smiled. "Yeah, probably." She climbed into her house and gave me a sly grin. "But we probably won't anyway. Because I think we're both a bit addicted to the past. I'll see you later."

I fell backward onto my bed and groaned because I knew she was right.

CHAPTER 17
Elizabeth

So you're seeing that Tristan Cole guy, huh?" Marybeth asked at the book club meeting.

I arched an eyebrow as I held *Little Women* in my grip. "What?"

"Oh, honey, you don't have to be shy about it. Everyone in the neighborhood has seen the two of you hanging out. And don't worry, you can tell us all about it. This is a safe place," Susan promised.

Yeah right.

"He just cuts my grass. We hardly know each other."

"Is that why I saw you climbing out of his bedroom window at one in the morning the other night? Because he was cutting the grass?" asked a woman I'd never even spoken to.

"I'm sorry, who are you?"

"Oh, I'm Dana. I'm new to the neighborhood."

It took everything in me to not roll my eyes. She would fit right in.

"So is that true? Were you climbing out of his window? I told Dana I didn't believe it because you just lost your husband and it would be insulting to his memory for you to already be moving on with another man,"

Marybeth explained. "It would be like a slap in the face of your marriage. Almost as if your vows were only written in sand and not in your heart."

My stomach twisted in knots. "Maybe we should talk about the novel," I offered.

But they kept asking me questions. Questions I didn't have answers to. Questions I didn't *want* to answer. The night went on and on, and it all felt like slow motion. When the end of the night came, I couldn't have been happier.

"Okay, bye, ladies!" Susan said, waving to Emma and me as we left her house. "Remember, in two weeks make sure you've read *Fifty Shades of Grey*! And bring notes!"

I waved goodbye to everyone. By the end of the night, we hadn't spoken one word about *Little Women*, but I felt extremely belittled by these women.

August 23.

It was just a date to most people, but to me, it was more.

Steven's birthday.

One of the big moments.

I was supposed to be better at the big moments. The little moments were what was supposed to hurt me the most.

I leaned against the tree in my backyard and looked up at the bright sky, the sunrays shining overhead. Emma was playing with Zeus in the small plastic swimming pool I'd bought her, and Tristan was working outside his shed building a dining-room table.

Out of nowhere, a white feather came floating past me. A small, tiny feather that somehow stung my soul. An overwhelming feeling of loss flew through me as I hit the palm of my hand against my head repeatedly. My heart was pounding against my chest as memories of Steven came flooding in, suffocating me, drowning me. I couldn't breathe as I slapped myself repeatedly and slid down the tree trunk, my body shaking uncontrollably. "I'm sorry," I cried, to myself. *To Steven.* "I'm sorry I couldn't…" I howled, shutting my eyes.

Two hands landed on my shoulders and I jumped in fright. "Shhh, it's me, Elizabeth," Tristan whispered, falling to the ground and wrapping his arms around me. "I got you."

I pulled on his T-shirt, pressing my body against him as I soaked him with my tears. "I couldn't save him, I couldn't save him," I wailed into his shirt. "He was my world, and I couldn't save him. He fought for me and—" I couldn't talk anymore. I couldn't get my scrambled thoughts to leave my choking heart.

"Shh, Elizabeth. I got you. I got you." His voice soothed me as I fell apart, having the first breakdown in a long time. I held on to him, silently begging him to never let me go.

That was when he held on tighter.

Then I felt two tiny hands wrap around me, and Emma pulled me close to her.

"I'm sorry, baby," I whispered, shaking against Tristan and my little one. "Mama's sorry."

"It's okay, Mama," she promised. "It's okay."

But she was wrong.

It wasn't okay.

And I wasn't sure if it ever would be.

That night, it began to rain. For a while I sat in my night robe, just watching the deluge of raindrops hitting hard against the ground. I cried with the rain, unable to hold myself together. Emma was sleeping in the other room, and Tristan allowed Zeus to stay the night with her.

Make it stop, I begged my heart. *Make the pain go away*, I pleaded.

I crawled out my window and over to Tristan's. I was soaked within seconds, but I didn't care. I tapped lightly on his window, and he wandered over, shirtless, staring at me. His arms held the edge of the windowsill, showcasing his toned arms.

"Not tonight," he said, his voice low. "Go home, Elizabeth."

My eyes still burned from all the crying. My heart still hurt from all the longing. "Tonight," I argued.

"No."

My fingers wrapped around the string holding my robe together and I untied it, dropping the fabric to the ground, standing in the rain in only my bra and panties. "Yes."

"Jesus Christ," he muttered, sliding his window open. "Get inside."

I did as he said. A puddle of water formed around my feet, and I shook from the cold. From the hurt. "Ask me how I want it tonight."

"No." His voice was stern, and he wouldn't make eye contact with me.

"I want it like you love me."

"Elizabeth—"

"You can do it hard if you want."

"Stop."

"Look at me, Tristan."

"No."

"Why not?" I asked, walking close to him as he turned his back to me. "Don't you want me?"

"You know the answer to that."

I shook my head. "You don't think I'm beautiful? Am I not as pretty as her? Am I not as good as—"

He shot around and placed his hands on my shoulders. "Don't do this, Elizabeth."

"Fuck me, please…" I cried, running my fingers against his chest. "Please make love to me."

"I can't."

I hit his chest. "Why not?!" I cried, my vision becoming blurry. "Why not?! I let you touch me when you wanted her. I let you screw me when you needed it. I let you…" My words faded off, becoming sobs. "I let you… Why not…"

He grabbed my fists, stopping me from pounding all my anger against his chest. "Because you're broken. You're extremely broken tonight."

"Just make love to me."

"No."

"Why not?"

"Because I can't."

"That's not an answer."

"Yes, it is," he said.

"No, it's not. Stop being a coward. Just tell me why not. Why the hell not?!"

"*Because I'm not him!*" he shouted, my body shaking in his grip. "I'm not Steven, Elizabeth. I'm not what you want."

"You can be, though. You can be him."

"No," he said sternly. "I can't."

I shoved him. "I hate you!" I shouted, my throat burning as tears fell against my lips. "I hate you!" But I wasn't talking to Tristan. "I hate you for leaving me! I hate you for leaving me. I can't breathe. I can't breathe." I lost myself in Tristan's arms.

I fell apart in a way I'd never experienced in my life.

I shook, I screamed, and a part of me died.

But Tristan held me, making sure not all of my soul disappeared that night.

CHAPTER 18
Elizabeth

I waited two weeks before I could face Tristan again. I was embarrassed, ashamed of the way I'd broken down in his room, but when he called me over to talk about the possibility of me doing the interior design for his home, I felt as if I had to suck up my fears.

"Are you okay? You seem off," Tristan said as he walked Emma and me through his house. I was still so extremely uncomfortable with what I'd done, the way I'd fallen apart in front of him.

"No, I'm fine," I said. "Just taking everything in." I gave him a fake smile he saw straight through.

"Okay, well, you can do pretty much anything you want with the place. There's the living room, dining room, bathroom, my bedroom, and the kitchen mainly. And I would love for the study to not look like a complete mess."

I walked into the study, where boxes were stacked on top of boxes. His desk was covered with items, and as he walked Emma and Zeus out of the room, I stayed paused, staring at a receipt partially hidden under some paperwork. I picked it up and read it.

Five thousand white feathers.

Overnight shipping.

I opened one of the boxes on his desk and my heart skipped as I saw more bags of feathers. He hadn't found the white feathers at Mr. Henson's shop. He'd ordered them. He'd ordered thousands of them, just so Emma's heart wouldn't be broken.

Tristan…

"You coming, Elizabeth?" I heard him shout. I closed the box and hurried out of the room.

"Yup, I'm here." I cleared my throat and gave him a smile. "What about your shed?" I asked, catching up to Tristan. "I can fix that up for you too."

"No, the shed is off-limits. That's…" He paused and frowned. "It's just off-limits."

I narrowed my eyes in understanding. "Okay… Well, I think I've got everything I need for now. I'll draw up some different ideas and make some boards with fabrics and colors for us to go over together later on. I better get going."

"You're in a hurry."

"Yeah, well, you know." I glanced over at Emma, who was playing with Zeus, living in her own world. "Emma has a sleepover tonight that I have to get her ready for."

Tristan stepped closer to me and spoke softly, "Are you angry with me? For the night you came over?"

"No." I sighed. "I'm angrier with myself. You did nothing wrong."

"Are you sure?"

"Truly, Tristan. You held me when I needed you the most." I smiled. "But maybe it's best we don't use each other to remember any-more… Obviously I can't handle it."

He frowned and looked at the ground, almost as if he were disappointed, but within a second he held his head up and gave me a small grin. "I want to show you and Emma something."

He led us to the back of the house and held the back door open. I listened to the nightly crickets chatting amongst themselves. It was a comforting sound…peaceful even.

"Where are we going?" I wondered out loud.

He nodded toward the darkened woods as he picked up a flashlight from the back hallway. I didn't ask any more questions. I grabbed Emma's hand and walked beside Tristan. We walked into the night, and he led us deeper into the woods.

The skies were star-filled and the sweet air greeted us as we stepped in and out of the shadows between the trees. The branches swung back and forth as we pushed our way through the woods. "We're almost there," Tristan insisted.

But where?

When we reached it, I knew instantly that it was where he wanted to take us just based on the beauty. My hands covered my mouth to keep from making any sound. There was this odd fear that if I made a peep, all the beauty would vanish. A small river flowed before us. The stream was quiet, as if all the creatures who traveled by the small waves were resting peacefully. Across the river lay what seemed like an old stone packhorse bridge. Through the cracks of stones, flowers were growing, making the view perfect under the moonlight.

"I found this place with Zeus," Tristan said, walking over to the bridge and taking a seat. "Whenever I need to clear my head, I come here to refocus my mind."

I sat beside him, took off my shoes, and slipped my feet into the chilled water. Emma and Zeus splashed in the water joyfully, freely.

He turned and gave me a smile that made my own lips turn up. Tristan had a way of making people feel worthy just by smiling and looking them in the eye. I wished he smiled more often.

"When I first moved out here, I was angry all the time. I missed my son. I missed my wife. I hated my parents, even though I shouldn't have. For some reason, I found it easy to blame them, as if it were their fault that I lost my wife and son. It felt easier to be mad at them than to be sad. The only time I didn't feel angry was when I came out here and breathed with the trees."

He was opening up.

Please stay open.

"I'm glad you found something that can make you feel a bit of peace."

His eyes danced across me, and a knowing smile found his lips. "Yeah. Me too." He ran his fingers against his beard, which was growing in fast. "Since we aren't using each other anymore, you can use this place if you want. To help you find peace."

I smiled. "Thank you."

He simply nodded in response.

Emma jumped into the river and made huge splashes, pretty much soaking us all. Even though I wanted to scold her, the smile on her face and the excitement in Zeus made me happy.

"Thanks for bringing us here, Tick! I love it!" she shouted, tossing her hands up in excitement.

"Anytime." Tristan smiled.

"I'm glad my daughter likes you. Otherwise I would've never spoken to you again."

He laughed. "I'm glad my dog likes you. Otherwise I would've been convinced that you were a psycho. A person should always trust their pet's instincts. Dogs are better at judging the character of a person than people are."

"Is that so?"

"It is." He paused and ran his fingers through his hair. "Why does your daughter keep calling me Tick?"

"Oh… Because the first time we met I called you a dick, and she asked what a dick was, and seeing as how I'm an awful parent, I told her I said *tick* and explained to her that a tick is a bug."

"So she thinks I'm a parasite that lives on the blood of mammals?"

"I think it's actually an ectoparasite, seeing as how they live on the outside of the mammals as opposed to in the interior. And they live on some amphibians too."

He snickered. "Well, that makes me feel better."

I laughed. "It should."

"Well, Emma, if you're going to call me Tick, I think it's only right for me to call you Tock!" Tristan smiled.

"Like a clock!" Emma beamed, jumping up and down. "Tick and Tock! Tick and Tock!"

"I think she approves," I said.

"Elizabeth?" He turned my way with a serious stare.

"Yes?"

"I know we can't do what we were doing before anymore, but can we be friends?" he asked timidly.

"I thought you didn't know how to be a friend?"

"I don't." He sighed, rubbing his neck. "But I was kind of hoping you could show me."

"Why me?"

"You believe in good things, even when your heart is broken. And I can't remember what good things are like."

That saddened me. "When was the last time you were happy, Tristan?"

He didn't reply.

That saddened me even more. "Of course we can be friends," I said.

Everyone deserved at least one friend they could trust with their secrets and fears. With their guilt, with their happiness. Everyone deserved a person who could look into their eyes and say, "You're enough. You're perfect, scars and all." I thought Tristan deserved that more than most, though. In his eyes, he held such sadness, such pain, and all I wanted to do was wrap my arms around him and let him know he was good enough.

I didn't want to be his friend because I felt bad for him, though. No. I wanted his friendship because, unlike most, he saw past my own fake happiness, and he would sometimes stare at me as if he were saying, "You're enough, Elizabeth. You're enough…scars and all."

Tristan's brow furrowed, and he looked at me as if he was seeing me for the first time. I stared at him as if I would never see him again. Neither of us wanted to blink. The seriousness of the moment started making us both uncomfortable. As he cleared his throat, I cleared mine. "Too much?" I asked.

"Too much indeed. So, on another note…" He ran his hands through his hair. "I noticed a certain *Fifty Shades of Grey* book in your hands when I last cut the grass."

My cheeks reddened, and I shoved him. "Don't judge me; it's for my book club. Plus, it's good."

"I'm not judging. Okay, well, I am. Only a little, though."

"Don't knock it till you've tried it." I smirked.

"Oh? And how much of it have you actually tried?" He gave me a smug look, and I swore my cheeks were on fire.

Snickering, I started walking back toward our houses. "You're such an ass," I muttered. "Come on, Emma, let's get you cleaned up and get you to your sleepover."

"You're going the wrong way," Tristan remarked.

I paused, turned around, and walked past him again, going the opposite way. "You're *still* an ass." I smiled. He smiled back and walked beside me as Emma and Zeus followed our lead.

It was ten thirty at night when I heard the banging. I dragged myself out of bed to answer the door. Susan was standing there with her arms crossed beside Emma, who was still in her pajamas, holding her overnight bag and Bubba.

"Susan, what's going on?" I asked, alarm filling me up. "Emma, are you okay?" She didn't reply; she just stared at the ground, almost embarrassed. I turned back to Susan. "What happened?"

"What happened," she hissed. "What happened was that your daughter thought it was okay to tell stories about zombies to the rest of the girls, making them all freak out. Now I have ten girls at my house who won't go to sleep because they're afraid of nightmares!"

I frowned. "I'm sorry. I'm sure she didn't mean any harm. I can come over and talk to the girls if you want. I'm sure it's all a misunderstanding."

"A misunderstanding?" She huffed. "She started walking like a zombie and said she wanted to eat brains! You told me she didn't suffer any trauma from Steven's death."

"She didn't," I said, anger building in my stomach. I looked down at Emma and saw tears falling from her eyes. Bending down, I pulled her into a hug. "It's okay, honey."

"Well, obviously she's not okay. She needs professional help."

"Emma, honey, cover your ears really fast," I said. She did. My insides tightened and I stood tall, facing Susan. "I'm going to say something, and I mean this in the nicest way possible. If you say one more thing about my daughter, I will literally kick your ass, pull out your hair extensions, and tell your husband that you've been screwing the checkout boy at the grocery store."

"How dare you!" she cried, horrified by my words.

"How dare *I*? How dare *you* think it's appropriate to walk up to me and tell me things about my daughter in such a rude, demeaning fashion? I think it's time for you to go."

"I think it is! Perhaps you should stay away from our book club too. Your energy and lifestyle is toxic to our group. Keep her away from my Rachel," Susan ordered, walking off.

"Don't worry," I shouted. "I will!" There was something that happened to the sanest people when others talked about their children: you turned into a beast and would do anything and everything to protect your children from the wolves of the world. I wasn't proud of the words I'd said to Susan, but from the bottom of my heart, I meant every single one.

I walked Emma into the living room and we sat down. "Mama, the girls said I was a freak because I liked zombies and mummies. I don't want to be a freak."

"You're not a freak," I promised, pulling her closer to me. "You're perfect the way you are."

"Then why did they say that?" she asked.

"Because..." I sighed, trying to find the right answer. "Because sometimes others have a hard time embracing people's differences. You know that zombies aren't real, right?" She nodded. "And you didn't try to scare the other girls, did you?"

"No!" she said quickly. "I just wanted them to play with me as the characters from *Hotel Transylvania*. I didn't want to scare them. I just wanted to have friends."

My heart is breaking.

"You want to play with Mama?" I asked.

She shook her head. "No."

"Well, how about we watch a cartoon on Netflix and have our own sleepover?"

Her eyes lit up, and the tears stopped. "Can we watch *Avengers?*" she asked, loving superheroes almost as much as her father had.

"Of course," I said.

She fell asleep right as the Hulk appeared on screen. I placed her in her bed, kissing her forehead. She began to smile in her sleep, and then I went to bed to find my own dreams.

CHAPTER 19
Elizabeth

T ristan," I faintly muttered. My breaths were uneven, heavy.

His hand brushed against my cheek. "Suck it slow," he ordered, running his thumb against my bottom lip. He slid his finger into my mouth, allowing me to suck it gently as he rocked it in and out of my mouth before pulling it away from me and running the wetness down my neck, against my bra strap, down my cleavage. My nipples were hardening from his touch, longing for his mouth to find its way to each one.

"You're beautiful," he said. "You're so fucking beautiful."

"We shouldn't," I moaned, feeling his hardness pressed against my panties. *We should*, I thought to myself. "We're not supposed to do this anymore..." My breaths were heavy, hungry for him to be inside me, hungry for him to take me deeply. I wanted him to turn me around, lift my legs, and take me hard. He ignored my protest—as I wanted him to—twisting my hair in one hand and moving his other down my body, landing at my black lace panties.

"You're wet," he said, bending in closer to me, running his tongue against my cheek before he slipped his mouth over mine. He whispered as he slid his tongue between my lips. "I want to taste all of you," he hissed. His fingers rolled against my panties, my breaths catching as his thumb circled my clit through the faint fabric.

"Please," I begged. I arched my back, longing for his hand to remove the thin barrier.

"Not here," he said, lifting me up to a sitting position. He slid my panties to the left and bent down, allowing his tongue to taste my wetness. My hips involuntarily arched in his direction as my hands ran through his hair. When he lifted his head, he rested his mouth against mine, allowing me to taste myself, to taste him. "I want to show you something," he muttered against my lips.

Anything. Show me anything.

My eyes fell to his erection hidden beneath his boxers, and a smile came to my lips. He lifted me off the bed and pressed me against the closest door. "How bad do you want it?" *Bad*, I thought, unable to speak. My heart was racing, and I was almost afraid it would give up on me, unable to keep up with my wants, my desires. I wanted to explode for him. I wanted to lose myself to him. His hips rocked toward me as he pushed his hardness against my body.

"I want to show you the room," he whispered against my ear, flicking his tongue up and down before sucking my lobe.

"Mmm," I replied as he carried me down the hallway. There was a room to my left, which I hadn't noticed when I'd first arrived. "What is…?"

He shushed me, placing his hand over my lips. "It's my green room," he muttered, pushing the door open.

"Your what?" Before he could reply, I turned around and saw a room filled with all green furniture. Green whips, green dildos, green *everything.* "What the…" I shut up and kept looking around. "This is kind of weird, babe…"

"I know," he said with a deep tone of voice. When I turned back to him, my throat burned as a scream escaped me. I was staring at a huge, green man who was holding me against his body. His eyes were glowing green and he held me up. *"Incredible Hulk wants to smash you!"*

"Holy shit!" I screamed, shaking myself from a very weird, twisted nightmare. Within seconds, Tristan was standing at his bedroom window, looking at me.

"Are you okay?"

I looked down to see I was wearing a white tank top with white panties and no bra. I screamed again, covering my chest with a blanket. "Oh my God, go away!" I hissed, freaking out.

"I'm sorry! I heard you scream and…" He paused and raised an eyebrow, looking into my eyes. "Did you just have a sex dream?" He started chuckling, covering his mouth with his hand. "You just had a sex dream."

"Go away!" I said, leaping up from my bed and closing my window shades.

"Okay, okay, you nasty woman, you. I told you about those books."

My cheeks blushed over, and I collapsed back on my bed, pulling the cover over my head.

Freaking *Incredible Hulk.* Freaking *Tristan Cole.*

CHAPTER 20
Elizabeth

"You've been avoiding eye contact with me all day," Tristan said as he moved some items around in Needful Things. I sat at the counter, watching Mr. Henson make me an herbal tea mixture. Emma and Zeus were running around on a hunt for random objects in the store. We'd been coming to Mr. Henson's shop weekly now for tea, hot cocoa, and every now and again a tarot reading. I was beginning to love the place. "You don't have to be shy about it; I'm pretty sure it happens to everyone," Tristan explained.

"What are you talking about? I'm not avoiding you. And I *don't* know what happens to everyone because nothing happened to me." I huffed, totally avoiding his stare. Each time I looked at him, I couldn't stop blushing and imagining his shirt bursting open as he transformed into a beast.

"It was just a sex dream," he said.

"It *wasn't* a *sex* dream!" I vocalized, sounding a little too guilty.

Tristan turned to Mr. Henson with a smug smirk on his face. "Elizabeth was having a sex dream last night."

"Shut up, Tristan!" I screamed, slamming my hands against the table. My face was beet red, and I couldn't stop it from heating up.

Mr. Henson looked at me and then at my tea mixture, and added a few more herbs. "Sex dreams are normal."

"Was it a good sex dream?" Tristan badgered me. I was five seconds away from figuring out a way I could beat him up.

My lips parted to deny the dream, but I couldn't. My hands cupped my face, and I sighed heavily. "We aren't talking about this."

"Come on, you have to tell us now," he said, walking over to sit on the stool beside me.

I twisted away from him.

He took my stool and twisted me back toward him.

"Oh, crap," he muttered, looking at me with eyes filled with understanding.

"Shut up, Tristan!" I muttered again, unable to look at him for too long.

"You had a sex dream about *me*?!" he hollered, and I slugged him in the arm as a reflex at his words.

Mr. Henson chortled. "Plot twist."

A wicked smile spread across Tristan's face, and it was official: *I. Am. Dying!* He leaned in and whispered, "Did I do that thing with my tongue to your lips?"

I blushed. "Which lips are we talking about?" I whispered back.

His wolfish grin deepened. "You filthy, filthy girl."

Pushing myself off my stool, my eyes met Mr. Henson's. "Can I get that in a to-go cup?"

"Oh, come on, Elizabeth. I need to know more!" Tristan said, laughing at my embarrassment. I ignored him and took my tea, which Mr. Henson had transferred to a to-go cup.

"I'm not talking to you," I said, moving to leave the store. "Come on, Emma, let's go."

"Just a few more details!" he begged as I held the front door open.

A heavy sigh left me, and I turned his way. "You took me to a green room where you transformed into a green monster and started smashing me around the room. And I mean 'smashing' in every possible sense of the word."

Blinking eyes. Blinking eyes. Blank stare. Blank stare. "Come again?"

His paramount confusion almost made me burst into laughter. "You wanted to know."

"You're a really, *really* odd woman."

Mr. Henson smiled. "Ah, the same thing happened to me during the summer of 1976."

"You had a sex dream?" I asked, confused.

"Dream? No, honey. I was tossed around a green room and smashed."

Awkward moment number five thousand four hundred and forty-two of my stay in Meadows Creek. "On that note, I'm leaving. Thanks for the tea, Mr. Henson."

"I'll be by to cut the grass later today," Tristan said.

I knew there was nothing dirty about his words, but still, I blushed as if there was.

That afternoon, Faye came over because I wanted her help picking out the best designs and paint colors for Tristan's house. She always had such a solid eye for the tiny details.

We sat on the front porch with the three design boards I'd created, but instead of her focusing on the task at hand, she was watching the handsome man cutting my grass. Standing on his feet, helping him push the lawnmower was Emma, who was convinced she could cut grass better than Tristan. She argued with him the whole time, telling him how he was doing a terrible job. He just smiled and sassed her back. Faye stared at Tristan, almost awestruck at his transformation. She hadn't seen him since he'd cut off all of his hair and revealed his strong bone structure. She also hadn't ever seen him smile until today. His beard was already growing back in, and honestly I was happy about that. I loved his beard almost as much as I loved his smile.

"I can't believe it." Faye sighed. "Who would've ever thought that that wild, dirty hippie, asshole thing would ever become something so...*hot*?"

"We're all a little wild, and we're all a little something."

She turned to me, a silly grin finding her lips. "Oh shit. You like him."

"What? No. He just helps around the house. Mostly with the lawn."

Her voice took on a loud shout—she had no clue how to whisper. "Are you sure it's just the lawn? Or does he help unclog your drains too?"

"Faye! Shut up."

"Does he wash your dirty dishes? Your dishes were always so, so filthy."

"I'm not doing this with you." I blushed. "Anyway, I need your input. Which layout do you like the best for the living room and dining room area? I want to incorporate his wood pieces that he makes. Tristan builds a lot with wood and I think—"

"Is his wood good? Thick? Does Tristan have thick, long wood?"

I stared at her with narrow eyes. "Is your mind always in the gutter?"

"Always, babycakes. Always. You like him, though. I can tell."

"Not at all."

"You like him."

With a whisper and a turn of my stomach, I stared at Tristan, who was staring back at me. "Yeah. I like him."

"Jesus, Liz. Only you would fall for an asshole dude who ends up looking like Brad Pitt circa *Legends of the Fall*. Get it?" She smiled. "*Legends of the Fall*—character's name was Tristan?"

"Well, aren't you clever?"

"It's almost ridiculous."

I laughed. "Almost."

She stepped in closer and studied my face. "What's that?"

"What's what?"

"That weird, goofy grin you're giving me—holy face full of sex! You slept with him!"

"What? No, I—"

"Don't try to outsmart the sexoholic, Liz. You totally boned him!"

Like a little girl who'd just gotten her first kiss, I squirmed. "I totally boned him!"

"Sweet Jesus! Yes!" She stood up on the front porch and started chanting. "YES! YES! YES!!! The drought is over!"

Tristan turned our way and raised an eyebrow. "Everything okay, ladies?"

I pulled Faye back down to sit and giggled. "Everything's fine."

"Including that sweet ass of his," Faye muttered with a smirk. "So, how was it?"

"Well, let's just say I gave his thing a nickname."

Tears formed in her eyes, and her hands flew over her heart. "My little girl is growing up. Okay, what's the name?"

"The Incredible Hulk."

She cringed. "I'm sorry, what?"

"The Incr—"

"No, no. I heard you the first time. You mean that green monster thing? Liz, are you fucking a guy with a green penis? Because if you are, you need a tetanus shot." She eyed me up and down, cringing. "And higher standards."

I laughed. "Can I tell you the truth about Tristan and me without you giving me a scolding?"

"Absolutely."

"We used sex with each other to remember Steven and Jamie. It's kind of like…we used each other to have the feeling we used to get with them."

"You mean you, like, envision Steven while Tristan's screwing you?"

"Yeah. I mean, well, at first I did. We don't do it anymore, though. I got way too emotional and couldn't handle it."

"But now you like him."

"Yeah. Which is bad, because he was just seeing Jamie when he was with me."

Faye's eyes glanced over at Tristan. "Bullshit."

"What?"

"He sees you, Liz."

"What are you talking about?"

"Listen, coming from a girl who has slept with a ton of different guys and has envisioned Channing Tatum for most of those guys, I can tell the difference between when a person is thinking about you and when they are thinking about someone else. Look at the way he's staring at you."

I glanced over at Tristan to find his stare, once again, on me. Did he really think about me when we were together?

And if it were true that he did, why did the idea of that make me so happy? I shook my head back and forth, not wanting to really face the fact of what was happening between Tristan and me. "So what's the deal with you and Matty? How's that going?"

"Terrible." She sighed, slamming her hand against her face. "I need to break things off with him."

"What? Why?"

"Because, like a loser, I went ahead and fell in love with him."

My eyes lit up. "You're in love."

"I know, it's awful. I drink every night to try to forget about it. Now shut up and let's go back to talking about Tristan's wood."

I smiled, and after a few hours and about a hundred dirty comments, Faye and I picked out the colors for each and every room in his house.

CHAPTER 21
Elizabeth

A few days passed before Sam called me up on Friday to ask if I was interested in hanging out with him. I'd figured he had forgotten that months before, he'd said he'd show me around the town, but I guessed some people were just a little slower getting around to things. On Friday night he pulled up to my house in his family's work truck. I watched him from the living-room window as he hopped out of his truck and fixed his bow tie. He started stepping toward the house, and then he paused and stepped backward. This went on for about five more rounds before he finally made it up the porch, where he debated knocking or not.

Tristan leaned behind me and studied Sam's movements. "*Oh*, you got a hot date tonight? Is that why you're wearing that cute little dress?" For the past few days, Tristan had been staying in our guest room since his house was being painted. That night we'd been going over my ideas for his house, and I'd been showing him different boards I'd created with ideas for the space. He seemed less than interested, but I was just happy to be doing what I loved once again.

"It's not a date," I said. "Sam just wanted to show me around Meadows Creek a bit, to get me out of the house." Tristan cocked an eyebrow. "What? What's wrong with that?" I asked.

"You do know that he thinks this is a date, right?"

"What?" I stood up a tad. "No, he doesn't. He just doesn't want me sitting around the house." Tristan gave me a bullshit-it's-totally-a-date look. "Shut up, Tris."

"All I'm saying is I doubt Stalker Sam knows that it's not a date."

"What does that mean? What do you mean *Stalker* Sam?" I asked, my voice timid. Tristan gave me a wicked grin and started walking away. "Tristan! What do you mean *Stalker Sam*?!"

"Ever since he moved into town, he has a history of coming on a little strong sometimes, that's all. I'd watch him follow girls around in town when I would be out running. Did he say where he was taking you?"

"Yes, and it's not really a place where dates happen, so I think you're wrong."

"The town hall meeting?"

"Exactly!" I said, pleased with the idea. "The town hall meeting isn't a place you take someone you think you're going on a date with." Tristan's lips pressed together as if he was trying to hold in a chuckle. "Stop it," I argued. There was one knock on the door. "He doesn't really think this is a date, does he?"

"I bet ten dollars Stalker Sam leans over to you during Sheriff Johnson's speech about the town fair and asks you if you want to go down to the barn house where there's always a fish fry, dancing, and karaoke after the town meeting."

"You don't want to pay me ten dollars."

"You're right, I don't. But it doesn't matter because I'm going to win the bet," he joked cockily. "Stalker Sam is going to woo you."

Knock number two.

"Stop calling him Stalker Sam!" I whispered, feeling my heartbeat increase. "He's not going to ask me to the barn house."

"You bet money on it?" he said, holding his hand out.

I shook his hand. "Fine. Ten dollars that this isn't a date."

"Ah, easiest money I ever made, Lizzie."

The nickname left his mouth as if it was effortless. When I pulled my hand back from his, I tried not to show how much the simple nickname affected me.

Knock number three.

"What's wrong?"

"You called me Lizzie."

His brow furrowed with confusion.

"It's just…no one called me that except for Steven."

"Sorry," he said, nodding a little. "It slipped out."

"No, no. I like it." *I've missed it.* I gave him a small smile. We stared at each other, standing still as if the soles of our shoes were superglued to the floor. My eyes traveled to the small unfinished tattoo on his left hand, and I forced myself to take it in, instead of his stare; sometimes it was too much looking him in the eyes. "I like it."

"Then I'll keep saying it."

Knock number four.

"You should probably…" Tristan's head nodded in the direction of the door. I shook my head and agreed, rushing to open the door to Sam, who was giving me the biggest smile and holding a bunch of flowers in his hands.

"Hey, Elizabeth." Sam smiled, stretching his hands out to me with the flowers. "Wow. You look beautiful. These are for you. I was sitting out here and realized I didn't bring you anything, so I don't know. I just picked them from the front of the house for ya." His eyes moved to Tristan, who was standing a few feet from us. "What's that asshole doing here?"

"Oh, Sam. This is Tristan. Tristan, Sam," I said, introducing the two. "Tristan's house is being painted, so he's staying with Emma and me for a few days."

Tristan held his hand out toward Sam with his beautiful smile. "Nice to meet ya, Sam."

"You too, Tristan," Sam said warily.

Tristan patted him on the back, his wolfish grin in full force. "Oh, no need to be so formal with my name. By all means, call me Asshole."

I giggled to myself. *What a jerk.*

Sam cleared his throat. "Anyway, sorry about the flowers. I should've thought to grab some from town, but—"

"Don't worry about it, buddy," Tristan said, knowing he was making him feel extra levels of discomfort. "How about you come on in and take a seat in the living room while Elizabeth and I find a vase or something to toss the flowers in?"

"Oh, okay, yeah, sounds good," Sam agreed, allowing me to take the flowers from his grip. "Careful," he said. "They have thorns."

"I think I can handle it. Thanks, Sam. Take a seat and I'll be right back."

The moment I stepped into the kitchen, Tristan was already giving me a smart-ass grin. "If you keep looking at me like that, I will beat you up, Tristan. This doesn't mean it's a date." He snickered. I narrowed my eyes. "It doesn't!"

"He stole flowers for you from the front of your house. It's much more serious than I thought. He loves you. That's like a Bonnie-and-Clyde-type love."

"You're an ass." He started filling up a vase with water for the flowers. As I passed them to him, a thorn landed in my finger, and I cursed under my breath as blood started to appear. "Crap."

Tristan took the flowers, tossed them into the vase, and then took my hand in his, examining the small bit of blood. "It's not too bad," he said, grabbing a rag and holding it against my finger. My stomach was building with butterflies that didn't have a place in my life. I tried my best to ignore them, but the truth was, Tristan's touch was nice, gentle, and wanted. "Stalker Sam was right about one thing, though," Tristan said with his stare on my finger.

"And what's that?"

"You do look beautiful." Our hands stayed together, and he stepped in closer to me. I liked how close he was. I loved how close he was. His breaths were heavy. "Lizzie?"

"Yes?"

"Would you be mad if I kissed you? And by kiss you, I mean you, not the memory of Jamie." His eyes studied my lips. My heart was pounding against my rib cage as he moved in closer and brushed a fallen piece of hair behind my ear. Our hands stayed attached for a second longer before he cleared his throat and pulled away from me. A wave of embarrassment filled his eyes. "Sorry. Ignore me." I blinked a few times and tried to shake the nervous feeling away. It wouldn't leave. He knotted his hands together before resting them on the back of his neck. "You better get back to your date."

"It's not a—" I started to say, but when I noticed his lips turning down a bit, I dropped the subject. "Have a good night."

He nodded once. "You too, Lizzie."

I stared up at the podium where Tanner was speaking about why Needful Things should be closed down. It made me sick to my stomach listening to him tear into Mr. Henson, who was sitting a few rows back at the town meeting. Mr. Henson didn't seem fazed by Tanner's words at all, though. He just sat and smiled.

I'd never truly seen that side of Tanner—the business-driven side of him. The one who would say and do pretty much anything to get his way, even if that meant throwing a nice old man under the bus.

It left me with such a taste of disgust.

"Tanner has some great reasons why Mr. Henson should give up his store. He says it's a waste of space since nobody ever goes into the place," Sam said.

"I think it's a great store."

He raised an eyebrow. "You've been in there?"

"Many times."

"And you haven't grown warts or anything? Mr. Henson practices voodoo and stuff in his back room. Turns out when the Clintons' cat Molly went missing, someone saw her wander into Mr. Henson's store, and I kid you not, Molly came out as a pit bull dog. Even answered to the name and all. It's freaky."

Chuckling, I said, "You don't believe that, do you?"

"Heck yeah, I do. I'm surprised you didn't come out with a third eye or something after going into that place."

"Oh, I did. I'm just really good with makeup."

He chuckled. "You make me laugh, Elizabeth. I like that about you." His eyes locked with mine, and he gave me a longing stare. *Oh no...*

I broke our stare and pointed to someone else. "What about them? What's their story?"

He didn't get a chance to tell me because Sheriff Johnson was walking up to the stage.

The moment Sheriff Johnson stepped up to the microphone to speak about the town fair, I knew I owed Tristan ten dollars. Right on cue, Sam leaned over and whispered in my ear, "You know, I was thinking maybe we can go to the fish fry after this. It's real good, and there's a lot of dancing and stuff that goes on. It's a great time."

I smiled. I wasn't sure how to turn him down. He looked so hopeful. "Well…" His eyes widened with a sparkle of excitement. "I would love that."

He took his baseball cap off his head and slapped it against his knee. "Woo! Awesome, awesome, awesome!"

Sam couldn't stop smiling wide, and I couldn't stop feeling as if going with him was a major mistake. Plus, I was out ten bucks, which sucked.

Sam and I sat in two chairs watching everyone else dance around drunkenly and freely as he told me the backstory of each and every person in the room. He turned to face me and said, "I hope you're having fun."

"I am." I smiled.

"Maybe we can go on another date at some point?"

My jaw tightened. "Sam, you're a wonderful person, but I don't really think I'm in a place to be dating. You know what I mean? My life is currently a mess."

He released a nervous chuckle and nodded in understanding. "I get it. I just…" He placed his hands on his knees, and our gazes met. "I had to try. Just had to put myself out there."

"I'm glad you did."

"So you said you're not ready to date? Are you sure it has nothing to do with your feelings for Tristan?" he asked.

"What?"

A smile found his lips. "I read people, remember? I saw the way you looked at him at your house. He makes you happy. I think that's nice."

"We're just friends," I argued.

He kept smiling but didn't say another word about it.

I nudged him in the shoulder and said, "Are you sure you don't want to get out there and dance?"

He wrung his fingers together and looked at the ground. "I ain't much of a dancer. I'm more of a watcher."

"Come on," I said, holding my hand out toward him. "It will be fun."

Sam hesitated for a while longer before he reached out and took my hand. We walked to the dance floor, and I watched as his nerves built up more and more. His stare was trained on his tennis shoes, and I could see him counting his steps in his head.

One.

Two.

Three.

One.

Two.

Three.

"Eye contact helps," I offered. He didn't comment. He just kept counting as his face got more and more flushed with nerves. "You know what, I could really go for some water," I said. Sam's eyes met mine, and he gave me a grateful smile.

"I can get some for you," he said, thankful that he wouldn't have to dance anymore. I returned to my seat, and when he came back with the water, he handed it to me and sat. "This is nice, isn't it?"

"It is."

He cleared his throat and pointed out to someone else on the dance floor. "That over there is Susie. I guess she was the hot-dog-eating champion for years at the town fair. And over there is—"

"What about you, Sam? Tell me something about you."

There was hesitation in his eyes before he blinked and shrugged his shoulders. "There's not much to me."

"I'm sure that's a lie," I offered. "Why are you working at the café if your dad offered you a full-time spot at his business?" He studied my face, and I stared at his. His eyes were so handsome, but I could tell he was uncomfortable for some reason.

He broke the eye contact. "My dad wants me to take over the family business, but it's not what I want."

"What do you want to do?"

"Be a chef," he said. "I figured working at the café would be a start to learning a bit more about it until I could save up for school, but I'm never allowed back by the kitchen, so it's kind of a bust."

"I can talk to Matty about letting you get in the kitchen some-times," I offered.

A genuine smile rose on his lips and he thanked me but declined the offer, saying he would figure it out on his own. He pushed himself to a standing position. "Well, this is getting a bit too Dr. Phil for my liking, so I'm going to head over and get me some more catfish. Do you need anything?" he asked. I shook my head and watched him walk away.

"Oh thank God, you're still alive," muttered a voice next to me. I turned as Tristan slid into Sam's seat.

"What are you doing here?" *I'm so happy you're here. I like when you're here. Ask me the kissing question again.*

"Well," he began to explain. "When a friend goes on a date with Stalker Sam, it's your responsibility to check in on that friend."

Friend.

I'd been friend-zoned. *Ask me the kissing question! Please.*

"And since when are you the responsible friend?" I asked, playing nonchalant about the fact that my stomach was doing cartwheels and somersaults while unicorns and kittens danced around inside of me.

"Since about..." He glanced down at the invisible watch on his right wrist. "Five seconds ago. It sounded like fun to come and watch you and Sam make complete fools of each other." He tapped his fingers against his kneecaps, avoiding eye contact with me.

Oh my gosh...

He was jealous.

I wouldn't mock him about it, though. "Dance with me?" I asked.

When his hand reached out for mine, my heart skipped a beat. I placed my hand in his, and he led us to the dance floor. He spun me around once before pulling me closer to his body. My breaths were short and fast as I stared into his eyes. *What are you thinking, stormy eyes?* He stood inches over me, never letting his hold on me falter. I could feel the eyes of every person in the place staring at us. I could almost hear their judgments, their whispers.

My head lowered, my stare falling to the ground. I felt his finger lift my chin, and he forced my stare to meet his, which was fine. I liked looking at him, and I liked the way he looked at me. Even though I wasn't certain what it meant—the two of us staring at each other the way we were.

"You lied to me," I said.

"Never."

"You did."

"I'm not a liar."

"But you lied."

"About what?"

"The white feathers. I saw the receipt for them. You said you found them at Mr. Henson's shop."

He chuckled and frowned. "I might have lied to you about that."

I leaned in closer to his lips, seconds away from kissing him, seconds away from our first kiss where he was him, and I was me.

My hands fell against his chest, and I could feel his heartbeat against my touch. I could almost see his soul within his eyes. The song stopped, but we stayed close, our breathing patterns matching each other's. Our breaths heavy and nervous. Excited and scared. His thumb ran alongside my neck, and he stepped in closer. I liked how close he was. I feared how close he was. He tilted his head slightly as he gave me the smallest crooked smile, staring at me as if he was promising to never look away.

They all warned me about Tristan, begging me to stay away. *"He's an asshole, he's wild, and he's broken, Liz,"* they would say. *"He's nothing but the ugly scars of his yesterdays,"* they swore.

But what they didn't see, what they chose to ignore, was the fact that I was also a little wild, a bit crazy, and completely shattered too.

I was damaged goods at best.

But when I was with him, at least I remembered to breathe.

"Mind if we switch partners?" A familiar voice interrupted me from falling into Tristan's taste. I looked up to see Tanner smiling toward me with Faye in his arms.

I smiled, even though I kind of wanted to frown. "Of course."

As Tanner took my hand, Tristan took Faye's. I missed him even though he was only a few steps away from me.

"Don't look so disappointed," Tanner said, pulling me close to him. "I know I have two left feet, but I can still move my hips pretty well," he joked.

"I happen to remember a certain holiday party where you won the award for the best *worst* dancer."

He crinkled up his nose. "I still think that my shopping cart dance should've won the best dancer, but with your husband as the judge, I knew I would be screwed over."

I laughed. "The shopping cart. How did that one go again?"

With two steps back, Tanner started pretending that he was pushing a shopping cart and placing items into said shopping cart. He then started to invisibly place his items on a checkout lane where he scanned his food and bagged it up. I couldn't stop laughing. He smirked and moved back to me, falling into our much slower and easier dance routine.

"Perfect. You really should've won the best dancer that night."

"Right?!" He bit his bottom lip. "I was screwed."

"Don't worry. I'm sure there are plenty of holiday parties in the future where you can reclaim your victory."

He nodded in agreement and combed my hair behind my ear. "God. I missed you, Liz."

"I missed you too. Gosh, I've missed everyone. It just feels good to…feel again."

"Yeah. Man, that has to be great. So this is the point where I clear my throat and take a leap of faith, asking you if you want to maybe get dinner with me at some point."

"Dinner?" I asked, taken back by his question. "Like a date?" Out of the corner of my eye, I saw Tristan dancing with Faye.

"Well, not *like* a date. But an actual date. Me and you. I know this probably seems weird and all, but—"

"I'm kind of seeing someone, Tanner."

His face dropped, confusion in his stare. "Seeing someone?" He stood straighter, uttering his fogged thoughts. "Are you seeing Sam? I know you two came together, but I didn't think he was your type. I didn't think—"

"It's not Sam."

"It's not?" His stare moved across the room, landing on Tristan and Faye. When he looked back at me, the playfulness I'd seen moments before was gone. All color was drained from his face, where a new, vibrant irritation now existed. "Tristan Cole?! You're seeing Tristan Cole?!" he whisper-shouted. I cringed. I wasn't exactly seeing Tristan. I truly had no clue how he even felt about me, but I knew I had these feelings for him—and I couldn't ignore them much longer.

"You come back to town, and you pick the absolute worst person to start dating."

"He's not as terrible as everyone thinks."

"You're right; he's even worse."

"Tanner." I placed my hands against his chest. "I didn't mean for this to happen, I didn't mean to feel whatever it is I'm feeling for him, but you can't help who you fall for."

"Yes. You can. Tristan and Mr. Henson are not the kinds of people you want to be associated with."

"What's your problem with Mr. Henson's shop, anyway? Mr. Henson is one of the kindest men I've ever met."

He pinched the bridge of his nose. "You're wrong, Liz. And I'm terrified that Tristan is going to hurt you."

"He won't." He didn't believe me. He somehow convinced himself that the idea of me and Tristan was a terrible thing. Just like the rest of the town. "Tanner, he won't. Now, come on," I said, pulling him closer to me, feeling how stiff his body was. "Just dance with your friend and stop worrying so much about me."

"I'm worried about your heart, Liz. After Steven, you were destroyed. I don't want your heart to get broken again."

Oh, Tanner.

I lay my head against his chest, and he combed his fingers through my hair. "I'll be okay. I promise."

"And if you're not?"

"Well, I guess I'll just need you to hug me sometimes."

CHAPTER 22
Tristan

I don't think we have properly met," Faye said as we danced together. "So you're the penis that's been inside my best friend's vagina."

Well, that's one way of putting it. "And you're the highly inappropriate best friend."

She smiled wide. "That's me. So listen, this is the part where I tell you if you hurt Liz, I will kill you."

I laughed. "She and I are just friends."

"You're kidding, right? Jesus. The two of you are two of the dumbest human beings on the planet. You honestly can't tell that my best friend is falling for you?"

"What?"

"Look at her!" Faye said, glancing at Elizabeth. "She can't take her eyes off of us because she's terrified that you might make me laugh, or I might touch your balls, or the wind might blow your penis into my mouth!"

"Wait, what?"

"Oh my freaking gosh, do I really have to spell it out for you? She's jealous, Tristan!"

"Of us?"

"Of anyone and everyone who looks at you." Faye grew sober. "Just, be easy with her, okay? Don't break her heart. It's already in a million pieces."

"Don't worry." I shrugged. "So is mine." My eyes locked with Tanner, who was giving me a hard stare. "What about him? Is he jealous and secretly in love with me too?"

Faye stared at Tanner with a look of distaste. "No. He just hates your guts."

"Why?"

"Because for some reason Liz chose you over him. Can you keep a secret?"

"Probably not, no."

She smiled. "Oh well, I guess I can't either because I'm about to tell it to you. The night before Liz and Steven's wedding, Tanner came stumbling over to Liz's place. Luckily I answered the door and Liz was sleeping, but he told me that Liz was making a big mistake, that she should've been marrying him and not Steven."

"He's been in love with her all this time?"

"Love, lust, I don't know, wanting what you can't have? Anyway, it's probably killing him that when she finally came back to town, she didn't even bat her eyes at him once. He probably had his mind made up that Liz would finally pick him; what a blow to the ballsack when she came back and picked the biggest asshole there was." She paused and smiled. "No offense."

"Some taken."

I swung her around once and pulled her close to me. "For the record, though." Faye's grin switched wider. "I don't think you're a complete jerk anymore, so in a few weeks we are having a birthday party for Liz and you're invited. It's just going to be about getting her to dance on bar counters and be free from the mind demons that take over her for a little while, and I am giving you full permission to touch her vagina that night."

I laughed. "That's really kind of you."

"What can I say?" She smirked. "I'm a solid friend."

After the dance with Faye, I found a seat in the back corner of the room and tried to absorb everything I'd been told. I watched Elizabeth talking to Sam before she hugged him and he headed out of the building. I guessed their night together was over. *Good.* When Elizabeth walked over, I couldn't even deny the way my heart skipped.

"It looked like you and Faye were getting along well," she said, sitting beside me.

"The same could be said about you and Tanner," I replied.

"That's not the same. Tanner and I are just friends. So what…did she ask you to have sex with her? I bet you said yes. But I don't think you should with all the issues you're dealing with." She bit her bottom lip. "But did she ask you?"

I cocked an eyebrow at her sassy expression. "Is that a real question?"

"I'm just saying, I don't think sticking your penis inside a woman is a great way to cope with the stress of your life."

"But isn't that what you and I were doing?" I argued.

"And it didn't work out too well, did it?"

Faye was right. Clarity filled my head as I took in Elizabeth's features. Her face was flushed, and she kept running her hands against her legs. Our gaze met. I edged my chair closer to her and placed her legs in between mine. Leaning in toward her, I whispered, "I get it now."

I watched a sigh roll from her lips as she studied our proximity. "Get what?"

"You're jealous."

She huffed loudly and laughed. "Jealous? Don't be ridiculous, Narcissus."

Giving her a soft, therapist tone, I took her hands into mine. "You don't have to be embarrassed. It's completely normal to at some point develop feelings for one's neighbor. Why would you think that's ridiculous?"

She yanked her hands from mine, and it took everything in me to not crack up laughing in her face at how red she was turning. "Why? You want all the reasons why? Well, for starters, lately you haven't shaved, and you look like a lumberjack, which is repulsive. With your beanie hat and your thick beard, I'm semi-surprised you're not wearing plaid. Do you even shower?"

"I shower. If you want, we could go back to my place and shower together to save water."

"Look at you being an environmental activist and all."

"Not really. I just love making you wet." Her cheeks blushed as I studied the few freckles dappling her face. She was so damn beautiful. "Plus," I said, trying to break my thoughts away from the fact that I was feeling for her everything I hoped she was feeling for me. "I saw the Timber app on your cell phone. You don't have to hide your love for lumberjacks. No one's judging you out loud. Mostly it's silent, side-eye judgment, but really, that doesn't even count."

"The app was a trending topic on the side of my Facebook page, Tristan! Faye made me get it, and I was curious, *that's all*!" She was getting redder and redder by the second, and my body was starting to react to being so close to hers. I wanted to press my hands against her heated cheeks to feel her warmth. I wanted to lay my fingers against her chest and feel her heart pound from nerves. I wanted to taste her lips...

"What's the deal with you and Tanner?" I asked once more.

"I told you, he and I are just friends."

"It looked like more from the way he held you."

She laughed, looking at the ground. "Who's jealous now?"

"I am."

"What?" Her head rose, and she met my stare.

"I said I'm jealous. I'm jealous of the way his hand lay against your back. I'm jealous of the way he made you laugh. I'm jealous of the way his words filled your ears. I'm jealous that for those few moments he got to stare into those eyes, and I had to stand back and watch it all unfold."

"What are you doing?" she said, her breaths short, confused. My lips were lingering inches away from hers. Her hands were resting against my jeans. My hands were lying against her fingers. We were so close I was almost certain she was sitting in my lap, and I could hear her heartbeat.

The room around us was loud as always. People were getting drunk, people were eating, and people were discussing mediocre shit in a mediocre way. But my eyes...they were trained on her lips. On the curves of her mouth. On the color of her skin. On *her*.

"Tris, stop," she whispered against my skin, but she inched her body closer. It seemed she was as confused as I was, her body going against what her mind was demanding she do.

"Tell me you don't want this," I begged her. *Turn me away.*

"It's... I..." She was stuttering, her eyes on my mouth. Her voice was shaking, and I could hear her fears loud and clear, but somewhere within those fears and doubts was a small whisper of hope. I wanted to hold on to that as long as I could. I wanted to feel the hope she kept locked away deep in her soul. "Tristan... Do you..." She chuckled nervously and ran her fingers back and forth against her forehead. "Do you ever think of me? I mean..." Her tongue stumbled, and she went silent. Her nerves were eating at her thoughts, jumbling them. "Do you ever think of me in a way that is more than a friendship?" When she looked into my eyes, she had to see the answer. I felt her soul staring deep into mine. Her eyes were full of wondering interest, and her beauty was softened by an air of mystery.

I blinked once. "Every second. Every minute. Every hour. Every day."

She nodded, closing her eyes. "Me too. Every second. Every minute. Every hour. Every day."

Pull away, Tristan.

Pull away, Tristan.

Pull away, Tris...

"Lizzie," I said, pulling her closer. "I want to kiss you. The real you. The sad you. The broken you."

"That would change things."

She was right. It would be crossing that invisible line that was dangling right in front of us. I'd kissed her before, but that was different. That was before I started falling for her. Falling and falling hard. I exhaled the breath I'd been holding and felt her do the same against my skin. "And what would happen if I didn't kiss you?"

"I would hate you a little," she said softly as I rested my lips millimeters away from hers. "I would hate you a lot."

My lips pressed into hers as she arched her back and grabbed my

T-shirt, pulling me closer. A light moan left her as I slid my tongue into her mouth and made love to her tongue. She kissed me hard, almost sliding into my lap, almost giving me all of her. "I want you to let me in," she muttered against me. It took everything in me to not wrap my arms around her and take her back to my house and explore every inch of her body. I wanted to feel her wrapped around me. I wanted to feel myself deep inside her. I tugged on her bottom lip, and she kissed me gently before pulling away. "I want to know who you are, Tristan. I want to know where you go when you get lost in your mind. I want to know what makes you shout in your dreams. I want to see the darkness in you that you fight daily to keep hidden. Can you do something for me?" she asked.

"Anything."

Her hands fell to my heart, and she watched my inhales and exhales against her fingertips. "Show me the part of you that you try to keep buried. Show me where it hurts the most. I want to see your soul."

CHAPTER 23
Elizabeth

He took me to the shed.

For the longest time, I'd wondered what it was he did inside those walls. After he unlocked it, he swung the two doors wide open. The space was dark, and I couldn't see anything until he pulled on a lamp cord, turning on a light. The room lit up as he led me inside.

"Charlie…" I muttered, staring around at a room that was set up like a mini library. The shelves were filled with novels, both children's books and more classic tales such as *To Kill a Mockingbird* and a huge Stephen King collection. The bookshelves were all hand built, and I could tell Tristan was the one who'd built them.

There was one bookshelf that held only toys—dinosaurs, cars, toy soldiers.

Yet the toys and the bookshelves weren't what shook me the most. I stared at the walls of the shed and studied the words carved into the wood. It looked as if he had filled the walls up with notes, with memories—with apologies.

"Every time I missed him, every time I thought of him, I carved it into the wood," he explained as my fingertips ran across the painful words Tristan had only shared with himself...until now.

I'm sorry I left you.

I'm sorry I wasn't there.

I'm sorry I didn't let you read certain books.

I'm sorry I never took you fishing.

I'm sorry you'll never fall in love.

I wish I could forget.

I miss you...

"Plus," he whispered, "Jamie always wanted me to build her a library; I always put it off for tomorrow. I thought I had more time, but sometimes tomorrow never comes, and you're only left with the memories of yesterdays."

When I found his stare, he tried his best to blink his emotion away. I could see the pain that still lived fresh in his mind, in his heart. I stepped toward him. "It wasn't your fault, Tristan."

He shook his head in disagreement. "It was. If I hadn't been running around trying to start a stupid career, I could've been there. I could've kept them alive."

"What happened? What happened to them?"

His head lowered. "I can't. I can't talk about that day."

I lifted his face to find his stare. "That's fine. I get it. But I just want you to know that it wasn't your fault, Tristan. I need you to understand that. You were the best father and husband you could be." His eyes told me he didn't believe me. I hoped one day he would. "What was the hardest part for you when you lost them? What was your lowest moment that first week?"

A hesitation hit him as his lips parted to speak. "The day before their funeral I tried to kill myself," he whispered, extremely raw and uncut. "I sat in my parents' bathroom and I tried to end my life."

Oh, Tristan...

"I remember staring at myself in the mirror, knowing that my heart had died right along with them. I knew I was dead. I've been dead ever since, ya know? I was okay with that. I was okay with being mean and callous because I was convinced that I didn't deserve to have people care for me. I pushed my parents away because I was my own ghost. I wanted so much to be dead because I felt like it would be better, easier. But then you came, and I started to remember what it felt like to exist." His lips lay against mine, and my heartbeats sped up. His voice was giving me chills. "Elizabeth?"

"Yes?"

"It's easier with you."

"What's easier with me?"

His hand found my lower back. My hips arched toward him, our bodies slowly becoming one. He ran his fingers against my neck as I closed my eyes, and he spoke softly into my soul. "Being alive."

I took a deep breath. "You're good, Tris. You're good enough. Even on the days you feel worthless."

"Can I see your soul now?" he asked. I nodded nervously, and I led him inside my house.

"Love letters?" he asked, sitting on my couch as I opened the heart-shaped tin box.

"Yes."

"From Steven to you?"

I shook my head. "My mama wrote them to my dad, and he wrote them back to her, almost every day since they met. After he passed away, I would read these every day. Just as a way to remember him. But then one day, Mama threw them out. I found them…and I still read them all the time."

He nodded in understanding as he picked one up and read it.

"You're sleeping beside me, and each second I love you a little more.—HB."

That one always made me smile. "They weren't always happy like that. There were some things I didn't even know about my parents until I started reading these letters." I went digging into the box for a certain one. "Like this one. *I know you think you're less of a woman. I know you think you're less of a woman and blame your body for our loss. I know you think you're less of a woman because of what the doctors said. But you're wrong. You're strong, wise, and unbreakable. You are more than a woman. You are everything beautiful in the world, and I am a mere man lucky to call you my goddess.—KB.* I didn't even know they lost a child before me. I didn't know…" I smiled tightly at Tristan, who was taking it all in. "Anyway. My parents are where I first saw true love. I just wish Steven and I had written each other letters. It would've been nice."

"I'm so sorry," he said.

I nodded, because I was too.

I closed the tin box and moved closer to him on the couch.

"How did your mom handle losing him?" he asked.

"She didn't. She used men to forget. She lost herself the day she lost my father. It's just sad because, well, I miss her."

"I miss my parents. After Jamie and Charlie passed away, I ran away from them because they were comforting, and I didn't think I deserved their comfort."

"Maybe you could give them a call."

"I don't know..." he whispered. "I'm still not sure I deserve their comfort yet."

"Soon, though."

"Yeah. Maybe soon. So..." he said, changing the subject. "What was the hardest part for you that week? What was your lowest?"

"Um, telling Emma. I didn't even do it right away either. The first night I lay in her bed holding her, and she asked when Daddy was coming home. I broke down crying, and that was when it became real for me. That's when I knew my life would never be the same again." Tristan reached out and ran his thumbs under my eyes, wiping away the tears I hadn't known had fallen. "It's okay," I promised. "I'm good."

He shook his head. "You're not."

"I am. I'm good. I'm good."

His eyes narrowed. "You don't have to be good all the time. It's okay to be hurt sometimes. It's okay to feel lost like you're wandering around in the dark. It's the bad days that make the good ones so much better."

My hands ran through his hair, and I set my lips against his. "Kiss me," I whispered, placing my fingers against his chest, taking in the feeling of his heart resting in my hands.

He hesitated. "If I kiss you, we can't go back. If I kiss you, I'll never want to stop."

My tongue slowly danced across his bottom lip, and then I used it to part his mouth as I spoke in a whisper, "Kiss me." His hands moved to my lower back, and he pulled me closer to him. He started to rub my back in a circular motion. We were so close together that it was hard to tell if we were two separate people or one soul discovering its inner flame for the first time.

"Are you sure?" he asked.

"Kiss me."

"Lizzie…"

A small smile spread across my mouth as I laid a finger against his lips. "I'm only going to tell you this one last time, Tristan. Kiss—"

I didn't have to finish my words, and I hardly remembered him carrying me to my bedroom.

My back lay against my dresser as he boxed me in. He tightened his grip around my waist, and our lips met within a moment's time. His mouth tasted every inch of mine as he deepened our connection. His fingers traveled up my spine, sending chills throughout me. He leaned in closer, and his tongue parted my lips, finding my tongue ready to dance with his. His arms wrapped tighter around me, and I dug my fingers into his back, holding on to him as if he was my favorite thing in the world. *He is.* My head tilted to the side as my hands became tangled in his hair, forcing him to kiss me deeper, harder, faster…

"*Tristan*," I moaned against him, and he growled into me. My hand fell to the bottom of his shirt, and I slid it up, feeling the tight body he hid underneath. I loved how he felt. I loved how he tasted. *I love how I am falling in love with him.*

I didn't know it was possible. I didn't know the broken pieces of a heart could still beat for love.

He lifted me up, his hands clasping around my behind, and he sat me on the edge of my mattress. His breaths were rushed, his hunger clear. "I want you so much, Lizzie." He sighed as his mouth sucked on my ear before he rolled his tongue across my chin and landed his lips against mine. The way he tongued my mouth as if he was trying to find every inch of me, every taste, made me moan into him as he began to slide his hands under my dress. I watched as he slid my panties down my hips and tossed them to the side of the room. He edged me closer to his body and spread my legs, allowing me to feel his hardness. The longing look in his eyes made me smile. I knew right then that he would always make me smile.

His fingers gripped the edge of my dress, and he slowly moved it up, studying every inch of me, every curve. "Arms," he ordered in a deep snarl, and I lifted my hands up as he took the dress off and tossed it next to my panties. "*Beautiful*," he muttered before bending down and kissing my neck. Each time his lips connected to my skin, I felt my heartbeat racing. His tongue followed the curve of my bra as he reached behind me, unhooking it and throwing it to the pile. He sent shivers through my body as his thumbs circled my hardening nipples.

I started raising his shirt, revealing his toned abs. "Arms," I ordered. He held them up, and I let it drop on top of the growing pile. He didn't waste any time lowering his mouth to my chest again, sliding his tongue across my breasts. His lips kissed me hard and sucked me harder. My breaths grew heavier and heavier, hungrier and hungrier for him to touch me, taste me. "Tristan, just… Oh my God," I muttered, my head falling back from the way his tongue knew how to control my body.

"Lie down," he ordered. I did as he said and closed my eyes, running my fingers across my chest. The anticipation of his next touch made me nervous yet thrilled. When would he touch me, and where?

My hips arched up when I felt the wetness of his tongue sweep against my inner thigh. "I want to taste you, Lizzie. I want to taste every inch of you," he whispered against my skin. His hands gripped my ass, and he pushed my hips up toward him as his tongue fell deep inside me. He licked me slowly and steadily as my body shook in his hold. He licked me harder and wilder as my body begged for more. He licked me deeper and longer as I tangled my fingers in his hair, wanting nothing more than him inside of me.

"Tristan, please," I begged, my hips wiggling as he slid two fingers inside me. He continued rolling his tongue in and out of my wetness. "I want you…"

Once he pulled away, he stood up and began to unzip his jeans. "Tell me how you want it. Tell me how you want me," he said, his eyes never leaving mine.

"I don't want it gentle," I whispered, short of breath. My eyes met his hard erection standing against his boxers as he stepped out of his jeans. My fingers wrapped around the edge of his boxers and within seconds, they were off. "Show me the shadows that keep you up at night. Kiss me with your darkness."

He lifted me off the bed and placed me facing my dresser, my hands falling against the drawers. With haste, he reached for his jeans pockets, pulled out his wallet, and grabbed a condom, ripping it open with desperation and rolling it on his hardness. Within moments he was standing behind me, his body pressed against my naked soul. His finger trailed down my back until he hit the curves of my ass, and he grasped it in his hold. "Lizzie," he said, his breaths matching the speed of my own. "I won't hurt you," he promised as he grabbed my left leg and held it up in his arm.

I know, Tristan. I know.

In one thrust, he slid into my tightness with force, making me cry out as my back arched from the sensation of him entering me. As his left hand held my leg up, his right wrapped around to my front to massage my breasts.

His breaths were rough as he spoke. "You feel so good, Lizzie…

God… You feel so…" His words faded as he continued to thrust into me. Being so close to Tristan—not only physically but deep within both of our darkness—made tears form in my eyes. He was beautiful. He was scary. He was real.

This isn't a dream. This is real.

He slid out from me and twisted me around so I was facing him.

His hands grasped around my behind, and he lifted me, forcing me to wrap my legs around his waist, his body the only thing that kept me from falling. Our foreheads fell against each other's as he slid back inside me. "Don't close your eyes," he begged. His eyes were filled with lust, with passion, with…love?

Or maybe it was my own love I was seeing shining through him. Either way, I liked the feeling it created in me. He kept entering me hard and pulling out slow. My core was shaking, my eyes wanting to close, but I couldn't. They had to stay open. I had to see him.

I was seconds away…

Seconds away from my body giving way to him. Seconds away from losing myself and finding myself with Tristan Cole inside me. "I'm going to…" I muttered, my body shaking as the orgasm overtook me, my words falling away. My eyes closed, and I felt his lips press against mine as my body shook against him.

"God, I love that, Lizzie. I love it so much when you lose yourself against me." He smiled against my lips as I moaned into him.

"I want all of you," I begged. "Please."

"I'm yours."

That night we fell asleep in each other's arms. In the middle of the night, we woke up, and he slid inside me again, finding ourselves together, losing ourselves together. Early the next morning, we touched each other again. Every time he entered me, it was as if he was apologizing for something. Every time he kissed me, it was as if he was begging for my forgiveness. Every time he blinked, I swore I saw his soul.

CHAPTER 24
Elizabeth

When I woke up, I rolled over and noticed Tristan was missing from my bed. A part of me wondered if the night before had been a dream, but when my fingers landed on the pillowcase beside me, I picked up a note.

You're so beautiful when you snore.—TC

I held the paper to my chest before I reread it over and over again. The sound of a lawnmower was the only thing that stopped me from reading the note again. I tossed on a pair of shorts and a tank top, wanting to go watch Tristan cutting my grass and kiss his lips gently, but once I stepped onto my porch, I stopped.

He wasn't mowing my grass.

He was cutting his lawn.

To everyone else in the world, it wouldn't have seemed like a big deal, seeing a man cutting his grass. But I knew it meant more. I knew Tristan Cole had spent months sleepwalking through life, and today, he was slowly waking up.

Tristan and I started leaving Post-it Notes around each other's houses for one another. Unlike Mama and Dad's, ours weren't as romantic. Most of the time, they were corny and silly—which kind of made me love them even more.

> I think you have a cute butt.—EB

> Sometimes when I'm cutting the grass and you're sitting on your porch reading your dirty books, I see your face blush when you get to a really good part. That Mr. Darcy must have done some crazy shit to Elizabeth's body.—TC

> I don't know if I should be worried or turned on that you know the names of the characters from *Pride and Prejudice*—EB

> You. Are. So. Fucking. Beautiful.—TC

> Knock knock.—EB

> Who's there?—TC

> Me. Naked. At midnight. In my bed. Join me. Bring an Incredible Hulk costume and your huge green monster.—EB

Please, please, please never call my
penis a green monster. On a scale of
1–10, that's a solid "fucked up."—TC

P.S. I won't argue with the word "huge," though.
I even think you should look into other words
like: Enormous. Massive. Gigantic. Heaven-sent.

I want you to hold me tonight.—EB

You know that place in between nightmares and
dreams? The place where tomorrows never come
and yesterdays don't hurt anymore? The place
where your heart beats in sync with mine? The
place where time doesn't exist, and it's easy
to breathe? I want to live there with you.—TC

CHAPTER 25
Elizabeth

Weeks began to pass, and if Tristan wasn't kissing my lips, he was in a sassy argument with Emma. They fought over the weirdest things but would always end up laughing together.

"I'm telling you, Tock , Iron Man is the best Avenger," Tristan said, throwing french fries at Emma from across the table.

"No way! He doesn't have a cool shield like Captain America, Tick! You don't know anything about anything."

"I know something about something, so take that!" he said, sticking his tongue out at her.

She laughed and stuck her tongue out at him. "You don't know ANYTHING!"

A conversation like this happened each night, and I was starting to love our new normal.

One night after I put Emma to bed, Tristan and I lay on the living-room floor, books in our hands. I held on to Harry Potter, while his eyes were fixed on the Bible. Sometimes I would turn to glance at him, and I would catch him staring at me with a small smile on his face before he went back to reading.

"Okay," I said, laying the book in my lap. "Your thoughts on the Bible so far."

He laughed and nodded. "It makes you think. It makes you want to know more about *everything*."

"But?" I asked, knowing there was a "but" coming.

"But…I don't understand at least ninety-six percent of it." He chuckled, placing the book down.

"What do you want to be, Tristan?"

He turned to me and narrowed his eyes, uncertain what I meant. "What?"

"What do you want to be?" I asked again. "We never really talk about what we want, and I'm just curious."

He rubbed the bridge of his nose and shrugged, unable to answer. "I don't know. I mean, in the past I was a father. A husband. But now… I have no clue."

My lips released a quiet sigh, and I frowned. "I wish you could see in yourself what I see when I look at you."

"What do you see?"

"A fighter. Strength. Courage. Someone who loves deep and loves hard. Someone who doesn't run when things get messy. When I look at you, I see endless possibilities. You're smart, Tristan. And talented." He cringed. I shook my head. "You are. And you can do anything. Anything you set your mind to, you can do. Your woodwork is amazing; you could do something with that."

"I was," he said. "My dad and I were starting our business up, and the day of the accident, he and I were flying to New York to meet with a few people interested in being our business partners."

"And nothing came of it?"

He shook his head. "We didn't even make it to New York. We had a layover in Detroit, and when we touched down and turned on our cell phones, we had a ton of messages about Jamie and Charlie."

"That's so—"

"It was the worst day of my life."

Before I could reply, I heard the sound of footsteps running down the hallway.

"Mama! Mama! Look!" Emma said, holding her camera in one hand and two white feathers in her other hand.

"You're supposed to be sleeping, missy."

She groaned. "I know, Mama, but look! Two white feathers!"

"Oh, it looks like Daddy is giving you a few kisses," I said.

She shook her head. "No, Mama. These aren't from Daddy." Emma walked over to Tristan and handed him the feathers. "They are from Tristan's family."

"For me?" he asked, his voice shaky.

She nodded and whispered, "It means they love you." Emma held her camera up. "Now, take a picture. Mama, get in the picture with him!" she ordered. We did as she said. When the Polaroid picture printed, she handed it to Tristan, and he thanked her over and over again.

"Okay, time for bed. How about I read you a story so you can sleep?" I asked.

"Can Tristan read it to me?" she asked, yawning.

I looked over at him with questioning eyes. He nodded, standing from the ground. "Of course I can. What should we read?" he asked her, lifting my tired girl into his arms.

"I like *The Cat in the Hat*," Emma replied. "But you have to read it like a zombie."

His smile stretched as the two of them walked down the hallway and he said, "That's one of my favorite ways to read it."

Outside of Emma's bedroom, I sat on the floor with my back against the wall, listening to Tristan read to her, listening to her giggle at his terrible zombie voice. She sounded so happy, which in an instant made my life light up with joy. As a parent, there was nothing better than knowing that your child was smiling. I couldn't thank Tristan enough for bringing those smiles to Emma's face.

"Tick?" Emma said with a heavy yawn.

"Yes, Tock?"

"I'm sorry about your family."

"It's okay. I'm sorry about your dad."

I peeked into the room to see Tristan lying on the floor beside Emma's bed with the book against his chest. Zeus lay against Emma's feet. She yawned again. "I miss him."

"I bet he misses you too."

She closed her eyes and curled into a ball as she began to fall asleep. "Tick?" she whispered, almost falling into her dreams.

"Yes, Tock?"

"I love you and Zeus, even though your zombie voice was really bad."

Tristan pinched the bridge of his nose and sniffled before standing up and pulling the cover over her. He slid Bubba into her arms and tucked her in. "I love you too, Emma." As he turned to leave the room, he caught me staring his way and gave me a small smile. I gave him one back. "Come on, Zeus," he called. Zeus wagged his tail but didn't move. Tristan arched a brow. "Zeus, come on. Let's go home."

Zeus whimpered and curled in closer to Emma.

I laughed. "What a traitor you have on your hands."

"I can't really blame him. Is it okay if he stays the night?"

"Absolutely. I think the two of them became used to each other after you and Zeus stayed a few days at our house."

He leaned against the door, watching as Zeus snuggled into Emma's arms, where Bubba was. Emma hugged him tight and smiled in her dreams. Tristan crossed his arms. "I see why you didn't fall completely apart like I did. You had Emma, and she's…she's wonderful. She's everything good in this world, isn't she?"

"Yeah." I nodded. *She is.*

The second week of November, a huge rainstorm moved through Meadows Creek. I sat on the porch, staring out at the rain that was hitting the grass at crazy speeds. I was surprised we hadn't had any snow yet, but I was sure that within a few weeks, everything would be covered in white.

The sky was darker by the minute, and the thunder rolled through, followed by big flashes of light. Emma was sound asleep inside, and I was thankful that she was such a heavy sleeper because otherwise, the storms would've spooked her. Zeus sat beside me on the porch, staring out at the raindrops as his eyes opened and closed. He was trying his best to fight his tiredness, but he was losing the battle.

"Elizabeth!" Tristan shouted, running from the back of his house. Every part of me began to panic when I saw him getting closer and closer. "Elizabeth!" he yelled. He was soaked from head to toe when he reached the bottom step of the porch. The palms of his hands fell to his knees as the rain continued to wash over him, and he tried to catch his breath once more.

"What's going on?" I asked, my voice shaking with fear. He looked freaked out. I stepped down the porch and joined him in the rainfall, placing my hands against his chest as he rose up. "Are you okay?"

"No."

"What's wrong?"

"I was sitting in my shed and you crossed my mind." He laced his fingers with mine and pulled me closer to him. My heart pounded in my chest, my nerves skyrocketing as I stared at his lips, taking in each word that fell from his mouth. "I tried to stop you from crossing my mind. I tried to shake you from my thoughts. But I kept thinking about you, and my heart skipped. And then..." He moved in closer, his lips millimeters away from mine, his mouth slowly brushing against my bottom lip. The heat from him canceled out the chill of the rain. He was a kind of warmth I'd never known existed, a protective blanket that sent away the past hurts and sadness. Tristan's voice shook as he kept speaking. "And then, I accidentally fell in love with you."

"Tristan..."

His head shook back and forth. "That's bad, right?"

"It's..."

His tongue danced across my bottom lip before he sucked it gently between his own. "Awful. So right now, Lizzie...if you don't want me to love you, tell me and I'll stop. I'll walk away and I'll stop loving you. Push me away, if you want to. Tell me to go, and I will. But if there is any small part of you that is okay with this, any part of you that is okay with me accidentally falling in love with you, then pull me closer. Take me into your house, lead me to your bedroom, and let me show you how much I'm falling in love with you. Let me show each and every inch of your body how crazy I am for you."

A level of guilt settled in my stomach. I glanced at the ground. "I don't know if I'm ready to say it back yet..."

He lifted my chin up with his finger and stared into my eyes. "That's okay," he promised, his voice low. "I'm pretty sure I have enough love for the both of us."

My eyes closed, and each breath I took was more peaceful than I'd thought they would ever be. I'd never thought I would hear the word "love" from another man, but with Tristan, when he said it, I felt whole again.

He breathed against my lips; the air he exhaled became the inhales that healed me. We stayed in the rain for a second more before my footsteps led us both inside the warmth of the house.

CHAPTER 26
Tristan

I need your shit," Faye said, standing on my porch in all black, wearing black cloth gloves and a black hat. It was late at night, and I'd just gotten back from working at Mr. Henson's shop.

I arched an eyebrow. "What?"

"Well, not your shit exactly. But your dog's shit."

My hand brushed against the back of my neck, looking at her with the same confused look. "I'm sorry, but you said that as if it made common sense."

She sighed, smacking the palm of her hand against her face. "Look, normally I would go to Liz with my issues, but I know she's probably putting Emma to bed and being a grown-up or something stupid like that. So I figured why not try to reach out to her boyfriend and ask him for a favor."

"A favor is giving you my dog's shit."

She nodded. "Absolutely."

"Do I want to know what you're doing with it?"

"Duh, tonight is 'do it yourself' spa night at my house. Dog shit works fantastic for a facial," she said. The blank stare I delivered her made her smirk. "Dude. I'm putting the shit in a brown paper bag and burning it on my boss's porch."

Another blank stare from me. "If you don't want to tell me the truth, that's fine."

She reached into her back pocket and pulled out a brown paper bag. "No. Seriously."

"How long is this going to take?" Faye asked as we lapped around the neighborhood with Zeus on a leash for the fourth time.

"Hey now, you're lucky that Zeus is even offering up his poop to you. He's very selective about who he lets have it."

While we took a few more laps, Faye told me her opinion on pretty much everything. "P.S. I think it's stupid you named that little-ass dog Zeus."

I smirked. "My son, Charlie, named him. We read *Percy Jackson and the Olympians: The Lightning Thief*, and Charlie was just in love with the whole Greek god idea. After reading the book, we spent months studying the gods. He fell in love with the name Zeus, but then he fell in love with a medium-sized dog from the pound, who didn't exactly fit the name of such a huge god. I remember he said, 'Dad, the size doesn't matter. He's still Zeus.'"

Her face frowned for a second before she went back to her playful self and rolled her eyes. "Geez, did you really just play the dead son card on me, leaving me feeling extremely bad and awkward?"

I laughed because I saw the playfulness in her eyes. "I think I did."

"Jerk," she muttered before turning away to try to hide a tear glistening in the corner of her eye. I saw her, but I didn't say anything about it.

Zeus paused in front of a fire hydrant and started doing his "time to poop" moves. "Here we go!" I said, clapping my hands together.

Within seconds, Faye was scooping Zeus's fresh poop into the bag and dancing around the street corner with it. "Way to go, you Olympic god, you!" she shouted. I'd never seen someone get so excited by what I honestly considered to be the nastiest stuff ever.

"Okay, let's go," she said, walking back toward my house.

"Go? Go where?"

"Um, to my boss's house so I can be an adult and set this shit on fire and watch it burn."

"I thought you were joking about that."

She rolled her eyes. "Tristan, I joke about penis size, not about tossing shit on my boss's porch."

"But why do I need to be included with this? And aren't we a little...old for these kinds of antics?"

"Yes!" she shouted, her voice cracking. "Yes, it's completely immature of me to want to throw shit at my boss's house. And yes, it's completely immature of me to think that it will make me feel better, but if I don't do this I'm just going to be pissed off and sad. And I can't be sad because that means he wins. It means that when he called me tonight to tell me he was getting back together with his ex-wife, I realized he'd always had the upper hand, even though I thought I did. It means that the asshole allowed me to fall in love with him and trust him, only to rip my heart out. I don't fall in love! I don't get hurt!" Tears filled her eyes, but she refused to blink because she knew that would make them fall. Tears were a form of weakness to her, and I could tell the last thing Faye ever wanted to feel was weak. "But now all I feel is this breaking inside. I can literally feel every inch of me seconds away from falling apart, and I can't even go to my best friend about it because she lost her fucking husband and had a really shitty year. I shouldn't have come to you because it turns out you had an even shittier year, but I didn't know what to do! I'm fucking heartbroken.

"I mean, why would someone do this?! Why do people fall in love if it means there is a chance of feeling this way? What the fuck is wrong with humans?! HUMANS ARE FUCKING SICK AND TWISTED! I mean, I get it—it feels good, you know? Being in love, being happy." Her body trembled as the tears fell faster than she could take breaths. "But when that magical rug is ripped out from under you, it takes all the happy and good feelings with it. And your heart? It just breaks. It breaks, and it's unapologetic. It shatters into a million pieces, leaving you numb, blankly staring at the pieces because all your free will, all the common sense you once had in your life, is gone. You gave up every-thing for this bullshit thing called love, and now you're just destroyed."

I was quick to wrap my arms around her. She sobbed into me, and I held her tighter. We stood on the street corner for a while as she cried and I rested my chin on her head. "I think Zeus went to poop in my backyard today, and I'm pretty sure I forgot to pick it up."

She pulled away and cocked an eyebrow. "Really?"

I nodded.

We searched my whole backyard and added a nice collection of poop to the bag before she hopped into my car and I drove her to Matty's house. "This is going to be so good," she said, rubbing her hands together. "Okay, you keep the car running, and I'll drop the shit, light it up, knock on his door, dash back to the car, and we'll hit it!"

"Perfect." She hurried off, did exactly as she'd said she would, and when she jumped into the car, she giggled like a five-year-old. "Um, Faye?"

"Yes?" she laughed, tossing her head back in amusement.

"I think his wooden porch is on fire."

Her stare twisted to her window, where Matty's porch was definitely on fire. "SHIT!"

"Literally." She went to open her door to rush to put it out, but I stopped her. "No. If he sees you, he'll fire you."

She paused. "Shit! Shit! Shit!"

I wondered how many times she could say that before it became a tongue twister. "Get down, just in case he sees you. I'll be back."

Hurrying out of my car, I rushed to the porch. I stared down at the fire and said a small prayer before I started stomping the fire out, including the bag of poop, which unfortunately got all over my shoes.

"What the hell are you doing?" Matty asked, opening his door and staring at me. The smell of the poop hit him quickly, causing him to cover his nose with his hand. "Is that dog shit?!"

My mind blanked. I wasn't sure what to say or how to explain why my shoes were currently covered in my dog's poop. So I panicked. "I'm the town asshole! I randomly leave shit around because I'm the town asshole! So…fuck you!"

He stared at me.

I stared at him.

He raised an eyebrow.

I raised an eyebrow.

He threatened to call the cops.

I kicked off my shoes, ran to my car, and drove away.

"Holy crap!" Faye said, crying, but this time tears of amusement. "That was amazing. You literally stepped in dog poop to make sure I kept my job."

"I know. I'm regretting it." She laughed, and when I pulled up to my house, I put the car into park.

"He didn't really love me, did he? I mean, he said he did, but only at times when he wanted sex. And he told me he was over his wife, but only at three in the morning when he was texting me to come over."

"He sounds like an asshole, Faye."

She nodded. "I have a way of falling for those kinds. I just kind of wonder what it would be like to find someone who loves you the same amount that you love them. You know, that person who you see looking your way and smiling because they are just as wild for you as you are for them."

"Why do you sleep with these guys if you know they are jerks?"

"Because I hope they will someday fall in love with me."

"I think you can fall in love with your clothes on."

"Dream a little dream with me." She chuckled nervously, her eyes filled with self-doubt. "But I'm done with this love crap. Throwing in the towel."

"It's worth it, though, Faye." I stared into her eyes, which were red from crying. "The heartbreak is worth those few moments of happiness, and the pieces of the shattered heart can be put back together. I mean, there will be cracks and scars, and sometimes this burning memory of the past, but that burn? It's just a reminder that you survived. That burning is your rebirth."

"Have you been born again?"

My eyes moved to Elizabeth's house before they locked with Faye's stare. "I'm working on it."

She thanked me, then climbed out of the car to get into hers. "Tristan?" she said, wiggling her nose.

"Yes?"

"Tonight I was pretty immature and broken, but you handled it like a champ, kind of like a father to my childish ways. Charlie was lucky to have you as his dad."

I smiled. She had no clue how much that meant to me.

"Oh!" she exclaimed. "And I'm sorry for calling you an asshole."

"You didn't call me an asshole."

She nodded. "Trust me. I did. One more thing as a thank you..." She hurried over to Elizabeth's bedroom window and pounded on it. When Elizabeth opened the window, I couldn't help but smile. She was always so beautiful. Always. "Hey, Liz?" Faye said, looking at her sleepy best friend.

"Yes?"

"Give this guy a blow job tonight as a thank-you from me." She smiled, leaned in, and kissed Elizabeth's cheek. "Night, babe." With that, Faye hurried away, seeming much happier than when she'd been crying not too long before. Sometimes all a broken heart needed was a bag of shit and a little fire.

Elizabeth climbed out her window, walked over to me, and I wrapped her in a hug. "Did you do something good for my bestie tonight?" she asked.

"I think so."

"Thank you." She pulled me in closer and rested her head on my chest. "Babe?"

"Yeah?"

"What's that smell?"

"Trust me..." I looked down at my socks, which had at one point been white but were now semi-brown. "You don't want to know."

CHAPTER 27
Elizabeth

"Well, don't just stand there staring at me. Aren't you happy to see me?" Mama smiled, standing on my porch with a suitcase in her hand.

"What are you doing here?" I asked, confused. I glanced toward the BMW sitting in front of my house, wondering *what* in the world my mother had gotten herself involved with now—or more likely, *who*.

"What? Your mother can't come visit? You haven't been answering my calls, and I missed my daughter and granddaughter. Is that such a crime? You won't even give me a hug hello!" She huffed.

I leaned in to hug her. "I'm just surprised to see you. Sorry I haven't called; I've been busy."

Her eyes narrowed. "Is your forehead bleeding?"

I ran my fingers across my forehead and shrugged. "Ketchup."

"Why is there ketchup on your forehead?"

"I WANT TO EAT YOUR BRAINNNNNS!" Tristan said, walking past the foyer as he chased after a zombified Emma with spaghetti noodles in his hands and ketchup dripping from his face.

Mama's head tilted to the left, and her stare followed Tristan. "I guess you have been busy."

"It's not what it looks like—" I started, but Emma cut me off.

"Grandma!" she screamed, running to the door and jumping into Mama's arms.

"My little sweet pea," Mama replied, wrapping Emma in her arms and getting covered in ketchup. "Well, aren't you a messy thing today?"

"Mama, Tick and I were playing zombie and vampires!"

"Tick?" Mama turned to me and raised an eyebrow. "You let a man named Tick into your house?"

"Are you really judging the type of men I let into my house? Do you not remember some of the men who walked into yours?"

She smiled wickedly. "Touché."

"Tristan," I called. He came over, rubbing his fingers through his ketchup-filled hair.

"Yeah?" He smiled my way before turning to look at Mama.

"This is my mother, Hannah. Mama, this is my neighbor, Tristan."

His stare met mine, and I watched his lips turn down for a split second, almost as if he was disappointed in my word choice. Soon enough he was smiling and shaking Mama's hand. "Nice to meet you, Hannah. I've heard a lot about you."

"That's funny." Mama nodded. "Because I haven't heard a word about you."

Silence.

Awkward silence.

"So should I join you all in the awkward silence, or should I wait by the car?" a man joked, walking up the steps of the porch with a suitcase of his own. He wore glasses and a mustard button-down shirt tucked into dark jeans.

Mama must've been on a nerdy boyfriend kick. *I wonder if he's a wizard.*

Silence.

Extremely awkward silence.

The man cleared his throat and held his hand out toward Tristan, probably because he noticed Tristan wasn't giving him an intense look of confusion like I was. "I'm Mike."

"Nice to meet you, Mike," Tristan replied.

"What happened to Richard?" I whispered toward Mama.

"It didn't work out," she replied.

Shocking.

"So Mike and I were hoping we could stay the night here. I mean, we could get a hotel room, but…I thought it would be nice for us all to have a dinner together and hang out."

"Mama, tonight is my birthday party. Emma is going over to Kathy and Lincoln's place for the night." I frowned. "You should've called."

"You wouldn't answer." Her cheeks blushed over, and she fiddled with her fingers, almost as if she was embarrassed. "You wouldn't answer, Liz."

And just like that, I felt like the crappiest daughter ever. "We can still do dinner, though… I can cook your favorite meal if you want. And you can watch Emma. I can call and cancel the plans with Kathy."

Her cheeks rose, and her smile stretched. "That would be wonderful! Tick—er—Tristan, you should join us for dinner." Her eyes rolled over his body once with a look of disappointment. "Though maybe you should shower first."

"You still make the best chicken parmesan I've ever had, Liz," Mama complimented me as we sat around the dining-room table.

"She's not lying, this is amazing," Mike agreed. I gave him a tight smile and thanked them both. Mike seemed nice, which was a big improvement from the last creep I'd seen Mama with. Every now and then he would reach across the table and hold Mama's hand, which actually made me feel bad for the guy. He looked at her with such lovey-dovey eyes; I was sure it was only a matter of time before she hurt him.

"So, Mike, what do you do?" Tristan asked.

"Oh, I'm a dentist. I'm in the process of taking over the family business because my dad is retiring in a year."

That makes sense. Mama had a way of choosing men who had bigger wallets than most.

"Very cool," Tristan replied. Everyone kept chatting, but I stopped listening; my eyes were glued to Mike massaging Mama's hand. How did she never feel guilty about taking advantage of men the way she did? How did it never get to her?

"So how did you two meet?" I blurted out, making everyone's stare turn to me. My chest felt tight, and my mind felt tired from seeing Mama using yet another man. "Sorry, just curious. Because last I heard Mama was seeing a man named Roger."

"Richard," Mama corrected me. "His name was Richard. And frankly, I don't like the tone in your voice, Liz." Her face was turning red, either from embarrassment or from anger, and I knew she would scold me in private soon enough.

Mike squeezed Mama's hand. "It's okay, Hannah." Mama took a deep breath, as if his words were all she needed to hear to calm her down. Her shoulders relaxed, and the redness on her cheeks began to fade. "Your mother and I actually met at my office. Richard was one of my patients, and she came with him while he was getting a root canal."

"Figures," I muttered. She'd already been scoping around for another man while still dating one.

"It's not what you think." Mike smiled.

"Trust me, Mike. I know my mother; it is what I think."

Mama's eyes watered over, and Mike kept squeezing her hand. He looked at her, and it was almost as if they had a complete conversation without any words needed. She shook her head once, and Mike looked my way. "Anyway, that doesn't matter. What matters is right now, we are happy. Right now things are good."

"In fact, things are so good in that…we're getting married," Mama said.

"What?" I hollered, all color draining from my face.

"I said—"

"No, I heard you the first time." I turned to Emma and smiled brightly. "Baby, you want to go pick out some pajamas for tonight?" She complained for a while before hopping out of her seat and heading to her bedroom. "What do you mean you're getting married?" I said to the apparently engaged couple, completely flabbergasted.

There were two things Mama never did:

1. Fell in love.
2. Talked about marriage.

"We're in love, Liz," Mama said.

What?!

"It's kind of why we came down here," Mike explained. "We wanted to tell you face-to-face." He laughed nervously. "And now it's awkward."

"I think the word of the day is *awkward*." Tristan nodded.

I twisted toward Mama and whispered, "How much debt are you in?"

"Elizabeth!" she hissed. "Stop it."

"Are you losing the house? If you needed money, you could've asked me." My throat tightened and I narrowed my eyes. "Are you sick, Mama? Is there something wrong?"

"Lizzie," Tristan said, reaching out to touch my hand, but I snatched it away.

"I'm just saying"—I chuckled, running my hands through my hair—"I just can't think of any reason why you would rush into something like this if you weren't in debt or dying."

"Maybe because I'm in love!" she cried, her voice shaky. She pushed herself up from the table. "And maybe, just maybe, I wanted my daughter to be happy for me, but that seems to be too much to ask for. Don't worry, go to your party tonight, and when morning comes, I will be out of your hair forever!"

She stormed off to the guest room and slammed the door behind her. Mike gave me a tight smile before excusing himself to go check on her.

"Ugh!" I stood up from the table. "Can you believe her?! She's just so...*dramatic!*"

Tristan snickered.

"What's so funny?"

"Nothing. It's just..."

"Just? Just what?"

He laughed again. "It's just that you are so much like your mother."

"I am nothing like my mother!" I screeched, maybe a hair too loud, maybe a hair too dramatic.

He continued laughing. "The way your nose flares when you're pissed off or how you bite your bottom lip when you're embarrassed."

I stared at him with disgust. "I'm not going to listen to this. I'm going to get dressed." Storming off, I paused halfway. "And I am NOT storming off like she did!"

Though perhaps I did slam my door.

Within seconds, my door was opened, and Tristan leaned against the doorframe, calm as ever. "Almost identical."

"My mother uses men to forget her own issues. She's a mess. Mike is just another man who's going to be let down. She's unable to commit to anything or anyone because she never truly got over my dad dying. Watch, she'll probably walk down the aisle and have that poor guy thinking he actually has a shot at a happily ever after, when in all reality, happily ever afters don't exist. Life isn't a fairy tale. It's a Greek tragedy."

Tristan ran his fingers against the back of his neck. "But isn't that what we did? Didn't we use each other because we missed Steven and Jamie?"

"It's nothing like that," I said, my fingers tapping against my sides. "I'm nothing like her. And it's really rude of you to even think something like that."

"You're right. What would I know anyway?" He frowned and brushed his thumb against his jaw. "I'm just the neighbor."

Oh, Tristan.

"I… I didn't mean it like that when I said it earlier." I was the worst person alive, I was certain of that much.

"No, it's fine. And it's true. I mean, it was stupid of me to think…" He cleared his throat and stuffed his hands into his jeans pockets. "Look, Lizzie. We're both still mourning. We probably went at this thing—whatever this is between us—in completely the wrong way. And I hold nothing against you for just wanting to be my neighbor. Hell…" He laughed nervously and stared straight into my eyes. "If all I'll ever be to you is your neighbor, then that's good enough for me.

That'll be enough. It's a fucking honor to be your neighbor. But seeing as how I accidentally fell in love with you, I think it might be best if I clear my head and skip the birthday get-together tonight."

"Tristan, no."

He shook his head. "It's fine. Really, it is. I'm just going to say good night to Emma and then head home."

"Tristan," I said once more, but he walked out of the room. I hurried into the hallway. "Tristan! Stop!" I jumped up and down like a child, pounding my feet against the ground. "Stop, stop, stop!" He turned back to me, and I saw the pained expression that I'd caused to exist within his eyes. I walked to him and took his hands in mine. "I'm a mess. Each day, every day, I'm a complete mess. I say stupid things like I did today. I make mistakes as if 'Mistakes' is my middle name. I'm hard to handle, and sometimes I hate my mother because deep down inside I know I am my mother. And just like everything else in my life, that's hard for me to deal with." I held his hands against my chest. "And I'm sorry you had to witness the broken Elizabeth during dinner, but you are the one thing that makes sense to me. You are the one thing I don't want to mess up. And you are so, so much more than just my neighbor."

He placed his lips against my forehead. "Are you sure?" he questioned.

"I'm sure."

"Are you okay?" he asked.

"I'll get there." He hugged me, and I felt a little better already. "I should go get dressed." I sighed against him.

"Okay."

"And you should come help me."

So he did.

"Just for future reference, when I have a breakdown about my mother, you're supposed to agree with me no matter how much logic I am missing." I smirked, pulling my shirt over my head and sliding out of my jeans.

"Sorry, I missed that memo. Yes! Gah! Your mother, she's such a monster!" Tristan made a grossed-out face.

My lips curved up as I stepped into my dress. "Thank you! Now can you zip me?"

"Of course." His hands landed on my hips before his fingers moved up and zipped my red, curve-hugging dress. "And what's up with all that perfume she wears? Way too much Chanel."

"Exactly!" I swung around to him and playfully slapped his chest. "Wait. How did you know what kind of perfume she wears?"

His lips found my neck, and he softly kissed me. "Because her daughter wears the same kind."

I smiled. Maybe parts of me were extremely like Mama. "I should probably apologize to her for my freak-out, huh?"

He cocked a brow. "Is this a trick question?"

I laughed. "No."

"Then yes, I think you should, but not until after you have an awesome birthday tonight. Your mom loves you and you love her. I think you'll both be okay."

I sighed, kissed his lips, and nodded once. "Okay."

CHAPTER 28
Tristan

I should let you go in first," I said, rubbing my hands together. "It's your party, and I think you should have your moment." I stood tall in my dark-blue button-down shirt and dark jeans.

"We can go in together," she said.

I hesitated. "People will think we're a couple."

She held her hand out toward me with the most beautiful smile on her lips. "Aren't we?"

Man. With those two words from her mouth, I felt like such a damn giddy asshole.

God, I love her.

Even though we both were sure about each other, it didn't mean everyone else in Meadows Creek would be as okay with the idea. As we walked into the bar, everyone shouted "Happy birthday!" to Elizabeth, and I stepped to the side to allow all the hugs to begin.

She looked so happy from the love she was receiving.

Those were my favorite moments to take in.

It didn't take long for the music to turn loud and the drinking to begin. Shots were being taken left and right, and the gossiping ladies of Meadows Creek were growing louder and louder as they watched Elizabeth's and my every move.

After taking another shot of some nasty alcohol with her, I leaned in and whispered against her hair, "Are you okay? With the looks from people? Because if you're not comfortable, I can stop touching you."

"I love when you touch me. Don't stop touching me. It's just… hard. Everyone's judging us," she whispered with a frown. "Everyone's watching us."

"Good," I replied. My fingers touched her lower back, and her body relaxed, curving into mine. "Let them watch."

She smiled wide and looked at me as if I was all she could see. "Kiss me?" she asked.

My lips against hers were my answer.

The night went from a calm beginning to a quick trip down drunken lane. I knew Elizabeth was going to be pretty intoxicated, so I made sure to stop drinking hours before we were going to leave. I was quick to sober up, and one of the most annoying things about being sober was dealing with the drunk people. Every now and then, Elizabeth would get pulled into conversations with the book club ladies—who she hated. I overheard them talking to her, making her feel guilty about us.

"I can't believe you are actually with him. It seems way too soon," one judged.

"I wouldn't be able to date for years if I lost my husband," another echoed.

"It's just weird, that's all. You don't even know him. I would never bring another man around my kid," the last one explained.

Elizabeth handled it like a champ. Maybe because she could hardly stand up straight and was in a happy-drunk bubble. Even so, every now and then, she would look my way and give me the biggest eye roll followed up by her smile.

"So wh-wh-what's the deal with Liz and you?" Tanner said, plopping down on the barstool beside me, slurring his words. He'd been drinking more than most, and it hadn't gone unnoticed that he'd spent most of the night staring at Elizabeth.

"What do you mean?"

"Come on, man, everyone in town can tell you two have something going on. I can't blame you, though. Liz has one of the best set of tits I've ever seen."

"Knock it off," I said, growing annoyed with drunken Tanner. He had a way of getting under my skin, and ever since I'd found out that he'd had a thing for Elizabeth, I couldn't stand him that much more.

"I'm just saying…" He smiled, shoving me in the shoulder before he reached into his pocket, pulled out a quarter, and started flipping it between his fingers. "Back in college, Steven and I flipped a coin for her. I called heads, he called tails. I won, but the asshole went after her anyway. I guess she was too good in bed for him to pass up."

My eyes moved over to Elizabeth, who was wrapped up in a conversation with women I knew she hated. When she glanced my way, we exchanged the same "save me" facial expressions.

"Don't talk about Lizzie like that," I said. "I know you're drunk, dude, but don't talk about her like that."

Tanner rolled his eyes. "Take it easy. We're just having some good manly talk."

I didn't reply.

"So did you? Have you slept with her?"

"Fuck off, Tanner," I said, my fingers slowly forming fists.

"You *sonofabitch*, you screwed her, didn't you?" He shook his head. "Realistically, though, how do you see this unfolding, Tristan? Let's be honest. She's having a fun getaway with you, but a woman wouldn't want to stay with someone like you. One day, she won't be sad anymore. One day, she'll be the same Liz she used to, and she won't need the asshole neighbor to lose herself. She'll find someone better."

"Let me guess: Someone like you?"

He shrugged. "It's an option. Besides, I know her. We have a history together. Plus, she's too good for you. I mean, I have my own auto shop. I have a way to provide for her. But you? You work for Crazy Henson."

"Say one more word about Mr. Henson and you'll regret it."

He held his hands up in defeat. "Easy, slugger. That vein in your neck is popping out. You wouldn't want Liz to see that temper of yours, now would you? Like I said, she's too good for you."

I tried to ignore his words, but they were finding a way inside my head.

What was I thinking?

She's too good for me.

Tanner slammed his hands against my shoulders, rotated me around on the stool to face the dance floor, and pointed toward Elizabeth laughing with Faye. "What do you say? What if we do show her your temper? I think it's only right that she sees the true monster inside of you. You shouldn't be anywhere near Liz or Emma. You're a fucking beast."

"This is where I walk away," I said, pushing myself up from the stool.

"Hell, you probably should stay away from all people, actually. Didn't you have a wife and a child? What happened to them?"

"Don't, Tanner," I warned, my hands forming fist.

"What happened? Did you hurt them? Are you the reason they're dead? Shit. I bet you are." He laughed. "Are they buried in a ditch somewhere? Did you fucking murder your family? You're a psychopath, and I don't see why no one else can see it. Especially Liz. She's normally smart."

I huffed and turned to face him. "It must kill you that she's with me."

He was taken aback by my words. "What?"

"You stare at her as if she's your world, and she looks past you every time. I mean, it's actually funny." I laughed. "Because here you are pretty much throwing yourself at her, fixing her cars, showing up to have dinner with her, pretty much begging her to look your way, and she just doesn't see you, dude. And not only does she not see you, she chooses me, the town recluse, the one person you can't stand. It must be eating at you inside," I mocked. I was being mean and cold, but he'd brought my family into it. He'd made it personal. "It must be killing you to know it's my bed she's crawling into and it's my name she's moaning."

"Fuck you," he said with narrow eyes.

"Trust me," I replied with a wolfish grin. "She is."

"Do you not know who I am?" he said, pounding his finger against my chest. "Dude. I get what I want. I always get what I want. So enjoy the time you have with Liz because I'm getting her. And enjoy your time with Mr. Henson's shop because I'm taking that too." He patted me on the back. "Nice talking to you, psycho. Make sure to tell your wife and son I said hi." He paused and laughed. "Oh wait, never mind."

Everything in my head started to spin. Without hesitation, I swung around and slammed my fist into Tanner's jaw. He stumbled backward. I shook my head a few times. *No.* I felt Tanner's fist meet my eye before he sent me to the ground and started slamming his fists into me over and over again. I could hear everyone around us screaming, and I thought I saw Faye trying to pull Tanner off me, but I flipped him over and slammed him against the ground.

He wanted this. He wanted the beast to be unleashed, and he said all the right things to bring the beast to life. He had brought Jamie and Charlie into it. He'd gone too far and had taken me to the darkness. I slammed my fist into his face. I slammed my fist into his stomach. Over and over again. I couldn't stop. I wouldn't stop. Everyone was screaming around me, but I couldn't hear them anymore.

I fucking snapped.

CHAPTER 29
Elizabeth

O h my God!" I screamed. My eyes fell to Tristan as he stood over Tanner, slamming his fists into his face over and over again. His eyes were hard, his stare as cold as Tanner's, and he kept swinging. "Tristan," I said, walking over to him. Tanner was almost passed out, but Tristan wouldn't stop. He couldn't stop. "*Tristan!*" I said louder, reaching for his arm as it flew up in the air. The speed his arm was swinging at made me stumble backward, and when he saw me, he stopped. His chest was rising and falling, and I could see the anger in his eyes. I slowly approached him and placed my hands around his face. "It's over," I said. "It's over." *Come back to me.*

I watched his breathing slow as he climbed off Tanner, and he stared at his bloody hands. "Shit," he exhaled, crawling away from Tanner.

Tristan stood up, and as I reached for his hand he yanked his body away from mine. His eyes were wild, untamed, and I could see how far away from me he was.

What did Tanner do to you?

When I turned to Tanner, I felt awful for even thinking that it was somehow his fault. Tristan had almost knocked him out, and my gut was tangled up with guilt and confusion. Tristan stormed off, not turning around once to look back at me.

"Jesus," Tanner muttered. Faye rushed over to him to help him up. "I'm fine," he said, standing.

"What did you…" My voice shook. "What did you say to him?"

Faye's brow furrowed. "Liz. Seriously?"

"I just… He wouldn't just snap like that. He wouldn't just attack you. Tanner, what did you say to him?"

He huffed sarcastically and spit out blood. "Un-fucking-believable. I can hardly open my right eye and you are asking *me* what I said to *him*?"

My throat was tight, tears burning at the back of my eyes. "Sorry. I'm sorry. It's just, he's not one to just snap like that."

"Didn't he push you down a hill, Liz?" Faye frowned.

"It was an accident. I tripped. He would never hurt me." How could she even think something like that? Tristan had been there for her when she needed him! How could she turn on him so fast? Everyone stood around us, fear in their eyes. All of the ladies from the book club were whispering about Tristan, calling him a monster. Everyone was judging me for loving such a beast.

"Yeah. I'm sure this was an accident too," Tanner said, gesturing toward his bruised face. "He's a monster and he's dangerous, Liz. It's only a matter of time before he snaps on you too—or worse, on Emma. I'm going to show you, Liz. I'm going to find out the truth about that guy and show you his secrets. Then maybe you'll trust me."

I sighed. "I have to go."

"Go? Go where?" Tanner asked.

To find him.

To see what happened.

To make sure he's okay.

"I just have to go."

CHAPTER 30
Tristan

APRIL 5TH, 2014
TWO DAYS UNTIL GOODBYE

*Y*ou haven't eaten in days. Please, Tristan. Just take a few bites of a sandwich," Mom begged, sitting across from me. The sound of her voice annoyed me more and more each day. She slid the plate in front of me and asked me to eat again.

"Not hungry," I replied, pushing the sandwich back toward her.

She nodded once. "Your father and I are worried about you, Tris. You're not talking to us. You're not letting us in. You can't just keep all your emotions bottled up like this. You have to talk to us. Let me know what you're thinking."

"You don't want to know what I'm thinking."

"I do."

"Trust me, you don't."

"No. I do, honey." She reached out, placing her hand over mine, almost to comfort me.

I didn't want her comfort.

I wanted her to leave me alone.

"Okay. Well, if you can't talk to us, at least talk to some of your friends. They've been calling and stopping by every day, and you haven't spoken one word to them."

"I got nothing to say to anyone." Standing from the table, I turned to walk away but paused when I heard Mom cry.

"It's breaking my heart to see you like this. Please, just say whatever's on your mind."

"What's on my mind?" I turned to her, my brows knit, my stomach knotted, my mind clouded. "What's on my mind is the fact that you were behind the fucking wheel. What's on my mind is the fact that you fucking walked away with a broken arm. What's on my mind is that my family is fucking dead and you were the one driving the car—you were… YOU KILLED THEM! You did this! You're the reason they are dead! You murdered my family!" My throat tightened, my fists formed, and I stopped talking.

Mom cried more and more, her howls becoming louder and louder. Dad rushed into the room and wrapped his arms around her, bringing her some sort of peace of mind. I stared at her, feeling the distance between us. I felt the beast inside me growing more and more each passing moment. As I studied her tears, it should've sickened me that I didn't feel pity for her. It should've worried my soul that I didn't feel the need to comfort her.

I merely hated her.

Because of her, they were gone.

Because of her, I was gone.

I was becoming a monster inside, and monsters didn't comfort people. Monsters destroyed everything that crossed their path.

When I stepped into the shed, I slammed the door, locking it from the inside. "*Shit!*" I shouted, staring into the darkened space, staring at the scarred walls and bookshelves. The memories were rushing over me, choking my mind, suffocating my heart. I couldn't take any more.

I sent one of the bookshelves flying to the other side of the room, my heart beating at a speed I was certain would cause an attack. I leaned against the closest wall and closed my eyes, trying to take back the control of my breaths and my heart that had somehow been stolen from me.

There was a knock at the door.

I wouldn't answer it.

I couldn't.

I could've killed him. I could've killed him. I'm sorry, I'm sorry.

I knew Elizabeth would try to pull me back to her, pull me into the light. She would try to save me from myself. I couldn't be saved.

She kept tapping lightly, and my footsteps moved toward the sound of her knocks. My hands ran across each other before I stood in front of the door, placing my hands flat against it.

I assumed that her hands were resting on the other side of the door, her fingertips mirroring mine.

"Tris." She softly spoke eight words that made my chest tighten. "Every second. Every minute. Every hour. Every day."

I held my breath. Her words seemed more honest than ever before. She kept speaking, her voice filled with urgency. "Please open the door, Tristan. Please let me back in. Come back to me."

My hands fell from the door, and I rubbed my fingers against one another over and over again. "I could've killed him."

"You wouldn't have," she said.

"Go away, Elizabeth," I said. "Please, just leave me alone."

"*Please.*" She begged for me to open the door. "I'm not leaving until I see you. I'm not leaving until you let me hold you."

"*Jesus!*" I shouted, ripping the door wide-open. "Go away." My soul was wrung with a sudden, wild homesickness as I stared into her eyes. My stare faltered off toward the ground, unable to look at the one thing that made heaven almost seem real in my mind. "And then stay gone, Elizabeth." *I would just hurt you. You deserve more than me.*

"You…You don't mean that," she said, her voice cracking. I couldn't look at her anymore.

"I do," I said. "You can't save me." I closed the door and locked the shed once more. She pounded against it, screaming my name, begging for an explanation, begging for answers to all the unknown questions, but I stopped listening.

I stared at my hands, seeing the blood, unsure if it was Tanner's or my own, feeling it against my fingers, under my nails, *everywhere*. It was as if the walls were bleeding, and I couldn't see a way out.

I wanted him to know I was sorry. I wanted him to know I shouldn't have snapped. I wanted it all to be a dream. I wanted to wake up and have my family back. I wanted to wake up and never know how much hearts could truly break.

But mostly, I wanted to let Elizabeth know that I loved her. Every second. Every minute. Every hour. Every day.

I'm sorry. I'm sorry. I'm sorry.

When I found the strength to leave the shed many hours later, I opened the door to find a shivering Elizabeth on the ground, wrapped in her winter coat. "You should've gone home," I said, my voice low.

She shrugged.

I bent down and lifted her into my arms. She wrapped her arms around me and clung to my body.

"What did he say to you?" she whispered against my chest.

"It doesn't matter."

She held me tighter as I carried her into her house. "It does matter. It matters a lot."

I placed her in bed and turned to leave her room. She asked me to stay with her, but I knew I couldn't. My mind wasn't in a good place. Before I left her house, I stopped in her bathroom to clean the blood from my hands. As the water ran hot, I scrubbed my hands together aggressively, trying to get all the blood off. I couldn't stop. I kept scrubbing, adding more soap, even after all of the blood was gone.

"Tristan," Elizabeth said, breaking me from the trance I was in. She turned off the faucet, took a towel, and wrapped my fingers in the cloth. "What did he say to you?"

I leaned forward, placing my forehead against hers. I breathed in her scent, trying my best to not fall apart. She was the only thing still holding me together. "He said I killed them. He said it was my fault that Jamie and Charlie were dead, and he said I would end up doing the same to you." My voice cracked. "He was right. I killed them. I should've been there... I should've been able to save them."

"No," she said in a commanding tone. "Tristan. You didn't. What happened, whatever happened to Jamie and Charlie, was an accident. It wasn't your fault."

I nodded. "It was. It was my fault. I blamed my mom, but she... She loved them. It wasn't her. It was me. It's always been me..." Each word was harder to get out than the one before it. Breathing was becoming a chore. "I have to go." I stepped away from her, but she blocked the exit. "Elizabeth, move."

"No."

"Lizzie—"

"When I fell apart, when I hit rock bottom, you held me. When I lost it, you stayed. So take my hand and come to bed."

She led me to her bedroom, and for the first time, she unmade the right side of her bed for me to get under the sheets. I wrapped my arms around her as her head lay against my chest. "I ruined your birthday," I said softly as sleep grew heavy on my eyelids.

"It's not your fault," she replied. Over and over again, she said those words. "It's not your fault. It's not your fault. It's not your fault." As my heartbeat slowed to a normal pace, as my fingers caressed her skin, as I began to fall asleep, a part of me started to believe her.

For a few hours that night, I remembered what it felt like to not be alone. For a few hours, I stopped blaming myself.

CHAPTER 31
Elizabeth

I tiptoed to the kitchen around six in the morning, leaving Tristan resting. The whole house was silent, but I could smell the scent of freshly brewed coffee filling the rooms.

"You're a morning person too?" Mike asked, smiling my way with a mug of coffee in his hand. He seemed like such a friendly guy, and just seeing his smiling face made me feel awful for how I'd treated him and Mama the night before.

He pulled out another mug and poured a cup of coffee for me. "Sugar? Cream?"

"Black," I replied, taking the mug from him.

"Ah, something we have in common. I like to say your mom drinks her sugar and cream with a dash of coffee, but for me, the darker the better." He sat down on the stool at the island, and I sat beside him.

"I owe you an apology, Mike. Yesterday was terrible."

He shrugged. "Sometimes life is weird. You just have to deal with the weirdness and hope that you find some weirdos who will move forward with you."

"Is my mom your weirdo?"

He smiled wide.

She is.

His fingers wrapped around his mug, and he stared into the dark coffee. "Richard was an awful person, Elizabeth, and he did some terrible things to Hannah. When they came into my office that day, I watched him put his hands on her in the worst way. I sent him out of my office, where he left her crying. I canceled all my appointments that day and allowed her to just sit in my office for as long as she needed. I understand you thinking that this thing between her and me is fake. I know all about her history with men, her history of hurt, and I want you to know that I love her. I love her so much and will spend the rest of my days protecting her from any more hurt."

The mug shook in my hands. "He hurt her? He hurt her, and I said those terrible things to her last night..."

"You didn't know."

"That doesn't matter, though. I should've never said those things. If I were her, I wouldn't forgive me."

"She already forgave you."

"I almost forgot that both of you are early birds." Mama yawned, walking into the kitchen. She raised an eyebrow my way. "What's wrong?" I stood up and rushed over to her, wrapping her in my arms. "Liz, what are you doing?"

"Congratulating you on your engagement."

Her face lit up. "You'll come to the wedding?"

"Of course."

She hugged me back tighter. "I'm so glad, because the wedding is in three weeks for the New Year."

"Three weeks?!" I said, my voice rising. I paused, feeling the nerves in my gut. Mama didn't need my opinion right now; she needed my support. "Three weeks! Wonderful!"

Mama and Mike left a few hours later, after a game of Zombieland with Emma, complete with their own ketchup scars. Tristan, Emma, Zeus, and I sat on the couch for a while before Tristan pushed himself up on his elbows and looked my way. "Want to go shopping for my place?"

We still hadn't finished adding the small touches to his house—the things he claimed he didn't give a crap about, like throw pillows, paintings, and all the small decorative things I loved. "Yes!" I chimed, always looking for a reason to go shopping.

"Those are ugly, Tick!" Emma said, wrinkling her nose at Tristan's choice of purple and mustard-yellow throw pillows for his couch.

"What?! These are great!" he argued.

"They look like poop." Emma laughed.

I had to agree with her. "It's almost as if you thought, 'Ooh, let's make my house completely hideous after Lizzie and Emma worked so hard to make it amazing.'"

"Yeah." Emma nodded. "It's like you thought that." She flipped her hair over her shoulder. "You should just really leave this to the experts like Mama and me."

He laughed. "Tough crowd." Emma stood on the back of the shopping cart, and Tristan took her shooting around the corner, bumping straight into someone. "Sorry!" Tristan apologized quickly before looking up.

"Uncle Tanner!" Emma squeaked, jumping off the cart and running over to Tanner to wrap him in a hug.

"Hey, kiddo," Tanner said, giving her a squeeze before putting her down.

"What happened to your face?!" Emma asked.

Tanner looked my way. I stared at his bruises from the night before. Such a big part of me wanted to comfort him, but another part wanted to slap him across the face for what he'd said to Tristan about his family.

"Tristan, do you think you could take Emma over to the paintings and have her pick out some artwork for you?" I asked.

Tristan gently placed a hand on my forearm. "Are you okay?" he whispered.

I nodded. They walked off, but not before Tristan apologized to Tanner. Tanner didn't utter a word to him, but the moment Emma and Tristan left, it seemed he had a ton of comments to spit my way.

"Are you serious, Liz? Last night he attacks your friend and now you're running around the store with him as if you are some happy family? And you sent him off alone with your daughter?! What would Steven—"

"Did you say it was his fault his family is dead?"

Tanner narrowed his eyes. "What?"

"Tristan told me."

"Liz, look at my face." He stepped in closer to me. My throat tightened as I stared at his black-and-blue eye. He pulled up his shirt to reveal his left side, which was badly bruised. "Look at my ribs. The man you just sent off with your daughter did *this*. He fucking attacked me like a beast, and you're sitting here asking me what *I* said to *him*? I was drunk; I might have said some stupid things, but he snapped out of nowhere. I saw it in his eyes, Liz. He's completely mad."

"You're a liar." *He's lying. He's lying. Tristan is good. He's so good.* "You should've never said anything about his family. Never." The heels of my feet spun me away from Tanner, and I yipped when I felt his tight grip on my forearm. He forced me to face him once more.

"Listen, I get it. You're mad at me. Fine. Be mad. Fucking hate my guts. But I know there's something off about that guy. I know there's something wrong with him, and I'm not going to stop until I find out what it is because I care too much about you and Emma to let anything happen to you both. Yeah, okay, I said some shit I shouldn't have said, but did I deserve this? It will only be a matter of time before you say something wrong and he snaps on you."

"Tanner," I said, my voice low. "You're hurting me."

He dropped his tight hold from my arm, leaving red marks on my skin where his fingers had been. "Sorry."

When I reached the artwork section of the store, I found Tristan and Emma arguing over what to buy; of course, Emma was right. Tristan smiled my way and stepped toward me. "Are you okay?" he asked again.

I placed my hand against his cheek and stared into his eyes. His gaze was soft and gentle, reminding me of all the good things in the world. While Tanner saw hell in Tristan's stare, I only saw heaven.

It had been three weeks since my birthday, and slowly everything was going back to normal. That night we were driving to Mama's town for her wedding that weekend, and before we could leave, Emma had somehow talked Tristan and me into getting her ice cream in twenty-degree weather.

"I think mint ice cream is nasty!" Emma said as we walked back from the ice-cream shop, Tristan holding her on his shoulders. She was eating a plain vanilla cone, dripping ice cream into his hair every now and then.

As a few drops fell to his cheek, I leaned in and kissed them away, then gently kissed his lips.

"Thanks for coming with us," I said.

"Mostly I just came for the mint," he replied with a playful grin. The grin stayed on his lips until we walked closer to our houses. When his eyes met the steps of my porch, the playfulness left, and he lowered Emma off his shoulders.

"What are you doing here?" I asked Tanner, who was sitting on my porch with papers in his grip.

"We need to talk," he said, standing up. His eyes shifted to Tristan before moving back to me. "Now."

"I don't want to talk to you," I said sternly. "Besides, we are leaving in a few minutes to go visit my mom."

"Is he going with you?" he asked, his voice low.

"Don't start, Tanner."

"We have to talk."

"Tanner, look, I get it. You don't like that I'm with Tristan, but I am. And we're happy. I just don't see why you can't be—"

"Liz!" he shouted, cutting me off. "I get it, whatever. But I need to talk to you." His eyes were glassed over, and his jaw was tight. "Please."

I looked at Tristan, who was staring my way, waiting for me to decide my next move. It seemed as if Tanner truly had something to say, something that was eating at him. "Okay. Fine. Let's talk." He sighed with relief. I turned to Tristan. "I'll see you in a few, okay?"

He nodded and kissed my forehead before saying goodbye to me. Tanner followed Emma and me inside, and while Emma went to her room to play with some toys, we stood at the island in the kitchen. My hands gripped the edge of the counter.

"What do you want to talk about, Tanner?"

"Tristan."

"I don't want to talk about him."

"We have to."

Breaking away from his stare, I moved to the dishwasher and started to unload it, just to keep busy. "No, Tanner. I'm really sick of all of this. Aren't you tired of all of this?"

"Do you know what happened to his wife and kid? Do you know how they died?"

"He doesn't talk about it, and it doesn't make him an awful person that he doesn't talk about it. It makes him human."

"Liz, it was Steven."

"What was Steven?" I asked, tossing plates into the cabinets.

"The accident with Tristan's wife and kid. It was Steven. He was the car that drove them off the road." My throat closed up, and I looked his way. His eyes locked with mine, and as I shook my head, he nodded. "I went digging for information on the guy, and I'll be honest with you, I was just looking for crap to make him out to be a monster. Faye came into my shop and begged me to stop my witch hunt because she was certain it would ruin the little friendship I still had left with you, but I had to know what the deal was with this guy. I didn't find anything. It turns out he's just a guy who lost his world."

"Tanner."

"But I did find these articles on the accident." He held the papers out toward me, and I placed my hands over my chest. My heartbeat was erratic, my heart skipping beats and then speeding up whenever it chose to. "When Steven's car lost control, it slammed into a white Altima. The Altima had three passengers in it."

"Stop…" I whispered, my right hand cupping over my mouth, my body beginning to shake with horror.

"Sixty-year-old Mary Cole, who walked away from the accident."

"Tanner, please. Don't."

"Thirty-year-old Jamie Cole…"

Tears fell, my insides twisting into knots as he continued speaking. "And eight-year-old Charlie Cole, who both lost their lives."

Acid began to rise from my stomach, and I turned away from him, sobbing uncontrollably into my hands, unable to truly believe what he was telling me. Had Steven been the reason that Tristan lost his world? Had my Steven been the cause of Tristan's heartbreak?

"You can't be here right now," I managed to say. Tanner placed a comforting hand on my shoulder, and I slung it off. "I can't deal with this right now, Tanner. Go."

He sighed heavily. "I didn't want you to get hurt, Liz. I swear. But could you imagine if you both found out later on? Could you imagine if he didn't know until you two were in too deep?"

I turned to face him. "What do you mean?"

"I mean, you two can't stay together after this. There's no way." With hesitation, he rubbed the back of his neck. "You're going to tell him, right?" My lips parted, but no words came out. "Liz. You have to tell him. He has a right to know."

My hands brushed against my eyes. "I need you to go, Tanner. Please. Just go."

"All I'm saying is, if you love him, if there's any part of you that truly cares for this guy, then you'll let him go. You'll let him move on."

The last thing he said to me was he didn't mean to hurt me.

I had a really hard time believing him.

CHAPTER 32
Elizabeth

I didn't know how to tell Tristan what Tanner had told me. We drove to Mama's house, and he could tell Tanner had said something that bothered me, but he didn't pressure me to talk about it. I tried to put on my best smiles for Mama and Mike the night of their wedding reception; I tried my best to be happy for them, but inside my heart was so confused.

Emma dragged Tristan out to the dance floor. I couldn't help but smile when I heard a slow song come on and watched Emma step onto his feet. Mama came over to me in her beautiful ivory dress and sat beside me.

"You haven't said one word to me all night," she said. Her smile was the sad kind.

"I came, didn't I? Isn't that good enough?" Such a big part of me felt somewhat betrayed by her sudden rush to the chapel. She'd always had a way of rushing all of her relationships, but she hadn't been crazy enough to walk down the aisle with a man she hardly knew. I turned toward her. "What are you doing, Mama? Just be honest with me... Were you having money issues again? You could've asked me for help."

Her face reddened with embarrassment, maybe anger. "Stop it, Liz. I cannot believe you would say that to me, on today of all days."

"It's just... This is all so sudden."

"I know."

"And I know the man has a lot of money. Look at this wedding."

"The money has nothing to do with it," she disagreed. I cocked an eyebrow. "Really, it doesn't."

"Then what is it? Give me a reason you would rush into this crazy situation if it isn't for the money. What are you getting out of this?"

"Love," she whispered, her lips curving up. "I'm getting love."

For some strange reason, those words stung me. My heart was pained as she confessed to the idea of loving another man who wasn't Dad. "How could you?" I said, my eyes watering over. "How could you just throw the letters away like that?"

"What?"

"Dad's letters. I found them in the garbage bin before Emma and I moved away. How could you?"

She sighed heavily, folding her hands together. "Liz, I didn't just throw them away. I read each and every one of those letters every evening for sixteen years straight. Each night. Hundreds of letters. And then one day I woke up and realized that the security blanket I was wearing was really nothing but a crutch keeping me crippled from living my own life. Your father was a wonderful man. He taught me how to love fully. He taught me how to give in to passion. And then I forgot. I forgot everything he taught me the day he left. I lost myself. I had to step away from the crutch of those letters in order to heal. You are so much stronger than me."

"I still feel weak. Almost every day, I feel weak."

She took my face in her hands and placed her forehead to mine. "That's the thing, though. You're feeling. I was numb. I didn't feel anything. But you're *feeling*. One must know what it feels like to be weak in order to really find their own strength."

"Mike... He really makes you happy?" I asked.

Her face glowed.

She really did love him.

I hadn't known we were truly allowed to love again.

"Tristan," she said. "He makes you happy?"

I nodded slowly.

"And that scares you?"

I nodded once more.

She grinned. "Ah, then that means you're doing it right."

"Doing what right?"

"Falling in love."

"It's too soon..." I said, my voice shaky.

"Says who?"

"I don't know. Society? What's the amount of time you're supposed to have before starting to fall in love again?"

"People say a lot of things and give you all kinds of unwanted advice and tips on how to mourn. They tell you not to date for years, to let time pass, but that's the thing with love—time doesn't exist with it. The only thing love counts is the heartbeats. If you love him, don't get in your own way. Just allow yourself to feel again."

"There's something that I have to tell him. Something terrible, and I think I'll lose him."

She frowned. "Whatever it is, he'll understand if he cares for you the way you care for him."

"Mama." Tears fell from my eyes, and I stared into the eyes that mirrored mine. "I thought I lost you forever."

"I'm sorry I left, baby."

I pulled her into a hug. "It doesn't matter. You came back."

Tristan drove us home from the wedding after I had one too many glasses of wine, and Emma passed out in her car seat as soon as we left. We didn't speak to one another, but so much was said when my hand, which had been alone for so long, tangled with Tristan's fingers.

My eyes couldn't move away from staring at our touch. I lifted our hold up and lightly placed my lips against his hand. How could I tell him about Steven and the accident?

How do I begin to say goodbye?

He glanced over to me and gave me his half smile. "You're drunk?"

"A little."

"You're happy?" he asked.

"A lot."

"Thank you for inviting me. I think I'm a bit bruised from Emma stepping on my feet so much, but I loved it."

"She's crazy about you," I said, staring at his lips.

His eyes studied the darkened road as he replied, "I adore her."

Oh my heart. It stopped. Or sped up. Maybe both all at once.

I kissed his hand once more. My fingers traced every line that wound across his palm.

When we pulled up in front of my house, Tristan lifted Emma from her car seat and carried her to her bedroom. As he laid her down, I stood in the doorway watching. He took off her shoes and placed them at the foot of her bed.

"I should probably head home," he said, walking toward me.

"Yeah, probably."

He smiled. "Thanks again for tonight. It was great." He placed a small kiss on my forehead and stepped past me to leave. "Good night, Lizzie."

"Don't."

"Don't what?"

"Don't go. Stay tonight."

"What?"

"Stay with me."

He lowered his eyebrows. "You're drunk."

"A little."

"But you want me to stay?"

"A lot."

His fingers wrapped around my lower back, and he pulled me closer to his body. "If I stayed, I would want to hold you until the morning, and I know that scares you."

"A lot of things scare me. A lot of things completely terrify me, but being held by you isn't one of them anymore."

My mouth parted as he traced my bottom lip with his finger. He softly lifted my chin up so he could kiss me slowly and gently. "I adore you," he whispered against my lips.

"I adore you," I replied.

His fingers rested on my chest, and he felt my heartbeat. I placed my hands over his chest, feeling his. "I like this," he whispered against my lips.

"I like this too," I replied.

His eyes dilated, and he breathed me in. I breathed him in too, becoming slightly addicted to his entire being. He smelled like the wind that pushed through the most beautiful pine trees in the forest: refreshing, comforting, peaceful. *Like home.* It had been so long since I had felt like I was home.

We took in each other's breaths, silently begging for a little bit more. We headed to my bedroom, where our clothes fell off and our lips came together.

"Wait," I said, pushing him away for a moment. "Everyone in this town thinks this is wrong. Everyone thinks we are a ticking time bomb set to explode any second," I explained. "And I am completely positive that I'm going to somehow manage to mess this up. Then everyone will say, 'I told you so.'"

"For a second let's pretend that they are right. Let's pretend that at the end of this, we don't end up happy." He sighed against my skin, his lips rolling over my bare stomach. "But as long as air moves in and out of my lungs"—his tongue danced against the edge of my panties—"as long as I breathe, I will fight for you. I will fight for us."

CHAPTER 33
Elizabeth

I fell in love with the idea of him first. I fell in love with the idea of a man who could someday make me laugh, smile, and cry all at once. I fell in love with the idea of him loving me for my brokenness, for my pained heart. I fell in love with the idea of his kisses, his touch, his warmth.

And then, one chilly morning, I walked onto my front porch with a steaming coffee mug in my hand. He was lying in the snow-covered grass, making snow angels and looking up at the clouds with Emma beside him. They fought all the time but in the silliest of ways. That morning, they were arguing about what animal they saw. Tristan saw a giraffe cloud, while Emma swore it was a penguin, so after a while, he pretended to see the penguin too.

Emma's lips spread into a grin, and the two grew silent as they moved their legs and arms to perfect their snow angels.

It was in that silence that I knew. I loved him. I loved him so, so much. It wasn't a dream anymore, nor was it the simple idea of loving him.

It was real.

It was true.

He was love.

He made me smile. He made me happy. He made me laugh in a world that was determined to make me cry.

Tears formed in my eyes, and I tried to understand how—how could it be that I was allowed to love such a man who also loved me?

It was such a special feeling to love and be loved in return. To find a man who not only loved you but cherished the best part of you—your baby girl. I was blessed more than words could ever say.

Emma and I loved Tristan completely, and he loved us the same. Maybe he loved our scars the most. Maybe the truest form of love grew from the deepest kinds of pain.

It was funny how everything came to be. We first lied to one another, using each other to hold on to the past, and then we accidentally fell in love.

I knew I had to tell him about the accident. I knew I had to let him know, but I couldn't that morning. That morning, I needed him to know one thing and one thing only.

The two stood up from the grass. Emma hurried into the house for breakfast, and I stayed on the porch, leaning against the railing with a smile that was crafted just for Tristan. His hands were stuffed into his jeans. I was certain Emma had thrown the grass at him. As his foot hit the top step, he kept smiling my way and walked past me to enter the house.

"I love you," I said.

He turned to me and smiled even wider.

Because he already knew.

CHAPTER 34
Elizabeth

Late one night, I stood in my closet, staring at all of Steven's clothes. Inhaling deeply, I began to take them all off the hangers. I removed everything from the dressers. I took everything out of the drawers.

Exhaling slowly, I boxed them up to give away.

Next, I moved to my bed, and I turned my sheets down.

I was ready to fully let Tristan into my life, and I knew that meant I had to start letting go of Steven. In order to truly begin to move on, I knew I had to tell Tristan about the accident. He deserved to know and needed to know. If he truly meant the words he spoke about fighting for me—for us—then no matter what, we would be okay.

At least that was what I hoped. Yet a large part of me knew we wouldn't be okay after this. Our ticking time bomb was growing louder each day.

"We need to talk," I said to Tristan as we stood on my porch. "About when Tanner came over before the wedding."

"Did he hurt you?" Tristan asked. His hand brushed against my cheek, and he stepped into the foyer of the house, close to me. I stepped back. "What did he say?"

The words were on the tip of my tongue, right there, but I knew if I told him, those small touches would leave me forever. My lips parted to try to make him understand, but I knew if I told him what Tanner had found, I would lose him. I wasn't ready to let go of the dream we'd been dreaming.

"Baby...why are you crying?" he asked. I hadn't even noticed the tears falling against my cheeks. More tears began to form in my eyes, and he stepped closer to me. "Lizzie, what's wrong?"

I shook my head back and forth. "Nothing, nothing. Do you think... Will you just hold me for a few minutes?"

His arms wrapped around my body, and he held me tight. I breathed in his scent, almost certain that if I told him the truth—which I knew I had to do—I would lose that moment. I wouldn't be held by him anymore, I wouldn't be touched by him, I wouldn't be loved by him. Tristan's fingers slowly started rubbing my back in a circular motion as I pulled him closer, trying to hold on to something I felt as if I'd already lost.

"You know you can trust me, right? You know you can always tell me anything. I'm always here for you," he swore.

Pulling away from him, I gave him a tight smile. "I just need rest, that's all."

"Then let's go to bed." He nodded, slowly placing his hand on my lower back to guide me to my bedroom.

"I mean alone. I just need a night by myself."

The disappointment swimming in his stormy eyes broke my heart, but he gave me a sad grin. "Yeah, of course."

"We'll talk tomorrow," I promised. "I'll stop by Mr. Henson's shop."

"Yeah," he agreed. "Sounds like a plan." He apprehensively rubbed the back of his neck. "Are we okay?" he whispered, his nerves loud and clear in his tone. I nodded once. He wrapped his hands around my head and rested his lips against my forehead. "I love you, Lizzie."

"I love you too," I replied.

He flinched. "Then why does it feel like we're saying goodbye?"

Because I think we are.

CHAPTER 35
Tristan

APRIL 6TH, 2014
ONE DAY UNTIL GOODBYE

I'm dead," I whispered to myself, staring into the bathroom mirror. The pint of whiskey sat emptied on the counter, the orange pill bottle lay on its side, and my vision blurred. I could hear my parents outside the bathroom, talking about last-minute details for the day, the plans for the service, and our transportation from the church to the cemetery.

"I'm dead," I repeated. My tie hung around my neck, waiting to be tied. I blinked once, and when I opened my eyes, Jamie was standing in front of me, tying my tie.

"What's wrong, baby?" she whispered, as water filled my eyes. I lifted my hand and ran it against her soft cheek. "Why are you falling apart?"

"I'm dead, Jamie, I'm dead," I sobbed, unable to control my howls. "I want this to be over. I want this to stop. I don't want to be here anymore."

"Shh," she whispered, placing her lips near my ear. "Baby, I need you to breathe. It's okay."

"Nothing's okay. Nothing's okay."

I heard pounding on the bathroom door. "Tristan! It's Dad. Son, let me in."

I couldn't, though. I was dead. I was dead.

Jamie looked down at the sink and picked up the emptied pill bottle and whiskey pint. "Baby, what did you do?" My back slid down the wall, and I sat against the tub, sobbing. Jamie rushed over to me. "Tris, you have to throw up now."

"I can't... I can't..." My hands covered my face, everything a blur. My mind was playing tricks on me. I was fading. I could feel myself fading.

"Baby, think of Charlie. He wouldn't want you like this. Come on." She moved me to the toilet. "Don't do this, Tris."

I started to throw up. Everything inside me burned, and when the whiskey and pills rose up from my stomach, my throat was set on fire.

I fell back against the wall once I finished. My eyes opened, and Jamie was gone—she had never been there to begin with. "I'm so sorry," I whispered, running my hands through my hair. What was I going to do? How was I going to survive?

"Tristan, please, let us know you're okay!" Mom and Dad shouted from outside.

"I'm good," I managed to lie to them. I heard Mom's sigh of relief. "I'll be out in a few."

I could almost feel Dad's hand on my shoulder, trying to bring me comfort. "All right, Son. We'll be right here when you're ready. We're not going anywhere."

Elizabeth had said she would meet me at Mr. Henson's shop the next day, but at the last minute she had a change of plans. Five days passed without us actually speaking. Her window blinds had been drawn all week, and whenever I knocked on her door, it seemed as if she was on her way out or simply pretending I didn't exist.

I stopped in at Savory & Sweet to see if she was working and ran into Faye yelling at a customer about how the scrambled eggs were not super runny. "Faye, hey," I said, interrupting her argument.

She twisted around on her heels and placed her hands on her hips. I could see the uncertainty in her eyes. The last time we'd seen each other was when I attacked Tanner at the bar, and I could tell she was still unsure how to address me. I'd been hearing everyone in town whispering about me, and I was sure lies had somehow crawled their way into Faye's eardrums.

"Hey," she replied.

"Is Elizabeth working today?"

"She's out sick… She has been for a few days."

"Oh. Okay."

"Why didn't you just walk next door and check on her? Did you guys get into a fight or something?" She tensed up. "Is she okay?"

"We didn't get into a fight. At least, I don't think we did. She just…" I brushed my finger under my nose and cleared my throat. "She's just not talking to me, and I'm not sure why. Did she happen to say anything to you? I know you're her best friend, and…"

"I think you should go, Tristan." I could tell she didn't believe me. From the way every inch of her was alarmed, I could tell she didn't believe that I hadn't hurt Elizabeth.

I nodded, and as I opened the door to step outside, I paused. "Faye, I love her. I get why you're wary of me, and I understand why you might even hate me. For a long time I was a monster. After Jamie and Charlie died, I turned into this beast that I didn't even recognize. I'm sorry if I scared you the night of her birthday party, and I'm sorry I snapped, but...I would never hurt her. She's..." I pressed my fist against my mouth and bit the inside of my cheek to keep my emotions at bay. "Last year I died right alongside my wife and kid. I checked out of reality and left this world. I was fine being gone because being alive hurt; it hurt every fucking day. Then Lizzie came, and even though I was the walking dead, she saw past it. Even though I was death, she took the time to resuscitate me. She breathed life back into my soul. She brought me back from the shadows. Now she's not answering my calls or looking my way. I'm falling apart because I think she's hurting and I can't help her breathe like she helped me. So yeah, you should hate me. Please, hate the living shit out of me. I deserve it, and because of Elizabeth I can handle it. I'm alive again. But if you could just do me a favor and go check on her, if you could help her breathe for a little while, that would mean the world to me."

I walked out of the café and stuffed my hands into my jeans pockets.

"Tristan!" I turned around to see Faye staring my way. Her eyes were softer. Her strong stance was a mere memory.

"Yeah?"

"I'll check on her," she promised. "I'll help her."

When I headed to Mr. Henson's shop, I saw Tanner through the window, which made me hurry over. I knew he was probably giving Mr. Henson a hard time about selling his shop again. I wished the dude would give him a break.

"What's going on?" I asked, the bell over the door sounding.

Tanner turned to me with a sly smile on his face. "Just talking business."

I looked at Mr. Henson, who was red in the face. He hardly ever got upset, but I could tell Tanner had said something that bothered him. "Maybe you should go, Tanner."

"Give me a break, Tristan. I was just having a friendly chat with Mr. Henson here." Tanner picked up a deck of tarot cards and started shuffling them in his hand. "You think you can do a reading for me real fast, Mr. Henson?"

My friend stayed quiet.

"Tanner, leave."

He smirked and leaned in toward Mr. Henson. "You think the reading will say that you're giving me this space? Is that why you won't do it? You don't want to see the truth?"

My hand landed against Tanner's shoulder, and he flinched. *Good.* The way he was belittling Mr. Henson had my blood boiling. "It's time for you to go."

Mr. Henson sighed with relief at me taking hold of the situation, and he walked off toward the back room.

Tanner slung my hand off and dusted off his outfit. "Chill out, Tristan. I was just having fun with the old man."

"You need to go."

"You're right; I do. Some people have real jobs to do. But hey, I'm glad to hear that you and Liz were still able to work things out after she told you about the accident. That's cool. I mean, hell, you're a better person than me. I don't think I could even deal with being around a person who was involved in such a thing."

"What do you mean?" I asked.

He arched an eyebrow. "You mean, you don't know? Shit… Liz said she told you."

"Told me? Told me what?"

"That her husband was the one driving the car that slammed into your family's car." He narrowed his eyes. "She really didn't tell you?"

My throat dried out, and part of me considered that he could be lying. Tanner hated me because I loved Elizabeth. He was a sneaky asshole who made it his job to get underneath people's skin, and now he was determined to get underneath mine.

The last thing he said was that he was sorry and hadn't meant to start any trouble. He said he was happy that Elizabeth and I had found each other. He said all he wanted was for her to be happy, but I knew that all his words of comfort were full of shit.

That night, I sat on my bed with my cell phone in my hand, and I called my dad. I didn't say a word when he answered, but hearing his voice was good. It was needed.

"Tristan," he said. I could almost hear the relief in his tones. "Hey, Son. Mom said you called her a while back and didn't speak. She was also convinced that she ran into you when she went to Meadows Creek to see the market, but I thought it was just her mind playing tricks on her." He paused. "You're not going to talk, are you?" He paused again. "That's fine. I've always been a bit of a talker."

That was a lie—Dad had always been the quiet one of my parents, much more of a listener. I put the phone on speaker and lay back on my bed, closing my eyes as Dad caught me up on everything I'd missed. "Your grandparents are in town staying with your mom and me, and I think it's safe to say they are driving me crazy. They are having their house remodeled, and your mom thought it would be a good idea to have them stay at our place. They've been here for three weeks already, and I've been through more gin than I thought humanly possible."

"Oh! And your mom somehow talked me into taking a workout class with her because she worries about my healthy diet of Doritos and soda. So I showed up to the class—turned out I was the only man there. I ended up doing Zumba for an hour straight. Lucky for me, my hips don't lie, and I was a natural."

I snickered.

He talked to me late into the night as I moved from room to room, listening to him tell me stories, listening to him talk about sports and how the Packers were still the top team in the NFL. At one point he cracked open a beer, and I opened one too. It almost felt as if we were drinking together.

When it was past midnight, he told me he needed to get to bed. He told me he loved me and would always be on the other end of the line if I ever just needed someone to talk my way.

Right before I went to hang up, my lips parted. "Thanks, Dad."

I heard his voice crack and emotion take over him. "Anytime, Son. Call whenever you need to, day or night. And when you're ready to come back, we'll be here. We'll be right here when you're ready. We're not going anywhere."

The world needed more parents like mine.

CHAPTER 36
Elizabeth

Y ou have four seconds to open this door before I come busting in to find you, woman!" Faye shouted on my front porch. When I opened the door, she gasped. "For the love of God, when was the last time you showered?"

I was wearing pajamas, my hair was in the messiest bun of the century, and my eyes were swollen. I raised my arm a little and smelled my underarm. "I put on deodorant."

"Oh, honey." She frowned, stepping into my living room. "Where's Emma?"

"Friday-night sleepover," I explained, plopping down on the couch.

"What's going on, Liz? Your boyfriend came into the café saying you haven't been talking to him. Did he hurt you?"

"What? No. He's...he's perfect."

"Then why the silent treatment? Why do you look like a homeless person?" She sat down next to me.

"Because I can't talk to him anymore. I can't be with him." I went on to tell her about the accident, to explain why things with Tristan couldn't work out. The seriousness that filled her stare was something I didn't get often from Faye, which attested to how serious and real the situation was.

"Sweetie, you have to tell him. He's falling apart trying to figure out what he did wrong."

"I know. It's just…I love him. And I know because of this, I'll lose him."

"Listen, I don't know much about love, and when my heart was broken, I threw shit. Literally threw shit. After I got done throwing the shit, I was still heartbroken and sad. Someone told me that the heartbreak was worth it because in the end at least you got to experience the love."

I nodded and lay down, my head in her lap. "When does life stop hurting?"

"When we learn to tell life to fuck off and we find the littlest reasons to smile."

"I'm sorry Matty broke your heart."

She shrugged, pulling my hair tie out of my hair before starting to comb her fingers through it. "It's okay. He only cracked it a little. So what are we going to do for the rest of the night? We can be totally girly and watch *The Notebook* or some shit, or…we can order pizza, get some beer, and watch *Magic Mike XXL*."

Magic Mike won.

The next afternoon, Emma and I walked into Needful Things to find Tristan smiling behind the coffee counter. "Hey, you guys!" he said with the widest grin ever.

"Hey, Tick!" Emma exclaimed, climbing up into one of the chairs.

He bent down and bopped her on the nose. "Hey, Tock. Hot cocoa?"

"With extra marshmallows!" she yelled.

"With extra marshmallows!" he echoed, turning away. His happy demeanor was a bit off-putting. I wasn't sure what it meant or how to take it. We hadn't spoken in days, yet he was acting as if everything was perfect. "Elizabeth, can I get you something?"

He'd called me Elizabeth, not Lizzie.

"Just water," I said, sitting beside Emma. "Is everything okay?" I asked him as he poured me a glass of water and handed Emma her "semi-hot" cocoa, which he always added a few ice cubes to. She hopped out of her chair and hurried over to find Zeus.

"Everything's fine. Everything's good."

I raised an eyebrow. "We should talk. I know you're probably upset because I've been avoiding you…"

"Have you?" He smirked. "I hadn't noticed."

"Yeah, it's just—"

He started wiping off the counter. "That your husband killed my family? Yeah, no, that's cool."

"What?" My throat tightened and my ears rang as I replayed the words that had just left his mouth. "How did you…?"

"Your best friend Tanner stopped in for a bit yesterday. He wanted to, you know, try to talk Mr. Henson into closing his shop. So then he and I had a talk. He thought it was sweet how I was able to look past the fact that, you know, your husband killed my family."

"Tristan."

He placed the rag down on the counter, stood across from me, and leaned in. "How long have you known?"

"I—I wanted to tell you."

"How long?"

"Tris…I didn't know…"

"Dammit, Elizabeth!" he shouted, slamming his fist down. Emma and Mr. Henson turned toward us with looks of curious concern. Mr. Henson was quick to usher Emma into the back room. "How long? Did you know when you told me you loved me?"

I stayed quiet.

"Did you know at the wedding?"

My voice shook. "I thought…I thought I would lose you. I wasn't sure how to tell you."

He smiled a tight grin and nodded. "Awesome. That will be two dollars and twenty cents for the hot cocoa."

"Let me explain."

"Two-twenty, Elizabeth."

His stormy eyes were cold once again. There was a coldness I hadn't seen in his stare since the first day I'd met him. I reached into my pocket, pulled out some change, and placed it in front of me. Tristan picked up the money and tossed it into the cash register.

"We'll talk later this week," I said, my voice shaky. "If you let me, I'll explain everything the best I can."

His back was to me, and he gripped the countertop by the coffee machines. His head lowered, and I could see how red his hands were turning from his tight hold. "You need anything else?" he asked.

"No."

"Then by all means, stay the fuck out of my life." Tristan dropped his hold on the counter, called for Zeus, who came running out toward him, and then the two of them left the store, the overhead bell sounding their exit. Mr. Henson and Emma came out from the back room.

"What happened?" Mr. Henson asked, walking over to me. He placed a comforting hand on my shoulder, but it didn't stop my shaking body.

"I think I just lost him."

CHAPTER 37
Tristan

APRIL 7TH, 2014
GOODBYE

I *stood on the hilltop in the far back of the cemetery with Zeus by my
side. Everyone else stood around the side-by-side caskets, all dressed
in black, with tears in their eyes. Mom's body shook in Dad's hold. All of
Jamie's and my friends stood by, brokenhearted.*

Charlie's teacher showed up and cried the whole time.

*She was probably thinking that it was so unfair. It was so unfair that
Charlie would never have the chance to learn how to handle fractions
or what algebra was. That he would never learn to drive stick. That he
would never have to apply to college or fall in and out of love. That he
would never slow dance with his mother at his wedding. That he would
never get to introduce me to his firstborn. That he would never get the
chance to say goodbye…*

*I wiped my eyes and sniffled as Zeus moved closer to me and laid
his head on my shoe.*

Dammit, I couldn't breathe.

They lowered Jamie into the ground first, and my legs wobbled.

"Don't go…" I whispered.

They lowered Charlie next.

"No…" I begged.

My legs collapsed. I fell to the ground, and my hands covered my mouth as Zeus comforted me, licking my tears away, trying to make me believe that it was okay, that I was okay, that everything would somehow, someway, turn out okay.

But I didn't believe him.

I should've walked down and stood by my parents, but I didn't. I should've told both Jamie and Charlie I loved them both so fucking much, but my voice went mute.

I stood and turned away, Zeus's leash wrapped tightly in my grip.

I turned away from Jamie.

I walked away from my son.

And I learned how much it hurt to finally have to say goodbye.

"So you're running," Mr. Henson said to me a week later as I parked in front of his store to say our final goodbye.

I shrugged. "Not running. Just moving on. Things come and go; you should know that better than anyone."

He brushed his fingers against his gray beard. "But that's not what you're doing. You're not moving on; you're running again."

"You don't understand. Her husband—"

"Is not her."

"Mr. Henson…"

"My former love adored magic. He spent our whole life together trying to get me to support his dream of opening a tarot shop in this town. He believed in the power of energy, in the healing power of crystals. He believed magic had a way to make life more livable. I thought he was insane. I worked a nine-to-five job and hardly paid any attention to him. I called his dreams of owning his own shop ridiculous. We were already two gay men—life was already hard enough for us. The last thing we needed to be was two gay men who believed in magic.

"And then one day, he left. At first it seemed so out of nowhere, but as time went on, I realized it had been all my own doing. I hadn't valued him when I'd had him, so when I lost him, it hit me hard. After he left, I felt so alone; I realized he had probably always felt that way. No one should feel alone when they are in love. I quit my job and tried to make his dream of magic come to life. I studied the power of crystals and the healing herbs. I worked hard to understand his dreams, and by the time I did, it was too late. He had moved on to someone who loved him in the moment.

"Don't turn away from Liz because of something she didn't have anything to do with. Don't walk away from a chance at happiness because of an accident. Because at the end of the day, it's not about the tarot cards, or the crystals, or the special teas. That's not where the magic lives. The magic is in the tiny moments. The small touches, the gentle smiles, the quiet laughs. The magic is about living for today and allowing yourself to breathe and be happy. My dear boy, to love is the magic."

I chewed on my bottom lip, taking in all of his words, all of his thoughts. I wanted to believe him, and I thought a big part of me truly did understand his words. But another part of me, buried deep inside my soul, felt the guilt. Jamie deserved more. For me to even consider loving someone else after such a short period of time was selfish. "I don't know how to do it. I don't know how to truly love Lizzie, seeing how I never said goodbye to my past."

"You're going back to say goodbye?"

"I think I'm going back to learn to breathe again."

Mr. Henson frowned but said he understood. "If you ever need a place to rest your head and a friend to call on, I'll be here."

"Good," I said, pulling him into a hug. "And if you ever sell your shop to some asshole, I'll be back here to fight it tooth and nail."

He snickered. "Deal."

I opened the front door, listening to the bell ring overhead for the last time. "You'll watch after them? Emma and Lizzie?"

"I'll make sure their tea and cocoa is never too hot."

After we said goodbye, I headed out of the shop, jumped into my car, and started driving with Zeus. We drove for hours. I wasn't certain where I was going, or if I even had a place to go, but mindless driving made sense to me right then.

I pulled up to the house after three in the morning, and their porch light was still on. As a kid, I'd stayed out past curfew way too often and had made life a living hell for them. Despite that, Mom always kept the porch light on to let me know that they were still waiting for me to arrive back home.

"What do you say, boy? You say we go in?" I asked Zeus, who was curled up in the passenger seat of the car, wagging his tail. "Okay. Let's go in."

Once I stood on the porch, I knocked a total of five times before I heard the door unlock. Dad and Mom stood there in their pajamas staring at me, almost as if they were seeing a ghost. I cleared my throat. "Look, I know I've been a shit son this past year. I know I disappeared and didn't say a word. I know I've been lost and wandering around in my mind trying to find my way. I know I said some terrible things before I left, blaming you for what happened. But I…" My hand brushed over my mouth before I stuffed both hands into my jeans pockets. I started kicking around the invisible rocks on the ground. "I was just wondering if I could stay here for a while. Because I'm still lost. I'm still wandering. But I don't think I can do it alone anymore. I just need…um…I just need my mom and dad for a while, if that's okay."

They stepped onto the porch, wrapping their arms around me.

Home.

They welcomed me home.

CHAPTER 38
Elizabeth

What do you mean he left?" I asked Mr. Henson. My hands gripped the railing of the countertop in his shop as he stood making me a cup of tea on Friday afternoon. I'd just dropped Emma off at her grandparents' house for their sleepover, and seeing how I hadn't seen or heard from Tristan in a few days, I was at my breaking point. I needed to talk to him, or at least know that he was okay.

"He left two days ago. I'm sorry, Liz." Mr. Henson's bubbly personality was gone, which scared me.

"When will he be back?"

Silence.

My hands landed against my hips, and I tapped my shoe against the wooden floor. "Well, where did he go?"

"I don't know, Liz."

I sighed, nerves and worry building inside of me. "He won't answer my calls." My jaw shook as tears formed in my eyes. My shoulders rose and fell. "He won't answer my calls."

"Honey, you both have been through so much. And I know this has to be hard for you…"

"No. Not for me. I mean, I can deal with him not answering my calls. I can deal with him ignoring me. But I have a five-year-old wondering where Tick and Zeus are. She's wondering where her two friends went. She's asking why Zeus hasn't been over to play catch or why Tristan hasn't been reading to her at night. So yes, I'm sad that he's not talking to me, but I am beyond pissed off that he left Emma like that, without a word, without a thought. I'm pissed off that she's been crying because she misses them. And it is breaking my heart that I cannot even tell her where he is or if he's coming back. He said he would fight for us, but when it came down to it, he didn't even try." My voice crackled. "She deserves better."

He reached his hand out and placed it on top of mine. A slight wave of comfort flew through me. "You all deserve better than this."

"Okay, I better get going. Just, if you hear from him…" My words faded off. I wasn't certain if I wanted Mr. Henson to tell Tristan to come back or to go to hell. So I left the shop with a clouded mind.

That night, I was in bed before ten. Not sleeping, but just staring at the ceiling in my darkened room. I turned on my side and stared at the emptied space next to me. When I received a call from Kathy saying that Emma wanted to come home early that night, I would've been lying if I said I wasn't pleased.

When she came back, she lay beside me in my bed. I read her a few chapters from *Charlotte's Webb* in my best zombie voice, and her giggles reminded me of the important things.

After the story, we were both on our side, facing one another. I kissed the top of her nose, and she kissed mine.

"Mama?" she said.

"Yes?"

"I love you."

"I love you, babe."

"Mama?" she said once more.

"Yes?"

"Tick's zombie voice was good, but I like yours better." She yawned and shut her eyes. I combed my fingers through her wild, blond hair as she began to lose herself to sleep.

"Mama?" she whispered for the final time that night.

"Yes?"

"I miss Zeus and Tick."

I snuggled beside her, falling asleep only a few minutes after she did. I didn't say it to her, but I missed them too.

So, so much.

The next morning, I shot up from my bed at the sound of a shovel scraping against the sidewalk outside of my house. "Tristan…" I murmured to myself, tossing on my robe and slippers, hurrying to the front of the house. When I opened the door, the small bit of hope I held was demolished when I saw Tanner standing on my sidewalk, getting rid of the freshly fallen snow.

"What are you doing?" I asked, crossing my arms.

He looked up at me with an upside-down smile and shrugged. "I wanted to stop by and see how you and Emma were doing." He stopped shoveling and rested his chin against the handle bar. "Plus, I'm pretty positive you're mad at me."

I huffed.

Mad?

I was beyond mad—I was livid.

"You had no right to tell Tristan about the accident." My eyes tried to lock with his. Maybe if he stared into my eyes he could see how much he hurt me. Maybe if he stared into my eyes, he could see how he ruined things for Tristan and me. *Don't you feel bad at all?*

He wouldn't meet my stare. His eyes faltered to the ground, and he kicked snow around with his boots. "I thought you'd already told him."

"Tanner, you knew I didn't. I don't know what your deal is lately. Is this all because I wouldn't go out on a date with you? Is this because you were embarrassed? I've been playing it over and over in my head as to why you would do something so heartless, and nothing is coming to mind. I literally cannot understand why you would do this to me."

The palm of his hand ran across his mouth, and he muttered something.

"What?" I asked. "Speak up."

He didn't.

I walked down the steps on the porch and stood in front of him. "You've been in my life for years, Tanner. You were at my wedding. You are the godfather to my daughter. You held me at my husband's funeral. So if there's a reason you are acting weird, if there is a reason you broke Tristan and me up, then tell me. Because if there is a real, legit reason for why you don't think I should be with him, then maybe I can get over this feeling inside of me. Maybe I could figure out a way to look at you and not feel sick to my stomach."

"You wouldn't understand," he said with his head still lowered.

"Try me."

"But—"

"Tanner!"

"God dammit, I love you, Elizabeth!" he shouted, finally finding my stare. His words hit me hard, making me stumble backward as my heart stopped beating for a moment. He dropped his shovel, and then tossed his hands up in defeat. "I'm in love with you. I've been in love with you for years. Since I first met you. I hid my feelings for so long because my best friend loved you too. And you loved him. I stood by never speaking a word because I knew if there was anyone else worthy of your love, it was Steven. But after he died…" He started in my direction and combed my fallen hairs behind my ears. "I didn't plan to want you as much as I did once you came back to town. I buried my feelings down deep. But then, this Tristan guy came along, and I sat behind the scenes once more, watching someone else make you laugh, someone else make you happy, someone else loving you.

"So each day, I grew jealous. Each day I wanted you to want me. I wanted your laughs, your smiles, *you*. I wanted you, Liz. So I tried to rip Tristan and you apart. I know it was a shitty thing to do, and I know I cannot begin to ask for you to forgive me, but…" He sighed and laced his fingers with mine. "I just love you so damn much, and I'm not sure if my heart can take not having you."

His fingers were linked with mine, but instead of the warmth that Steven had always brought me, instead of the tenderness that Tristan supplied my way, I only felt coldness. Holding Tanner's hand made me feel more alone than ever.

"You deliberately broke us up," I said, flabbergasted. I dropped his hold on me and then ran my hands through my hair. "You literally interfered in my *life*, in my *choices*, because you *love* me?"

"He's not right for you."

I shook my head. "You don't get to decide that."

"He would've hurt you. He's a monster, I know he is. And look at what happened at the first sign of trouble: he disappeared. I wouldn't leave you, Liz. I would fight for you."

"Maybe you should, though."

He raised an eyebrow. "Maybe I should what? Maybe I should fight for you? I will, I promise you, I will."

"No." I crossed my arms, standing tall. "Maybe you should leave."

"Lizzie…"

"*Don't*," I hissed, my voice stinging his ears. "Don't call me that. You're insane if you think I would want anything to do with you. When you love someone, you don't go out of your way to hurt them. When you truly love someone, you want their happiness more than your own. Tristan isn't the monster, Tanner. You're the one people should be worried about. You're sick. Delusional. Now, leave me alone. Don't come back to my house. If you see me in town, look the other way. Because I truly want nothing to do with you."

"You don't mean that." His body was shaking, and all the color drained from his face. I began to walk up my porch steps, still listening to his shouts. "You don't mean that, Liz! You're mad, but we'll be okay. We'll be okay, right?"

Once my feet hit the inside of the house, I slammed the door and leaned against it. My heart was pounding against my rib cage, and I continued to listen to Tanner yelling outside about how we would figure things out—how we would be okay.

But we wouldn't.

The only way I would be okay was if I never saw his face again.

CHAPTER 39
Tristan

Weeks passed after I left Meadows Creek, followed by months. I spent most of my time in my parents' backyard, chopping wood and carving into it. I built things with my hands because building felt like the only thing I had left of myself.

When May came around, I was still thinking of Elizabeth. I was still missing Emma. I was still learning how to say goodbye to Jamie. I still wanted Charlie back. I hadn't known it was possible to lose my world twice in such a short period of time.

"Tristan," Mom said, stepping onto her back porch. "You want to come in for dinner?"

"Nah, I'm good."

She frowned. "Okay."

My hand rested against the axe in my grip, and I lowered my head. "Actually, I think I'll eat."

The level of excitement that overtook her almost made me smile. Even though I knew I wasn't anywhere near hungry, the joy it brought to her made me want to stuff my face. Mom had been through so much since the accident. I couldn't imagine the amount of blame she probably placed on herself, the number of daily struggles she dealt with from knowing she had been behind the steering wheel, and I hadn't made it any easier for her.

The least I could do was sit down and have dinner with her and Dad.

"Are you thinking of selling the house in Meadows Creek?" Dad asked.

"I don't know. Probably. I'll start all of that stuff next week or something."

"If you need any help, let me know. I don't know much about selling a house, but I can google better than most people my age," he joked.

I laughed. "I'll keep that in mind."

When I glanced up, I saw Mom staring my way with that same frown she'd worn outside. I shifted in my seat. "Dinner's great," I said, complimenting her skills.

She kept looking sad. "Thanks."

"What's wrong?" I questioned, rubbing the back of my neck.

"You're just… What happened to you? You seem so heartbroken."

"I'm okay."

"You're not."

Dad cleared his throat and gave Mom a stern look. "Come on, Mary. Give him time."

"I know, I know. It's just, I'm a mother, and the worst feeling in the world is knowing your child is hurting and you can't fix that hurt."

I reached out across the table and gripped her hand in mine. "I'm not okay. But I'll get there."

"Promise?" she asked.

"Promise."

I hadn't stopped by the cemetery since I'd returned to town. I spent a few too many hours in my car, trying my best to figure out what I was supposed to do with my life. How I was supposed to move forward. When I found myself sitting parked in front of the cemetery, I felt my stomach tighten into knots. It took everything in me to get out of the car and walk.

I hadn't been there since the burial. Standing in front of Jamie's and Charlie's tombstones made my eyes fill with tears as I lay against them.

"Hey, you guys. Sorry I haven't visited. Truth is, I was trying my best to run from you because I didn't know how to live without you. I abandoned you and went searching for a replacement. For someone who didn't even exist, because I couldn't imagine not having a family anymore. I couldn't imagine living in a world where you both weren't. I don't know how to do this without you. I don't know how to exist… So just tell me what to do. *Please.* I'm so fucking lost. I don't think I can do this without you." My heart pounded against my chest as I slid down to the ground, finally allowing myself to feel the loss of Jamie and Charlie. They were my world. Charlie was my heart, and Jamie was my soul, and I'd let them down by turning away from them both. By not mourning their memory the way they deserved. "Please wake me up. Wake me up. Wake me up and tell me I'm stronger than I think I am. Wake me up and tell me my heart isn't breaking anymore."

I stayed with them until the sun began to set. My arms were wrapped around my kneecaps, and I stayed still, staring at the words on the stones. Missing people, missing the ones who knew you better than you knew yourself left emptiness inside of you. I tried to fill that emptiness, but maybe it was supposed to be left hollow inside my heart.

Each day, I felt the hurt, the memories. Each day, they both crossed my mind; I guessed that was the blessing behind the broken heart.

"If I could tell you a secret, Jamie, I would tell you that I still love her. I would tell you that Elizabeth is something good and right in the world. I would tell you she's the reason I started to breathe again. So what am I supposed to do? How do I start to move on from her knowing that she can't be mine? I just wish…" I cleared my throat, uncertain what I was wishing for. Answers to the unasked questions, I supposed. "I just wish I knew you would be okay with this. I wish I knew it was okay for me to fall in love again." As I stood up to leave, I kissed my lips twice and placed my fingers against the gray tombstones.

Right before I turned to leave, a small white feather came floating down from above and landed against my arm. A wave of comfort washed over me as I nodded. "I'll be okay. I'll be good," I muttered, knowing that it was a kiss from my loved ones. I knew I would be okay one day because it was obvious that I wasn't alone.

"What are you looking at?" Mom asked me one afternoon as I sat at the dining-room table Dad had made her for Christmas a few years before.

I held on to the picture Emma had taken of Elizabeth and me with the white feathers many months before. I'd looked at it every day since I left. "Nothing."

"Let me see," she said, sitting beside me. I passed her the picture and heard a slight gasp fall from her lips. "That's her."

"That's who?"

"Kevin!" she shouted, calling Dad into the room. "Kevin! Come here!"

He hurried into the room. "Yeah?"

She passed the picture to Dad, and he narrowed his eyes as Mom began to explain. "The day of the accident, that's the girl. I was falling apart in the waiting room while Jamie and Charlie both went into surgery. I was sobbing uncontrollably, and this woman walked up to me and held me. She stayed with me the whole time, keeping me from falling apart, telling me it would be okay."

"That's her?" I asked, pointing to the picture. "Are you sure?"

She nodded. "I know without a doubt in my mind. That's her. When Jamie and Charlie came out of surgery, I didn't know what to do, who to check on first…so she sat with Jamie while I sat beside Charlie." She looked at me with confusion in her stare. "Why do you have a picture with her?"

I took the picture back from Dad and stared at a smiling Elizabeth, trying to get a grip on what was happening. *She stayed by Jamie's side.* "I don't know."

CHAPTER 40
Elizabeth

GOODBYE

No," I whispered, standing in the waiting room as a doctor stood in front of me.

"I'm so sorry. He didn't make it out of surgery. We did everything we could to stop the bleeding, but we were unable to..." His lips kept moving, but I couldn't hear him anymore. My world had just been stolen from me, and my legs gave out as I lowered myself to sit in the closest chair.

"No," I murmured again, covering my face with the palms of my hands.

How could he be gone so fast? How could he leave me here alone?

Steven, no...

Before the surgery, I held his hand. I told him I loved him. I kissed him one last time.

How could you be gone?

The doctor walked away after telling me how sorry he was, but I didn't care. Kathy and Lincoln showed up a few moments later, and *their hearts shattered right along with mine. We stayed at the hospital for the longest time, until Lincoln said we had to leave, we had to start planning.*

"I'll meet you back at your house," I said. "God. Emma's at Faye's house. Do you think you can pick her up?"

"Where are you going?" Kathy asked me.

"I'm just going to stay here for a little longer."

She frowned. "Honey."

"No, really, I'm fine. I'll be over soon. Can you just… Can you wait to tell her?"

Kathy and Lincoln agreed.

I stayed for hours in that waiting room, unsure what I was waiting for. It seemed that everyone in the waiting room was doing exactly that: waiting for an answer, waiting for a prayer, waiting for hope.

In the corner was an older woman crying her eyes out, completely alone, and I couldn't help but feel drawn to her. Her body was bruised, battered, as if she had just walked away from an ungodly event. Yet the pain in her stormy blue eyes was what haunted me the most. I shouldn't have stepped into her world of waiting, but I did. I held her, and she didn't push me away. I held her, and we fell apart together.

After some time, a nurse informed the woman that her grandson and her daughter-in-law were both out of surgery but in critical condition. "You can see them. You can sit in their rooms, but they won't be responsive. Just so you know. But you can hold their hands."

"How do I…" Her voice shook and tears fell. "How do I choose who to see first? How do I…?"

"I'll sit with one of them until you can," I offered. "I'll hold their hand."

She sent me to sit with her daughter-in-law. When I entered the room, a chill raced through me. The poor woman was drained of all of her color. She was almost a living ghost. I pulled up a chair beside her and took her hand into mine.

"Hi," I whispered. "This is weird, and I'm not even sure what to say. But, well, I'm Elizabeth. I met your mother-in-law, and she's super worried about you. So I need you to fight. She said your husband is on his way back from a trip, worried sick. So I need you to just keep fighting. I know it has to be hard, but keep going." Tears fell from my eyes as I stared at the stranger who seemed so familiar to my heart. I thought about how broken I would've been if I didn't get to at least hold Steven's hand before he passed away. "Your husband is going to need you to be strong." I leaned close to her ear and whispered, hoping my words would find her soul. "We have to make sure your husband's okay. We have to make sure he gets to hold you. We have to make sure he can say he loves you. You can't let go yet. Keep. Fighting."

I felt her fingers squeeze against mine, and my stare moved to our hands.

"Ma'am?" a voice said. I turned to the door to see a nurse staring my way. "Are you family?"

"No. I just..."

"I'm going to have to ask you to leave."

I nodded once.

And I let go of her hand.

"He keeps leaving these Post-it Notes." I sighed, sitting on the seesaw with Faye as Emma played on the monkey bars and went down the slide. "Every now and then I find a Post-it on my window, and I just don't know what to think about the messages. He says he still loves me and wants me, but then…nothing. I don't know what to think."

"He's playing mind games, and that's not cool. I just don't understand why he would do some crap like that to you. Do you think he's just being rude? Like, getting back at you for not telling him about the accident?"

"No." I shook my head. "He wouldn't do that."

"It's been months, Liz. He hasn't called once. He hasn't reached out except for some random pieces of paper every now and then. That's not normal."

"There never was anything normal about Tristan and me."

She pushed the seesaw down and looked up at me. "Maybe it's time to find a new normal, then. You deserve a normal life."

I didn't reply but thought maybe she was right.

I just wished the Post-its didn't bring me so much comfort that he might come back to me one day.

I just need time to figure things out.
I'll be back soon. I love you.—TC

Wait for me.—TC

Everyone was wrong about us. Just
please wait for me.—TC

"You have purple stuff on your lips, Sam," I said as I walked into the café for my shift. He was quick to run his hands over his mouth as I watched his cheeks redden. For the past few weeks, Matty had started tossing Sam into the kitchen for the lunch service to learn to cook the café's menu. He seemed so happy finally doing something he loved, and it turned out he was pretty amazing at it.

"Thanks," he said, lifting up a stack of plates to take back to the dish room. As he walked through the door, Faye walked out, and they did an awkward tango of who-gets-to-step-out-of-the-way-first.

When Faye saw me, she shouted my way, greeting me. I smirked. "Nice purple lipstick you have on, friend."

She smiled. "Thanks! I just bought it."

"I swear I've seen it before."

"Nope." She shook her head. "I just got it last night."

"No, I mean, I think I've seen it, like, five seconds ago on Sam's lips."

Her face flushed, and she twiddled her fingers together, rushing over to me. "Oh my gosh, shit! Creepy Sam wears the same lipstick as me? I need to find myself a new color."

I cocked an eyebrow. "You're so full of crap. So tell me."

"Tell you what?"

"Your nickname for his you-know-what."

She rolled her eyes. "Oh my gosh, Liz. We are almost thirty. Do you think we can not act like five-year-olds for one day?" The seriousness in her voice as she walked over to the counter to get a customer a cheese Danish made me wonder if she was truly growing up—until she shouted across the room, "Supersized Sam!"

I burst out laughing. "And to think, these past few months you convinced me that Sam was a creep."

"Oh, he is. He's a total creep. Like, he did this really creepy thing last night," she explained, pulling out a chair at an empty table and sitting. I was still completely confused how she managed to keep her job at that place.

"What did he do?" I asked, sitting across from her. *If you can't beat them, join them.*

"Well, for starters, he's always asking me how I'm doing, which is just weird. It's almost as if he wants to know about me."

"Dude. Okay, that's totally weirdo territory," I mocked.

"Right! And then! Last night, he came over to my place, and I asked him which room he wanted to bang in, and he was all like, 'No, I want to take you out somewhere fancy.' Like, what? And then after dinner and drinks, he walked me up to my porch, kissed my cheek, and said he would love to take me out some other time! He didn't even try to meet my vagina last night."

"WHAT A CREEP!"

"I KNOW!" She paused, glancing back at the kitchen where Sam was getting started on the griddle. A tiny smile played on her lips before she turned back to me. "He's not that creepy, I guess."

"No, I guess not. I'm so happy he gets to work in the kitchen too. I remember him telling me how much he wanted to do that."

"Yeah, plus, he's just freaking amazing in there."

"I'm surprised Matty let him cook."

She shrugged. "He kind of had to. I blackmailed him by threatening to send the video of him dancing naked to the Spice Girls to everyone who works here unless he gave Sam a chance."

"You're a terrible person, Faye." I pushed myself up from my chair and went to head back to work. "But a really great friend."

"It's that Scorpio in me. I love you until you do something to piss me off. Then I turn into your personal Satan."

I laughed.

"Oh crap," Faye shouted, leaping out of her seat, placing her hands on my shoulders, and rotating me around from facing the front windows. "Okay. Don't panic."

"About what?"

"Well, remember when your husband died and you disappeared for a year and then came back, but were super depressed and you started banging an asshole who turned out to not be an asshole but just a dude who was hurt because his wife and son died? And then you two like kind of fell into a weird sexlationship where you pretended you were both someone else but then one day you were like, 'But I want you to be you and me to be me,' so you fell in love. And then you found out that your husband was involved in his family's deaths, and then shit got weird and the dude left town, but for some reason thought it was okay to keep leaving you Post-it Notes that just left you even more confused and hurt and totally, 'Oh my gosh, it feels like I'm PMSing for four weeks out of every month and I can't even eat any more ice cream because my hot tears melt it every time I cry into the Ben and Jerry's.' Do you remember all of that?"

I blinked repeatedly. "Yes, I believe that sounds familiar. Thank you for the trip down memory lane."

"You're welcome. Well, okay, don't freak out, but here's the thing. That dude you fell in love with? He's across the street in the voodoo shop."

My body shot around, and I saw Tristan standing in the store with Mr. Henson. My heart skyrocketed from my chest to my throat, and I could feel my body tingling with nerves.

Tristan.

"You're freaking out," she said.

I shook my head. "I'm not."

"You're freaking out," she repeated.

I nodded. "I am." My voice trembled. "What is he doing here?"

"I think you should go find out," Faye said. "You deserve an answer for all of those damn Post-it Notes."

She was right. I needed to know. I needed closure. I needed to move on by letting go of any hope that he would someday come back for me—because I was definitely still waiting.

"Matty, Liz is taking a lunch break," Faye shouted.

"She just got here! And it's breakfast time!" he replied.

"Fine. She's taking a breakfast break."

"No way. She's working her whole shift." Faye started humming "Spice Up Your Life" by the Spice Girls, and Matty's face turned beet red. "Take all the time you need, Liz."

CHAPTER 41

Tristan

I pulled up to Mr. Henson's shop and hurried inside. He'd called me the day before and had sounded very distressed, telling me the shop was closing due to issues with the town asshole. I knew Tanner had something to do with it, and I knew Mr. Henson was probably falling apart. I had to check on him to see how I could help—after all, he had been one of the first to be there for me when I was completely lost.

When I walked into Needful Things, my eyes widened when I saw Mr. Henson packing up the store. It was as if everything magical about the place was gone. All the shelves emptied. All the mysterious items boxed away.

"What the heck is going on?" I said, moving toward Mr. Henson.

"Tanner is getting his wish. I'm closing down shop."

"What? I thought you called me here to try to figure this out." My fingers ran though my hair. "You can't close up shop. Did he do this at the town hall meeting? He can't do this!"

"It doesn't matter, Tristan. I already sold the shop."

"To who? I'll get it back. Whatever it takes. Who did you sell it to?"

"The town asshole."

"Tanner can't have this shop. You can't let him win."

"I wasn't talking about Tanner."

"Then who were you talking about?"

He turned my way and took my hand, placing a set of keys in my grasp. "You."

"What?"

"It's yours, every inch, every square," Mr. Henson sang.

"What are you talking about?"

"Well," he said, sitting on top of one of the boxes. "I've lived my dream. I've seen the magic this place can create. Now it's time I give it to someone else who needs a little magic in their life. Someone who needs a little dreaming."

"I'm not taking your shop."

"Oh, but see, that's the beauty in all of it. You are taking it. It's already yours. I set up all of the paperwork. All you have to do is cross a few t's and dot a few i's."

"What would I even do with it?" I asked.

"You have a dream, Tristan. The furniture that your father and you create would get a ton more people into this space than my old crystals ever did. Don't let anyone ever kill your dreams, my boy." He pushed himself up from his box, moved over to the counter, and picked up his hat. Placing it on his head, he began walking toward the front door.

"What about you? What are you going to do?" I asked, watching him open the front door, sounding the bell overhead.

"As for me, well, I'm going to go find a new dream, because you're never too old to dream a little dream, to discover a little magic. I hear there are rumors going around that the town might need some repairs, and I have a few dollars lying around. We'll chat through the details later on, but for now, I'll be seeing you." He winked, walking out the door.

I moved to the store door and opened it fast, glancing in the direction Mr. Henson had disappeared in.

My mind started to wonder if he was some kind of weird hallucination, but when I looked down at the keys in my hands, I knew he was real.

"What are you doing here?"

I turned around to see Elizabeth standing behind me, her arms crossed. "Lizzie," I muttered, almost stunned to see her standing so close. "Hi."

"Hi?" she huffed, barging into the store. I followed her inside. "Hi?!" she shouted. "You disappear for months, not giving me a chance to explain myself, and then randomly show up in town and all you can say is 'hi'? You're a...you're a...a DICK!"

"Lizzie," I said with narrowed eyes, stepping toward her. She stepped back.

"No. Don't come near me."

"Why not?"

"Because whenever you're near me, I can't think straight, and I need to think straight right now to say what I need to say." She stopped talking and took a moment to look around the store. "Oh my gosh. Where is everything? Why is it all boxed away?"

I placed my thumb between my teeth and studied her features. Her hair was longer, lighter too. She was makeup free, and her eyes still had the ability to make me fall in love with her. "You stayed with her."

"What?" she asked with her back leaning against the counter.

I walked closer to her, boxing her in as my hands rested against the countertop. "You stayed with Jamie."

Her breathing pattern became uneven, and she stared at my lips as I stared at hers. "Tristan, I don't know what you're talking about."

"The day of the accident, my mom was in the waiting room by herself because Dad and I were still flying back from Detroit. You saw her, and you held her."

"That was your mom?" she asked, her eyes narrowed.

I nodded. "And she said when Jamie and Charlie were out of surgery, you sat with Jamie. You held her hand." My lips hovered over hers, and I could feel the small exhales leaving her mouth. "What happened when you went into that room with Jamie?"

Her voice shook, and she blinked a few times before tilting her head back slightly to meet my stare. "I sat down beside her bed, held her hand, and told her she wasn't alone." My fingers rubbed against my forehead, taking in her words. "She wasn't in pain, Tristan. When she passed away, the doctors said there wasn't any pain."

"Thank you," I said. I needed to know that.

My left hand moved to her lower back, and I pulled her closer to me.

"Tristan, don't."

"Tell me not to kiss you," I begged. "Tell me not to do it."

She didn't say a word, but her body shook in mine. My lips brushed against hers, and I kissed her hard and deep, apologizing for everything I'd done, every mistake I'd made. When our mouths pulled away, she kept shaking against my hold.

"I love you," I said.

"No. You don't."

"I do."

"You left me!" she cried, yanking herself away from me. She crossed the room, ran her hands against her lips, and stood strong. "You left me without giving me a chance to explain."

"I didn't know how to handle everything that was happening. Jesus, Lizzie. Everything in the past months happened so fast."

"Don't you think I know that? I was living the same nightmares as you, but I wanted to explain to you what happened. I wanted to make it work."

"I still want to make it work."

She snickered with sarcasm. "Is that why you kept leaving the Post-it Notes? Was that your sign of wanting to make it work? Because it only confused me more. It only hurt me more."

"What are you talking about?"

"The Post-it Notes. The ones you left every week on my bedroom window for the past five months with your initials. The same notes we used to write to each other."

My eyes narrowed. "Lizzie, I didn't leave you any messages."

"Stop with the mind games."

"No, seriously. I haven't been back to town until today."

She looked at me as if she hadn't a clue who I was. I stepped near her, and she moved back. "Stop. Just—I don't want to play anymore, Tristan. I don't want to play your games anymore. Maybe if you had shown up two months ago, I would've forgiven you. Or maybe one month ago, but not today. Stop with the notes, and stop playing with my heart, with my daughter's heart." She turned and left the store, leaving me extremely confused. When I stepped outside, she was already walking back into the café across the street.

My stomach was in knots as I walked back into Needful Things. When the bell above the door rang, my body whipped around, hoping to see Elizabeth staring my way. Instead, I turned and saw Tanner standing in my doorway. "What are you doing back here?" he asked, urgency in his voice.

"Not now, Tanner. I'm really not in the mood."

"No, no, no. You can't be here. You can't be back here." He started pacing back and forth, rubbing his hands against the back of his neck. "You're going to ruin everything. She was coming back to me. She was warming up to me again."

"What?" The look on his face made my stomach turn. "What did you do?"

He huffed. "It's really kind of ridiculous. I mean, you storm off, leaving her for months and months, and the second you come back, she's already falling all over you. Kissing you as if you're her fucking Prince Charming. Well, hell, congratulations." He rolled his eyes and turned to leave. "It wasn't supposed to be like this," he muttered to himself as I followed him out of the store and across the street to his auto shop.

"Have you been leaving notes at Elizabeth's house?"

"What, I'm sorry, were you the only one allowed to do that?"

"You signed my initials."

"Come on, Sherlock. You can't really think that you are the only one with T and C as their initials." He went to one of the cars, opened the hood, and started tinkering with things.

"But you knew she would think they were from me. How did you even know that we gave each other notes?"

"Take it easy. It's not like I had little cameras spying on the two of you." He looked up toward me with an unsettling grin.

I charged toward him, gripping his shirt and slamming him against the car. "Are you fucking psycho? What the hell is wrong with you?!"

"What's wrong with me?!" he shouted. "What's wrong with *me*?! I won the coin toss!" he hissed. "And he took her from me! I called heads, he called tails, and the coin said heads! But he thought he could just take her and make her love him. He messed up our lives. She was mine. And he mocked me over and over again about it for years. Asking me to be his best man. Begging for me to be the godfather to their kid. Years and years of throwing it in my face when Elizabeth should've been mine. So I handled it."

"What?" I said, loosening my grip on his shirt. His eyes were wide, crazed, and he couldn't stop smiling. "Handled what?"

"He said his car was acting up. He asked me to check under the hood because he and Emma were going on a trip out of town for the day. I knew him coming to me that day was a sign—he wanted me to do it."

"Do what?"

"Cut the brake cord under his hood. He was giving Elizabeth back to me. Because I won the coin toss. And everything went great, except when he took the car onto the freeway, Emma wasn't in the back seat. She was home sick."

I couldn't comprehend his words. I couldn't believe what he was saying. "You tried to kill them? You rigged his car?"

"I WON THE COIN TOSS!" he cried, as if he were actually making sense.

"You're a lunatic."

He released a breath of air. "I'm a lunatic? You're sitting here in love with a woman whose husband killed your family!"

"He didn't kill them. You did. You killed my family."

He waved his finger back and forth. "No, Steven was behind the wheel driving the car. He was the one driving. I was just the mere mechanic under the hood."

I slammed him against the car over and over again. "This isn't some kind of game, Tanner. These are people's lives you're playing with!"

"Life is a game, Tristan. And I advise you to back off. Because I won her. It's now time for me to collect my prize, and the last thing I need is someone else to get in my way."

"You're sick," I said, walking away from him. "And if you come anywhere near Elizabeth, I will kill you myself."

Tanner laughed again. "Come on, buddy. You would kill me? When it comes to killing, I'm pretty sure I have you beat three times over. Four if you count later tonight."

"What?"

"Come on. You didn't think I could have Elizabeth with a little girl always reminding her of her dead husband, did you?"

"If you touch Emma," I warned, seconds away from slamming my fist into his face.

"What? What are you going to do? Kill me?"

I didn't even remember hitting him.

But I did remember him collapsing to the ground.

"Lizzie!" I shouted, entering the café. "We need to talk."

She hardly glanced my way, giving me the cold shoulder. "Tristan, I'm working. And I'm pretty sure we've already spoken enough."

I wrapped my hand around her forearm and slightly pulled her. "Lizzie, seriously."

"Let her go," Faye said, marching in front of us. "Now!"

"Faye, you don't understand. Lizzie, it was Tanner. All of this was him. He was behind the notes, the accident, he was behind all of it."

"What are you talking about?" Elizabeth asked, confusion floating in her eyes.

"I'll explain it all later, but for now I need to know where Emma is. She's in trouble, Lizzie."

"What?"

Faye gasped lightly. "What did you do to Tanner?" she asked, staring across the street. Two police officers were talking to him, and Tanner was pointing my way. *Fuck.*

"He's insane. He said he was going to hurt Emma."

Elizabeth was shaking, nerves taking her over. "Why would you say such a thing? I know Tanner has his moments, but he would never—"

She was interrupted as the cops came into the café. "Tristan Cole, you are under arrest for the attack on Tanner Chase."

"What?" Elizabeth gasped, running her hands through her hair, confusion in her eyes. "What's going on?"

The cop kept speaking as they went to handcuff me. "It turns out this guy was caught on Tanner Chase's auto shop security cameras attacking him." He began to speak to me. "You have the right to remain silent. Anything you say can and will be used against you in a court of law. You have the right to an attorney and if you cannot afford an attorney, one will be appointed to you."

They dragged me out of the shop, and Elizabeth hurried outside to follow us. "Wait, this is a misunderstanding. Tristan, tell them. Tell them it's a mistake," she begged.

"Lizzie. Check on Emma. Okay? Just make sure she's okay." I really hoped she would believe me. I really hoped she would make sure Emma was all right.

"I leave the shop with you for three hours and come back to find you locked behind bars," Mr. Henson joked.

"What are you doing here?" I asked, confused.

He cocked an eyebrow as a cop unlocked my cell door. "I think I'm paying your bail."

"How did you know I was in here?"

"Oh. I did a tarot card reading." I narrowed my eyes and he laughed. "Tristan, this is the most gossiping town of all towns. I overheard people talking about it. Plus," he said as we rounded the corner of the hallway, "this little birdie dropped me a line."

Elizabeth stood up from the bench in the front lobby and rushed over to me. "Tristan, what's going on?"

"Is Emma safe?"

She nodded. "She's with her grandparents."

"Did you tell them what's going on?"

"Not yet. I just asked them to watch her. I honestly don't even know what's happening, Tristan."

"Tanner did this, Lizzie. All of this is Tanner. He left you the notes these past five months, not me. He's the one who caused the accident with Steven's car. He told me it was him, Lizzie. You have to believe me. He thinks all of this is some kind of sick game, and I'm certain he's not going to stop until he gets the prize."

"What's the prize?"

"You are."

She swallowed hard. "What do we do? How do we prove that he's behind all of this?"

"I don't know. I don't know what the next step is, but we need to talk to Sam and get a few cops over to your place."

"What? Why?"

"Tanner said something about cameras. I think he might have put some around your house." Her hands started trembling, and I took hold of her. "It's okay. We're going to figure this out. Everything is going to be okay."

CHAPTER 42
Elizabeth

A team of cops came over to my house along with Sam and his father, and they searched the whole house for cameras.

Eight were found, including the final one, which was placed inside of my Jeep.

I'm going to be sick.

They were the same tiny cameras Sam had told me about when he'd first changed the locks in my house. "I can't believe this. God dammit, Elizabeth, I'm so sorry," Sam said, rubbing his brow. "Tanner was the only person in town we sold these new cameras to."

"How many did you sell him?"

He swallowed hard. "Eight."

"How could he do this? How could he get the cameras in here? He's been watching us this whole time?" I asked the cops who were collecting the cameras.

"It's hard to say how long he's been doing this, but we will find an answer. We'll run his fingerprints and see if anything comes up. We'll figure this out, ma'am."

After everyone headed out, Tristan wrapped his arms around me. "We should go get Emma. You should be with her."

I nodded. "Yeah, we should."

Tristan put his finger under my chin and tilted my head up so I could stare into his eyes. "We're going to figure all of this out, Lizzie. I promise you."

For the whole ride over to Kathy and Lincoln's house, I prayed that we would figure it all out.

"Liz, what are you doing here?" Lincoln asked, opening the front door. Tristan waited in his car for me.

"I know Emma's supposed to stay the night, but I would really feel more comfortable if she was home with me tonight."

Lincoln raised an eyebrow as Kathy walked over to greet me. "Liz, what's going on?"

"Just picking up Emma." I smiled. "I'll explain everything later, I promise."

"But Tanner just stopped by to pick her up. He said you were having car trouble and wanted him to drop her off at your house."

Oh my God.

I turned to look at Tristan. The worry in my eyes must have been clear as day because he pumped his fist against his mouth as I hurried back over to him. "Tanner has her."

"Call 911," he ordered as I hopped into the car and he drove off. I spoke with the cops and they said they were on their way to my house to meet us.

I couldn't stop shaking. My mind was shutting down on me, and I couldn't see through my tears. My head was growing more and more dizzy as each second passed. I was going to faint. I was going to pass out. I was going to—

"Lizzie," Tristan said sternly as he gripped my hand in his. "Lizzie! Look at me. Now!" he ordered. I sobbed, unable to stop as I turned his way. "I need you to take a breath for me. Okay? I need you to breathe."

I inhaled deep.

But I wasn't certain that an exhale followed.

"Can you think of any place he might have taken her?" a police officer questioned me.

"No. No." His partner stood by side him, taking notes. The process of everything was slow, and I didn't understand why they were taking their sweet time when they could've been out there searching. "I'm sorry, when are you going to actually start looking for her?"

Tristan handled calling everyone. He made sure everyone was up-to-date with all the information, and it wasn't long before Faye, Sam, Kathy, and Lincoln were standing in my living room, and Mama had already hit the road with Mike to be there soon.

"Ma'am, I know you're worried, but there is a process we have to go through when a child is missing. We'll need the most updated photos you have of her, and we'll need to know more details about her—hair color, eye color. Did she have any reason that maybe she ran away from home?"

"Are you kidding me?" I huffed, unable to believe the words that had just left his mouth. "We just found cameras hidden in my house, and then you have the nerve to question if maybe just maybe my daughter ran away instead of being kidnapped? Tanner Chase has my baby, so how about you just do your damn job and find her!" I screamed at them, not meaning to take it out on the officers but having no one else to blame. I felt so helpless. *I did this. This is my fault. My baby could be hurt or even worse…*

"Lizzie, it's okay. We'll find her," Tristan whispered against my ear. "It's okay."

But we didn't find her that night. The search went on and on, and we checked every inch of town, every inch of the wooded forest, but there was nothing to be found. Nothing at all. Mama and Mike showed up but weren't exactly sure what to say other than, "They will find her."

I wished the words brought more comfort, but they didn't. Everyone seemed just as terrified as I was.

I told everyone to go home, but they all refused and fell asleep in the living room. When I finally made it to my bedroom, Tristan was there to hold me. "I'm so sorry, Lizzie."

"She's just a baby… Why would he hurt her? She's my world."

He held me for a few minutes longer before we heard a tapping on my bedroom window. When we turned to look, there was a Post-it Note sitting against it.

So many books in this shed. I wonder what Emma would want to read?—TC

"Oh my God," I muttered.

"We have to call the cops," Tristan said, reaching for his phone. I looked out of the window and saw Bubba sitting on the ground.

"No, Tristan. We can't." I opened the window and climbed out. "We don't have time."

He followed after me and picked up the stuffed animal that had another Post-it Note.

Libraries and sheds are a weird mix. Sheds
seem better for cars, if you ask me.—TC

"He's by your shed," I said to Tristan, who placed his hand in front of me, refusing to let me go first.

"Stay behind me," he ordered as we walked toward his backyard.

"What a hero you are, Tristan," Tanner laughed, looking our way. His body looked like a shadow until he stepped closer to the light from the shed. "Taking care of Elizabeth."

"Tanner, what's going on?" I asked, confused and terrified.

"Do you hear that?" Tristan whispered to me. I stopped to listen, hearing the sound of a running car inside the shed.

"Emma's in there, isn't she?" I asked Tanner.

"You always were smart. That's why I loved you. Aloof as fuck but still, smart."

"You have to let her out, Tanner. The chemicals from the car will hurt her. They could kill her."

"Why did you choose him?" he asked. "I just don't understand."

"I didn't choose Tristan, Tanner. It just happened."

Tristan edged closer to the shed, and Tanner hissed. "No, no, no. Stop right there, Casanova. Or I'll shoot." He reached into the back waistband of his pants and pulled out a gun. *Oh my God.*

"What do you want from us?" I cried. My eyes moved to the shed where the car was still running. *My baby...* "Tanner, please let her out."

"I just wanted you," he said, waving the gun around. "From day one, I wanted you. And then Steven took you. I saw you first, and he didn't care. I won the coin toss, and he still took you away from me. And then he died, and I gave you time to mourn him. To miss him. I was here waiting for you, and out of nowhere, this guy shows up and steals you!" Tanner wiped his hands over his emotion-filled eyes. "Why didn't you pick me, Liz? Why didn't you come back for me? Why haven't you ever seen me?"

"Tanner," I said, walking cautiously toward him. "I do see you."

He shook his head. "No. You're just scared. I'm not stupid, Liz. I'm not stupid."

I stared into his panicked eyes and kept walking. It took everything in me to hold my fear inside my body. It took everything in me to seem somewhat calm. "I'm not scared of you, Tanner Michael Chase. I'm not." I stepped closer to him and lay my hand against his cheek. His eyes dilated, and his breaths became heavy. "I see you."

He closed his eyes, running his face against my hand. "Jesus, Liz. You're all I wanted."

My mouth hovered over his, and I felt his hot breath against me. "I'm yours. I'm yours. We can run away with each other," I said, my hands falling to his chest. "We can start all over."

"Just us?" he whispered.

My forehead fell to his. "Just us."

His free hand wrapped around my lower back, and I shivered at his touch. His fingers pulled up my shirt, and he felt my bare skin. "God. I've always wanted this." He sighed against my neck, kissing it lightly, sending chills throughout me. His tongue slipped from his mouth and landed against my skin, licking me slowly.

We heard the sound of the shed doors opening behind us, and Tanner's eyes shot open. "You bitch!" he hissed, looking betrayed by my closeness. He shoved me to the ground and held his gun up, seconds away from shooting toward Tristan, who had just disappeared into the shed. As Tanner went to chase Tristan, I grabbed his leg, making him fall to the ground with me.

The gun slipped from his grip, landing between us. We both leaped up to grab it, and we started wrestling. The gun was clasped in both of our hands, and Tanner shoved me with his elbow, slamming it against my eye. "Let it go, Liz!" he shouted, but I wouldn't. I couldn't. Tristan had to get Emma out safely. He had to save my daughter. "I swear to God, I'll shoot you, Liz. I love you so fucking much, but I'll do it. Just let go. Please!" he cried.

"Tanner, don't do this!" I begged him, feeling my hold on the gun slipping. "Please," I pleaded, wanting this terrible nightmare to come to an end.

"I loved you," he whispered, tears falling from his eyes. "I loved you."

The sound of the gun firing one time was what I heard first. We wrestled. The second fire, I heard next. Then a burning sensation crept into my gut, making vomit rise up my throat. My eyes were wide, terrified by all of the blood. Was I bleeding? Was I dying?

"Lizzie!" Tristan yelled, hurrying out of the shed with Emma in his arms.

I turned to him, my body in a state of shock, completely covered in blood that wasn't mine. Tanner lay under me, his body motionless as blood spilled from beneath him. *Oh my God.* "I killed him. I killed him. I killed him," I cried, shaking uncontrollably.

By that point everyone who'd been inside my house was standing in the backyard. I thought I heard yelling, shouting. Someone said to call 911. A hand landed against my shoulder, begging me to stand up. Emma wasn't breathing, someone said. Another voice told Tristan to keep doing CPR. My world was spinning. Everyone was moving in slow motion around me. The red, white, and blue lights in front of our house were burning into my soul. Professionals took over caring for Emma. Mama cried. Faye sobbed. Someone shouted my name.

There was so much blood.

I killed him.

"Lizzie!" Tristan said, knocking me back into reality. "Lizzie, baby." He bent down and placed his hands around my face. My tears fell against his hands, and he gave me a broken smile. "Baby, you're in shock. Were you shot? Are you hurt?"

"No, I killed him," I whispered, turning my head to look at Tanner, but Tristan refused to let me.

"Baby, no. No. It wasn't you. I just need you to come back to me, okay? Lizzie. I need you to put down the gun."

I stared down at my blood-covered hands, which were still clenching the gun. "Oh my God," I murmured, dropping the gun to the side. Tristan was quick to lift me up into his arms, away from Tanner's motionless body. My head fell into his shoulder as I watched cops and paramedics rush over.

"Where's Emma?" I asked, turning my head back and forth, searching the area. "Where's Emma?!"

"She's on her way to the hospital," Tristan explained.

"I have to go," I said, getting out of his grip. My legs were trembling, and I almost fell to the ground. "I have to go make sure she's okay."

"Lizzie," he said, shaking my shoulders. "I need you to focus for one second. Your eyes are bugging out, your heart rate is through the roof, and your breathing is chaotic. I need you to let this paramedic check you out."

His lips kept moving, and I narrowed my eyes, trying to hear his words, but they just turned to mumbles.

My body went limp, my eyes crossed.

Everything faded to black.

"EMMA!" I shouted, opening my eyes and sitting up. A sharp pain shot through me, and I lowered myself back down. My eyes glanced around the room, and I took in all the machines, cabinets, and hospital supplies.

"Welcome back, darling," Mama said, sitting beside my bed. I narrowed my eyes, confusion pulsing through my head. She bent forward and ran her fingers through my hair. "It's okay, Liz. Everything's going to be fine."

"What happened? Where's Emma?"

"Tristan's with Emma."

"Is she okay?" I asked, trying to sit up, but the pain shot across my side. "Jesus!"

"Relax," Mama ordered. "One of the bullets hit you in the side. Emma's okay; we are just waiting for her to wake up. She has a breathing tube in to help her a bit, but she's okay."

"Tristan's with her?" I asked. Mama nodded. My mind started to play catch up as I stared down at my body. My left side was wrapped in bandages, and my body was covered in blood, some that was mine, some that was… "Tanner… What happened to Tanner?"

Mama frowned. She shook her head. "He didn't make it."

I turned my head away and stared out the window. I wasn't certain if I was filled with relief or complete confusion.

"Can you go check on Emma?" I asked. She kissed my forehead and told me she would be right back. I hoped she wouldn't rush, though. Loneliness seemed right to me.

CHAPTER 43
Tristan

I sat beside Emma's bed, staring down at a little girl who had been through more than any five-year-old should ever experience. Her small lungs were working hard as she inhaled and exhaled, her chest rising and falling. The beeping machines around her reminded me of the day I last held Charlie's hand.

"She's not Charlie," I murmured to myself, trying my best not to compare the two situations. The doctors said Emma would be okay, that it might just take her some time to open her eyes, but I couldn't stop worrying and remembering the past hurts of my soul. I wrapped her small hand in mine and scooted closer to her bedside. I whispered, "Hey, Tock. You're going to be okay. I just want you to know that you're going to be fine, because I know who your mother is, and I know that so much of her strength lives within you. So you keep fighting, okay? You keep fighting and fighting, and then I want you to open your eyes. I need you to come back to us, Tock. I need you to open your eyes," I begged, lightly kissing her hand.

The machines around us started beeping quicker and quicker. My chest tightened as I looked around. "Someone help!" I called, and two nurses rushed in to see what was happening. I stood up and stepped back. *This can't be happening again. This can't happen...*

I looked away, covering my mouth with my hand, and I said a prayer. I was far from the praying type, but I had to try, just in case God was listening that day.

"Tick," a small voice whispered.

Turning on my heels, I hurried back over to Emma's side. Her blue eyes were open and she looked so confused, so lost. I took her hand in mine and turned toward the nurses.

They smiled, and one spoke. "She's okay."

"She's okay?" I echoed.

They nodded.

She's okay.

"Jesus, Tock. You scared me," I said, kissing her forehead.

Her eyes narrowed, and she slightly tilted her head to the left. "You came back?"

I held on to her hand tighter. "Yeah, I came back." She opened her mouth to speak, but her breaths were rough, and she began to cough. "Take your time. Take deep breaths."

She did as I said and lay back down against her pillow, her eyelids heavy. "I thought you and Zeus were gone forever like Daddy." She was falling back asleep and her words were breaking my heart.

"I'm right here, buddy."

"Tick?" she whispered, her eyes falling closed.

"Yes, Tock?"

"Please don't leave us again."

I brushed the palm of my hand against my eyes and blinked a few times. "Don't worry. I'm not going anywhere."

"Zeus too?"

"Zeus too."

"Promise?" she yawned, already asleep before I could reply.

But I did reply, softly whispering into her dreams. "Promise."

"Tristan." I turned to see Hannah staring my way.

"She just woke up," I said, standing up. "She's pretty exhausted, but she's doing okay."

Relief filled her eyes, and her hands landed over her heart. "Thank God. Liz is awake in the other room and asked me to come check on her."

"She's awake?" I asked. I started for the door to go see Elizabeth, but I paused, looking back at Emma.

"I'll stay with her. She won't be alone."

"You're up," I said, staring at Elizabeth, who was looking out the window. She turned toward me, and a small smile appeared on her lips.

"Is Emma okay?"

"Yeah." I walked over to her bed and sat beside her. "She's doing good. Your mom is with her right now. How are you doing?" I took her hand, and her stare fell to our fingers.

"I guess I got shot."

"You scared the crap out of me, Lizzie."

She pulled her hand away from mine. A tiny breath fell from her lips, and she closed her eyes. "I don't know how to deal with all of this. I just want to go home with my little girl."

My hand ran against the back of my neck, and I studied every inch of her. The bandage around her side. Her bloodstained body. Her frown. I wanted to make her feel better, I wanted to make her feel less alone, but I wasn't sure how.

"Can you find out when we can leave?" she asked.

I nodded. "Of course." As I stood up, I paused in the doorway. "I love you, Lizzie."

Her shoulders rose and fell before she turned her head away from me. "You can't just love me because I got shot, Tristan. You should've loved me before that."

Emma was able to go home before Elizabeth, and she stayed at the house with Hannah. I didn't leave Elizabeth's side until she was able to go home. When it was time to leave, she didn't pass up the offer of me driving her to her house, but she didn't speak a word to me.

"Here, let me help you," I said, hopping out of the driver's seat and rushing over to help her out of the car.

"I'm good," she whispered to me, not wanting my help. "I'm good."

I followed her into the house, and she told me I could leave, but I didn't. Hannah and Emma were both sleeping in Emma's tiny bed.

"Tristan, you really can go. I'm good, I'm good."

I wondered how many times she could say those words before she realized they were a lie.

"I'm just going to go take a shower and then head to bed." She walked toward the bathroom and took a deep inhale, gripping the doorframe. Her body went a bit limp, and I rushed over to help hold her up. She pulled away from me. "I don't need you, Tristan. I'm fine without you," she said coldly. But in the back of her tone I heard more fear than anything. "I don't need anyone except myself and my baby girl. We're good, I'm good. I'm good." She spoke softly, holding on to my T-shirt to keep herself from falling. "I'm… I'm…" She started crying, and I pulled her closer to my body. She cried into my shirt. "You left me."

"I'm so sorry, baby." I sighed. I didn't know what to say because I had left her and Emma. I ran away when things got real. I didn't know how to deal with the fact that I loved her because loving her meant that someday I could lose her, and losing people was the worst feeling in the world. "I got scared. I got mad. And I handled it all completely wrong. But I need you to hear me now: I'm not going anywhere. I'm here. I'm here, and I'm here to stay."

She pulled back, wiped her hand beneath her nose, and laughed lightly, trying to stop her tears. "Sorry. I just need a shower."

"I'll be here when you're done."

Her beautiful brown eyes locked with mine, and a tiny smile grew on her lips. "Okay."

She closed the bathroom door. I heard the sound of the shower coming on and I leaned against the bathroom door, waiting for her to finish.

"I'm good, I'm good," she told herself over and over again. Her voice started to shake as she said it, and I could hear her crying again. My hand wrapped around the doorknob, and I pushed it open to see her sitting in the bottom of the tub, her hands covering her face as she cried, dried blood washing out of her hair. Without thought, I climbed into the tub with her and wrapped myself around her. "Tanner's gone?" she asked, shaking against me.

"Yes."

"Emma's okay?"

"Yes."

"I'm good?" she wondered out loud.

"Yeah, Lizzie. You're good."

I stayed with her that whole night. I didn't lie beside her in her bed, but I sat in the chair at her desk, giving her the distance she needed but also letting her know that she wasn't ever going to be alone again.

CHAPTER 44
Elizabeth

I awakened to the sound of a lawnmower coming from the backyard. The sun was just waking, and there was no need for anyone to be cutting the grass at such a time. Walking toward my back porch, I looked at Tristan, who was cutting the grass around where the accident with Tanner had happened. My hand lay over my heart, and I moved down the steps, feeling the wet morning grass against my toes.

"What are you doing?" I asked.

He turned my way and shut off the lawnmower. "I didn't want you to have to see this when you came out to the backyard. I didn't want you to have to deal with what happened." He reached into his jeans pocket and pulled out a coin. "Tanner dropped his coin… I mean, did you ever see this?" He tossed it my way.

"It's a double-sided coin. It's always heads," I said, a bit shocked. "He never truly won the coin toss?"

"Never. I can't believe I didn't put the pieces together sooner. I can't believe he was almost able to hurt you and Emma… I should've known something was off. I should've known…"

He's my world. I wanted so much to overthink everything. I wanted to overthink him leaving us. I wanted to overthink his return. I wanted to doubt that he could ever be something that was mine, but my heart told my head to shut up. My heart told me to just allow myself to feel, to live in this moment in time because all we had was the here and now, and in the blink of an eye, that could be taken away. I had to allow myself to cherish the man in front of me. "I love you," I whispered, and his stormy eyes frowned in the saddest way.

"I don't deserve that."

Moving over to him, I wrapped my fingers around the back of his neck, pulling his lips closer to my lips. His hand fell to my lower back, and I jumped a little from the pain that shot through me. "Are you okay?" he asked.

I chuckled. "I've felt worse pain." My lips lay against his, and I felt his breaths weaving in and out of his mouth. As I inhaled his breath, he exhaled mine. The morning sun was rising behind us, lighting up the grass with a light we both craved. "I love you," I whispered again.

His forehead pressed against mine. "Lizzie…I need to prove to you that I'm not going to just run away again. I need to prove to you that I'm good enough for you and Emma."

"Shut up, Tristan."

"What?"

"I said shut up. You saved my daughter's life. You saved my life. You're good enough. You're our world."

"I'm not going to stop loving you both, Lizzie. I promise you that for the rest of my life, I am going to prove just how much I love you."

My face brushed against his thick beard, and my finger danced around his bottom lip. "Tristan?"

"Yes?"

"Kiss me?"

"Yes."

And then he did.

Emma and I sat on the front porch of the house the next morning, drinking the tea and cocoa that Mr. Henson dropped off for us. When a car pulled up to our house, Emma screamed with excitement as it parked and the driver climbed out and opened the back door. Zeus came sprinting out of the car and headed straight to Emma.

"Zeus!" she shouted with the biggest smile ever. "You came back!" Zeus wagged his tail, excitement overtaking the both of them as he knocked Emma to the ground and covered her in kisses.

My heart smiled as I walked over to the two older people who just climbed out of the car. "Sorry about that," I said, nodding toward Emma and Zeus. "It turns out they are old friends."

Before I could say anything else, the older woman wrapped me tight into a hug. "Thank you," she whispered. "Thank you."

When she pulled away, I smiled to the woman who was clearly Tristan's mother. "He has your eyes. I remember when I first met him, I felt like there was something so familiar about him, and that was it. He has your eyes."

"I don't think we've properly met. I'm Mary, and this is my husband, Kevin."

"It's so great to meet you both. I'm Elizabeth, and that's my daughter, Emma."

"She's beautiful," Kevin said. "She looks like you."

"Really?" I disagreed. "I think she looks like her father."

"Trust me, honey. She's a mini you. Come on inside. Tristan said

you redecorate his place, and I would love you to show me around."
Mary winked. We walked inside with Emma and Zeus following
behind us. "So did Tristan tell you about his shop? How Mr. Henson
left it to him?"

"I heard that. I think it's great. Tristan's amazingly talented. I think
he'll do so well." I smiled and turned to Kevin. "I hear you are running
it with him?"

"That's the plan," he replied. "I think it's great. A new beginning
for all of us."

As I showed them around Tristan's new-and-improved home,
Mary commented that I should consider going back into interior
design. For the first time in a long time, I was starting to consider the
possibilities of starting over. It didn't scare me the way that it used to.
The idea of beginning again inspired me. I was hopeful for the future,
and I was ready to make my daughter proud of me.

CHAPTER 45
Elizabeth

S o are you two like…together now?" Faye asked one night as we sat
on the seesaw in the park. Emma was running around with another
kid, playing on the slides and swings. It'd been a few months since the
accident with Tanner, and ever since then, Tristan had been back in
Mr. Henson's shop, turning it into his own dream.

"I don't know. I mean, we're good, but I don't know what it means.
I don't think I have to know what it means, either. It's just nice to have
him around."

Faye furrowed her brow. "Nope," she said, jumping off the seesaw
and sending me slamming against the ground.

"Ouch!" I said, rubbing my behind. "You could've given me some
warning about your leap of faith."

"Where's the fun in that?" She snickered. "Now, come on."

"Where to?"

"Tristan's shop. This whole 'I don't know what we are but I'm okay
with it' bullshit you're talking about is annoying, and we are going to

demand answers from him. Come on, Emma!" she shouted toward the slide.

Emma hurried over. "Are we going home, Mama?" she asked me.

"Nope. We are going to see Dick," Faye said.

"You mean Tick?" Emma asked.

Faye laughed. "Yeah, that's what I mean."

They started walking down the street, and I hurried behind them. "We should really do this another day. He's been stressed out with the store, working with his dad to get everything set up for the grand opening next week. I don't think we should bother him." They didn't listen, just kept up their brisk pace. When we got to the shop, all the lights were out. "See? He's not even here."

Faye rolled her eyes. "I bet he's just sleeping somewhere." She turned the doorknob—which was unlocked—and pushed her way in.

"Faye!" I whisper-shouted. Emma followed her inside, and I hurried behind her, closing the door. "We shouldn't be here."

"Well, maybe I shouldn't," she agreed, flipping on the light switch, illuminating thousands of white feathers sprinkled around the room. "But you definitely should be." She walked over to me and kissed my forehead. "You deserve to be happy, Liz." She turned and left the shop, leaving Emma and I standing still.

"Do you see all the feathers, Mama?!" Emma said excitedly.

I walked around the room, touching Tristan's wooden masterpieces, which were covered in white feathers. "Yes, baby. I see them."

"I'm in love with you," a deep voice said, forcing me to spin around. At the front door stood Tristan in an all-black suit with his hair slicked back. My heart skipped a few beats, but in the moment they didn't seem that important.

"I'm in love with you," I replied.

"You two haven't seen any of my pieces yet, have you?" he asked, walking around the room, looking at all of the wooden carvings that he and his father had created.

"No. It's amazing, though. You're amazing. This store is going to do great."

"I don't know," he said, sitting on top of a dresser. The knobs on the dresser drawers were carved with words, and the dresser drawers had different lines from children's novels carved into them. It was stunning. "My dad kind of backed out on the idea of opening the store with me."

"What?" I asked, confused. "Why? I thought this was a dream you both shared?"

He shrugged. "He said he just got his son back, and he didn't want to lose him by going into business together. I mean, I kind of understand, but I don't think I can do this alone. I just need to find a new partner."

"How do you even start looking?" I asked, sitting beside him while Emma ran around the room picking up white feathers.

"I don't know. It needs to be the right person. Someone who's smart. Who understands interior design a bit because I only know how to sell wood pieces, but I think the store would do better if we had more household items, you know?" My cheeks heated up as he kept speaking. "Do you happen to know anyone who might be into interior design? I need to hire someone soon."

I smiled wide. "I think I might know someone."

He slowly ran his finger across my bottom lip before he hopped off the dresser and stepped in front of me, placing himself between my legs. "I've made a lot of mistakes in my life, and I'll probably make more. I mess things up. I messed us up. I know you can never truly forgive me for what I've done, for how I left, and I don't expect you to. But I'm never going to give up. I'm never going to stop trying to fix this. To fix us. I love you, Lizzie, and if you give me the chance, I will spend the rest of my tomorrows proving to you that you have all of me. The good, the bad, and the ugly parts."

"Tristan," I whispered. I began to cry, and he wrapped his arms around me. "I missed you so much," I said, falling against his chest.

He pulled open the drawer on my left side; a small black box was sitting inside. Picking it up, he opened it, and I saw a beautiful, hand-crafted wooden ring with a large diamond in the center. "Marry me."

"I…" My eyes moved over to Emma. "I have baggage. I'm part of a package deal, Tristan. I wouldn't expect you to have to step up into Emma's life, but with me comes her."

He pulled open the drawer on my right side, which held a smaller black box. My heart melted right then and there. He opened it up, and I saw a smaller, almost identical ring.

"I love her, Lizzie. I adore her, and there is nothing about her that is baggage. Emma is a luxury. I'll take care of her for the rest of my life because it would be an honor. Because I love you. I love your heart, I love your soul, I love you, Elizabeth, and I'm never going to stop loving you or that beautiful girl of yours." He walked over to Emma, lifted her up, and sat her on the dresser beside me. "Emma and Elizabeth, will you both marry me?" he asked, holding the two ring boxes in his hands.

I was speechless, unable to find any words. My sweet baby poked me in the side with that big goofy grin upon her lips—the same one I was probably wearing on my face. "Mama, say yes!" she told me.

I did exactly as she said. "Yes, Tristan. Yes over and over again." He smiled.

"What about you, Emma? Will you marry me?"

She tossed her hands in the air and screamed the loudest yes I'd ever heard. He slid the rings onto both our fingers, and a few seconds later, the shop began to fill with all our best friends and family. Emma went rushing over to Zeus, who came dashing her way, telling the faithful dog that they were now each other's family.

Everyone began cheering and congratulating us on our future together, and I felt as if my dream had somehow turned into my new reality.

Tristan pulled me toward him, my lips connecting with his as he kissed me for the first time in what felt like centuries. He held his lips to mine, tasting all of me, and I kissed him back, silently promising to love him from that day forth. Our foreheads pressed against one another, and I sighed, staring down at the ring on my finger. "Does this mean you want to hire me?"

He swept me into his arms and kissed me deeply, filling me up with happiness, hope, and all of his love. "I do."

EPILOGUE
Tristan

FIVE YEARS LATER

Under the wooden dining-room table that Emma had helped me build, I saw the three of them sleeping. They'd transformed the table into a fort, the same way they did every Saturday night when we watched movies and camped out inside our house. Emma claimed to be too old to play make-believe anymore, but when her baby brother, Colin, asked her to play, she couldn't say no.

Colin was handsome and very much his mother's son. He laughed like her, cried like her, and loved like her too. Each time he kissed my forehead, I knew I was the luckiest man alive.

I crawled under the table next to my beautiful wife and placed my lips against her growing stomach. Within a few weeks we would be bringing yet another miracle into the world. We would be adding yet another beauty to our family.

For a long time, I just stared at Lizzie, Emma, and Colin. Zeus joined us underneath the table too, snuggling under Emma's arm. How had I gotten a second chance at life? How had I become so happy? I remembered the moment I'd died. I remembered sitting in the hospital room when the doctor told me Charlie was gone. I'd left that day too. Life stopped existing, and I stopped breathing.

Then Elizabeth came and resurrected me. She breathed life into my lungs, making the dark shadows flood with light. A light so bright that I slowly began to believe in happily ever todays. No more pains of yesterdays, no more fears of tomorrow. In that moment, I stopped replaying the past and didn't choose to reach for the future. Instead, I chose us as we were. I chose today.

Some days were still hard, and others, the easiest. We loved in a way that only brought more love. During the light days, we held each other close. During the dark days, we held each other closer.

I lay beside Elizabeth, wrapping her against my body, and she pulled in closer to me. Her brown eyes opened, and her sweet smile rose on her lips. "Are you good?" she whispered.

I kissed her earlobe and nodded once. "I'm good."

Her eyes fell closed, and I felt her exhale against my lips. With each exhale, I took in her breath, I drank her into me, realizing that she was mine. Forever and always, no matter what the future may hold. Each day, I longed for her. Each day, I loved her more. As my eyes closed and her hands lay against my chest, I knew life was never truly broken; it was simply bruised some days, and bruises healed with time. Time was able to make me whole again.

My children were my best friends. All of them. Charlie, Emma, Colin, and the unnamed angel resting within my beautiful wife's stomach. They were all so smart, so funny, and so deeply loved. I knew it made no sense, but sometimes when I looked into Emma's eyes, I could almost see Charlie smiling my way, telling me he and Jamie were okay.

Then there was Elizabeth.

The beautiful woman who loved me when I didn't deserve to be loved. Her touch healed me; her love saved me. She was more than any words could ever convey.

I treasured her.

I cherished her for everything she was, and everything she wasn't. I cherished her in the sunbeams and in the shadows. I cherished her loudly; I cherished her with whispers. I cherished her when we fought; I cherished her when we were peaceful.

It was quite obvious what she was to me; it was so clear why I always wanted her near.

She was simply the air I breathed.

As I fell asleep under that wooden table, my children snuggling against their mama and me, I laid my lips against my wife's and kissed her gently. "I love you," I whispered.

She smiled in her dreams.

Because she already knew.

Thank you for reading the first title in the Elements series!

Enjoy this brand new annotated chapter from Brittainy Cherry as as she takes you on a tour of the world of *The Air He Breathes*. An annotation guide has been provided for the numbers Brittainy has left next to certain notes for easy reading.

Let's cry together.[1]

CHAPTER 1

Elizabeth

JULY 3RD, 2015

Each morning I read love letters written for another woman. She and I had much in common, from our chocolate eyes to the blond tone of our hair. We shared the same kind of laugh that was quiet yet grew loud in the company of the ones we loved. She smiled out of the right corner of her mouth and frowned out of the left, the same way my lips did.

I found the letters abandoned in the garbage can, resting inside a heart-shaped tin box. Hundreds of notes: some long, some short, some happy, others heartbreakingly sad. The dates of the letters went far back in years, some older than my entire existence on this earth. Some letters were initialed KB, others, HB.

I wondered how Dad would've felt if he'd known Mama threw all of them away. He would be so sad![2]

Then again, lately it had been hard for me to believe she was the one who felt the way those letters said she felt.

Whole.

Complete.

A part of something divine.

Recently she seemed the complete opposite of all of those things.

Broken.

Incomplete.

Lonely all the time.

My heart hurts for Lizzie! [13]

I feel like this is me [4]

Mama became a whore after Dad died. There wasn't any other way to put it. It didn't happen right away, even though down the street Miss Jackson had been flapping her lips to everyone who would listen, saying Mama had always spread her legs, even when Dad was alive. I knew that wasn't true, though, because I'd never forgotten the way she'd looked at him when I was a kid. The way Mama stared was the way a woman gazed when she only had eyes for one man. When he'd go off to work at the crack of dawn, she would have his breakfast and lunch packed with snacks for the in-between hours. Dad always complained about getting hungry right after he was full, so Mama always made sure he had more than enough.

Dad was a poet and taught at the university an hour away. It wasn't surprising that the two left each other love notes. Words were what Dad drank in his coffee, and he tossed them into his whiskey at night. Even though Mama wasn't as strong with words as her husband, she knew how to express herself in each letter she wrote.

The moment Dad walked out the door in the mornings, Mama smiled and hummed to herself as she cleaned up around the house and got me ready for the day. She'd talk about Dad, saying how much she missed him, and would write him love letters until he came home at night. When he came home, Mama would always pour them both a glass of wine while he hummed their favorite song, and he'd kiss her against her wrist whenever she drew close enough to his mouth. They would laugh with one another and giggle as if they were kids falling in love for the first time.

"You're my love without end, Kyle Bailey," she'd say, pressing her lips to his. *BRB — sobbing*[5]

"You're my love without end, Hannah Bailey," Dad would reply, spinning her in his arms.

They loved in a way that made fairy tales envious.

So on that sizzling August day years ago when Dad died, a part of Mama left too. I remembered in some novel I'd read the author said, "No soul mate leaves the world alone; they always take a piece of their other half along with them." I hated that he was right. Mama didn't get out of bed for months. I had to make her eat and drink each day, just hoping she wouldn't fade away from sadness. I'd never seen her cry until she lost her husband. I didn't show too much emotion around her because I knew that would only make her sadder. *I want this kind of love!*[6]

I cried enough when I was alone.

When she finally did get out of bed, she went to church for a few weeks, taking me alongside her. I remember being twelve and feeling completely lost sitting in a church. We weren't really a praying kind of family until after bad things happened. Our church trips didn't last very long, though, because Mama called God a liar and scorned the townsfolk for wasting time on such deceit and empty promises of a promised land.

Pastor Reece asked us not to come back for a while, to let things smooth out a bit. *Reese should try harder*[7]

I hadn't known people could be banished from a holy temple until that very moment. When Pastor Reece said come one, come all, I guessed he met a different kind of "one" and a special kind of "all." *More Rain Clouds*[8]

Nowadays, Mama had moved on to a new pastime: different men on the regular. Some she slept with, others she used to help pay the bills, and then some she kept 'round because she was lonely and they kind of looked like Dad. Some she even called by his name. Tonight there was a car parked in front of her little house. It was a deep navy blue, with shiny metallic silver frames. The inside had apple-red leather seats, a man sitting with a cigar between his lips, and Mama in his lap. He looked like he'd walked right out of the 1960s. She giggled as he whispered something to her, but it wasn't the same kind of laugh she'd always given Dad. *I want to hug them?*

It was a little vacant, a little hollow, a little sad.

I glanced down the street and saw Miss Jackson surrounded by the other gossipy women, pointing at Mama and her new man of the week. I wished I were close enough to hear them so I could tell them to keep their yaps shut, but they were a good block away. Even the kids who were tossing a ball in the street, hitting it around with a few broken sticks, stopped their actions and stared wide-eyed at Mama and the stranger.

Cars that cost as much as his never traveled down streets that looked like ours. I'd tried to convince Mama she should move to a better neighborhood, but she refused. I thought it was mainly because she and Dad had bought the house together.

Maybe she hadn't completely let him go yet.

The man blew a cloud of smoke into Mama's face, and they laughed together. She was wearing her nicest dress, a yellow dress that hung off her shoulders, hugged her small waist, and flared out at the bottom. She wore so much makeup that it made her fifty-year-old face look more like a thirty-year-old's. She was pretty without all that gunk on her cheeks, but she said a little blush made a girl turn into a

I love Pearl necklaces [10]

woman. The pearls around her neck were from Grandma Betty. She'd never worn those pearls for a stranger before tonight, and I wondered why she was wearing them now.

The two glanced my way, and I hid behind the porch post where I was spying from. *hide + seek, anyone?* [11]

"Liz, if you're planning on hiding, at least do a better job at it. Now come on over and meet my new friend," Mama shouted.

Kind of rude, Liz [12]

I stepped from behind the post and walked over to the two of them. The man blew another puff of smoke, and the smell lingered around my nostrils as I took in his graying hair and deep-blue eyes.

"Richard, this is my daughter, Elizabeth. Everyone we know calls her Liz, though."

Richard eyed me up and down in a way that made me feel less like a person. He studied me as if I were a porcelain doll he wanted to watch shatter. I tried not to show my discomfort, but it seeped through as my eyes shifted to the ground. "How do you do, Liz?"

"Elizabeth," I corrected, my voice hitting the concrete I'd been staring down at. "Only people I know call me Liz."

"Liz, that is no way to speak to him!" Mama scolded, her slight wrinkles deepening in her forehead. She would've had a fit if she'd known her wrinkles were showing. I hated how whenever a new man came around, she was quick to back them up instead of standing up for me. *Richard's smoke* [13]

"It's all right, Hannah. Besides, she's right. It takes time to get to know somebody. Nicknames need to be earned, not given out freely." There was something so slimy about the way Richard stared at me and puffed on his cigar. I was wearing a pair of loose jeans and a plain, oversized T-shirt, but his eyes made me feel exposed. "We were about to go grab a bite to eat in town, if you want to join us," he offered.

Z Z zzz... [handwritten] [14]

I declined. "Emma's still sleeping." My eyes glanced back at the house, where my baby girl was lying on the pullout sofa she and I'd been sharing for one too many nights since we'd moved back in with Mama. *Liz's to do list: get a bed* [handwritten] [15]

Mama wasn't the only one who'd lost the love of her life.

Hopefully I wouldn't end up like her.

Hopefully I'd just stay in the sad phase. *over here life* [handwritten] *Still raining* [16]

It'd been a year since Steven passed away, and still each breath was hard to swallow. Emma's and my true home was back in Meadows Creek, Wisconsin. It was a fixer-upper place where Steven, Emma, and I had taken a house and created a home. We fell deeper in love, into fights, and back in love, over and over again.

It became a place of warmth just by us being within its walls, and after Steven passed away, a drift of coldness filled the space.

The last time he and I were together, his hand was around my waist in the foyer and we thought we had forever to keep doing things like that.

Forever was much shorter than anyone would ever like to believe.

For the longest time, life flowed in its accustomed stream, and one day it all came to a shocking stop.

I'd felt the suffocation of the memories, of the sadness, so I'd run off to stay with Mama.

Going back to the house would ultimately be me facing the truth that he was really gone. For over a year, I'd been living in make-believe, pretending he'd gone out for milk and would be walking through the door anytime now. Each evening when I lay down to sleep, I stayed on the left side and closed my eyes, pretending Steven was against the right.

But now, my Emma needed more. My poor Emma needed

This is so true! [handwritten] [17]

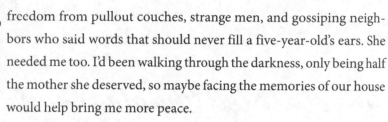

freedom from pullout couches, strange men, and gossiping neighbors who said words that should never fill a five-year-old's ears. She
needed me too. I'd been walking through the darkness, only being half
the mother she deserved, so maybe facing the memories of our house
would help bring me more peace.

I headed back inside the house and looked down at my sleeping
angel, her chest rising and falling in a perfect pattern. She and I had
much in common, from our dimpled cheeks to the blond tone of our
hair. We shared the same kind of laugh that was quiet yet grew loud in
the company of the ones we loved. She smiled out of the right corner
of her mouth and frowned out of the left, the same way my lips did.

But there was one big difference.

She had his blue eyes. *This is a blessing ♡ '8*

I lay beside Emma, placing a gentle kiss against her nose before I
reached into the heart-shaped tin box and read another love letter. It
was one I'd read before, yet it still tugged at my spirit.

Sometimes I pretended the letters were from Steven.

I always cried a little.

*With less rain
and tears 20*

*Better days are
on the way,
Liz. '9*

Annotatated Chapter Guide

Images and words on page 317: Drawing of hearts rising from the opening paragraph. Drawing of a daisy with a rain cloud over it. Drawing of three letters with hearts sealing the envelopes.

1. *Let's cry together.*
2. *He would be so sad!*

Images and words on page 318: Drawing of hearts along the top and bottom of the page. Drawing of a broken heart.

3. *My heart hurts for Lizzie!*
4. *"Words were what Dad drank in his coffee, and he tossed them into his whiskey at night." I feel like this is me.*

Images and words on page 319: Drawing of a rain cloud in bottom left.

5. *BRB—sobbing.*
6. *"They loved in a way that made fairy tales envious." I want this kind of love!*

7.   *Reece should try harder.*

8.   *More rain clouds.*

Images and words on 320: Drawing of stars along the top and middle of the page. Drawing of hearts along the bottom of the page.

9.   *I want to hug them.*

Images and words on 321: Drawing of a lit cigarette.

10.   *I love pearl necklaces.*

11.   *Hide & seek, anyone?*

12.   *"Only people I know call me Liz." Kind of rude, Liz.*

13.   *Richard's smoke.*

Images and words on page 322: Drawing of a rain cloud.

14.   *Zzzzz...*

15.   *Liz's to do list: get a bed.*

16.   *Still raining over her life.*

17.   *"Forever was much shorter than anyone would ever like to believe." This is so true!*

Images and words on page 323: Drawing of hearts along the top of the page. Drawing of a house with two trees at the bottom of the page.

18.   *"She had his blue eyes." This is a blessing.*

19.   *Better days are on the way, Liz.*

20.   *With less rain and tears.*

Acknowledgments

To my amazing group of critique partners who are easily some of the most amazing women I've ever came across. You all are beyond talented, and I'm glad to have you each in my life!

To Alison, Allison, Christy, and Beverly: Thank you for taking the time to beta read this novel for me! Your notes and comments have helped me so much, and I couldn't think of a better team of ladies to be working with!

Thank you to my amazing editor Caitlin at Edits by C. Marie: you are my superhero.

To my proofreaders Emily Lawrence and Stacy Kestwick: my fairy godmothers!

To CP Smith for formatting my novel last minute and being nothing but an angel the whole time, though! Thank you so much for your help! I'm so thankful that I know you!

To Danielle Allen and Olivia Linden: I love you, I love you, I love you some more.

To those who made my novel beautiful: my cover model, Franggy, for the lovely cover image, and my cover designer, Staci, from Quirky Bird.

A GIANT thanks to all of the bloggers and readers who spread the word of my novels and give them a chance! I cannot express how much you all mean to me! Thank you!

Lastly a big thank-you to my family—my life. Thank you for believing in me always. Mom: I love you to the moon and back.

About the Author

Brittainy Cherry is an Amazon bestselling author who has always been in love with words. She graduated from Carroll University with a bachelor's degree in theatre arts and a minor in creative writing. Brittainy lives in Milwaukee, Wisconsin, with her family. When she's not running a million errands and crafting stories, she's probably playing with her adorable pets.

Facebook: BrittainyCherryAuthor
Instagram: @BCherryAuthor